Collectors' Edition

THE
ROMANTIC
GLENCANNON

This Limited First Edition consists of nine hundred fifty copies of which this volume is Number 282

The Romantic Glencannon

by

Guy Gilpatric

First Edition
The Glencannon Press
Maritime Books

1999

The stories in this volume first appeared in *The Saturday Evening Post* as follows:

The Snyke in the Grass	October 25, 1930
The Ash Cat	February 27, 1932
A Nosegay For Mr. Montgomery	April 14, 1934
The Pearl of Panama	April 6, 1935
Three Lovesick Swains of Gibraltar	April 27, 1935
The Wailing Lady of Limehouse	May 23, 1936
The Mean Man of Genoa	June 5, 1937
The Donkeyman's Widow	January 29, 1938
At the Sign of the Brass Knuckle	April 23, 1938
The Scot From Scotland Yard	September 9, 1939
The Loving Cup	January 11, 1941

The Snyke in the Grass appeared in the book *Scotch and Water*; The Ash Cat in the book *Half-Seas Over*; A Nosegay For Mr. Montgomery, The Pearl of Panama and Three Lovesick Swains of Gibraltar in the book *Three Sheets in the Wind*; The Wailing Lady of Limehouse, The Mean Man of Genoa, The Donkeyman's Widow and At the Sign of the Brass Knuckle in the book *The Gentleman With the Walrus Mustache* and The Scot From Scotland Yard and The Loving Cup in the book *Glencannon Afloat*. These books were then incorporated in two of the omnibuses, *The Glencannon Omnibus* and *The Second Glencannon Omnibus* published by Dodd, Mead in 1937 through 1946.

The illustrations, including that on the front cover, are copyright © The Curtis Publishing Company and used with their permission.

First Edition. Copyright © 1999 by The Glencannon Press
All rights reserved.

ISBN 1-889901-10-5
Library of Congress Catalog Card Number: 99-73203

This Limited Edition is published by:
    The Glencannon Press
    P.O. Box 341
    Palo Alto, CA 94302
    Tel. 800-711-8985 Fax: 707-747-0311
    www.glencannon.com

TO
LOUISE

Contents

Preface xi
The Snyke in the Grass 1
The Ash Cat 15
A Nosegay for Mr. Montgomery 31
The Pearl of Panama 51
Three Lovesick Swains of Gibraltar 69
The Wailing Lady of Limehouse 89
The Mean Man of Genoa 115
The Donkeyman's Widow 131
At the Sign of the Brass Knuckle 151
The Scot From Scotland Yard 171
The Loving Cup 191

PREFACE

Affairs of the heart might seem a bit of a stretch for Mr. Glencannon, but we have managed to gather in this volume eleven stories depicting affection in all its many guises — compassion for a shipmate, romancing the wrong woman, marrying the wrong woman, several suitors vying for the same woman and others. In some cases Cupid's arrow strikes members of the crew, once even Mr. Hazlitt and a few times Mr. Glencannon himself. Of course, when our Scots chief engineer "falls in love" you can be sure there is a "muckle o' siller" somewhere in the offing. In fact, it can safely be said that when Mr. Glencannon falls in love, it is *always* with a woman who has a potential for profit.

Certainly, a woman who owns her own pub would be the lady of Mr. Glencannon's dreams. In "The Snyke in the Grass" he is smitten with Miss Myrtle Bootle, owner of the Shipwright's Arms. Her niece, Hortense, takes a fancy to him, and, to further complicate matters, Capt. Ball decides marriage is the last thing his chief engineer needs. He enlists the aid of Mr. Montgomery who decides marriage would be a sure way to be rid of his nemesis. Unknown to Mr. Glencannon, copies of his love poems are circulated far and wide and confusion reigns.

That green-eyed demon, jealousy, gathers Duncan Glencannon to her bosom, causing him to think that one of the *Inchcliffe Castle's* stokehold workers has claimed the barmaid of his affections. "The Ash Cat" is Radway, the "Yonkee Bruiser" and, physically, a match for the ham-fisted Duncan. Unfortunately, he's no match for the Glencannon family cunning. Thanks to Duncan, Radway misses the ship in Port Said, even though it was Minnie he courted, not Winnie.

In "A Nosegay for Mr. Mongtomery," the *Inchcliffe Castle's* mate is besmitten with a lovely lass who convinces him his nose should look more like that of the screen star Ronald Coleman. To win her, the mate orders a device guaranteed to give him a nose worthy of Apollo. Unfortunately, Mr. Glencannon intercepts the device with the result that love flies away on the wings of a vile odor — proving that a nose by any other name is not so sweet!

Mr. Hazlitt in love! Surely there is some mistake. But in "The Pearl of Panama" the hard-nosed manager of Clifford, Castle & Co., Ltd. takes a fancy to a demure miss he sees in a tea shop. Soon he is sporting new clothes, a toupee, and fancies himself quite the rake. Mr. Glencannon brings him back to his senses with the gift of a genuine "Pamana" (note the spelling) hat.

Then, there once was a sergeant major's daughter in Gibraltar who was wooed by three Scotsmen: Mr. Glencannon, Duncan Glencannon and Alf Chatterton — "The Three Lovesick Swains of Gibraltar." Of course, the fact that she was coming into a large inheritance may have had something to do with their ardor. Although compounded daily, none of their interest was enough to win the fair maiden's heart.

Mr. McFidd and Mr. Glencannon vie for the attentions of "The Wailing Lady of Limehouse." She settles for one, the wrong one, loses him, yet becomes the fish-and-chips magnate of the British Isles. Naturally, Mr. Glencannon would like to capitalize on this situation. And he would, were it not for the lady's secret love.

"There's no fool like an old fool," goes the saying. In this case, the old fool is "The Mean Man of Genoa" who fancies a series of charming young organists at the church in Genoa which he financially supports. Called in to repair the organ, Mr. Glencannon pulls out all the stops and puts a stop to the mean man's amorous endeavors.

The notion of love and romance might be stretched to include affection and stretched even further to include affection for a shipmate. In "The Donkeyman's Widow" Mr. Glencannon sets out to do the right thing for the widow of a deceased shipmate. Unfortunately, he succumbs to a bit of personal larceny and a lot of Duggan's Dew. The road to hell . . .

A chance encounter with Horace "Dumbell" Dillon at a sidewalk cafe in Marseilles causes Mr. Glencannon to become the sympathetic listener to Mr. Dillon's misguided lovelife. It also gives him a chance to collect an old debt, making him part owner of the "Brass Knuckle" pub in London. Unfortunately, the Brass Knuckle was really the Brass Knocker, Mr. Glencannon thinks it was the Physical Culture Cafe and that's just the beginning of the confusion "At the Sign of the Brass Knuckle."

"The Scot From Scotland Yard" is Constable Belcher, or is it Bellshear? In any case, he courts Mrs. O'Halloran, whom Capt. Ball thinks fancies Mr. Glencannon. Mr. Glencannon is bewildered. He sets out to clear the misunderstanding only to add to it, but, in the end, is best man at the wedding.

Only Mr. Glencannon could mistake a crematorium for a creamery. Summoned there by an old acquaintance in Cape Town, he agrees to take what he thinks are the ashes of his archenemy, MacCrummon, home to the grieving widow. Enroute, the opportunity to turn the funeral urn into a loving cup for Captain Ball, at a profit, of course, is too good a chance to pass up. He soon learns the joke is on him — the ashes held a smuggled diamond, MacCrummon is alive, and he has been duped. Mr. Glencannon laughs all the way to the diamond markets of

Antwerp leaving Captain Ball "The Loving Cup" and MacCrummon a knot on the head.

As always, we have retained the punctuation and spelling of the original stories as much as possible to faithfully reproduce the stories as they were written. A few terms and phrases might not be considered appropriate today, but they, too, have been left in, in the belief that the stories are evocative of their era and can be enjoyed in and of themselves.

So, wrap your hand around a bottle of Duggan's Dew o' Kirkintilloch, moisten the bottom of a tumbler 'til it overflows and stretch your feet before the fire. You're about to embark on a voyage of romance — swashbuckling, derring-do and many misguided affairs of the heart and of friendship. All ahead full!

Walter W. Jaffee
Editor

The Snyke in the Grass

O ver the way from the dockyard on West India Road, Poplar-on-Thames, there stands a house built of red bricks, the mortar between them painted white. Above the doorway swings a sign which bears the likeness of a four-bladed propeller and the legend "The Shipwright's Arms." In a region grown grimy through years of soft-coal soot belched from tall ships marching down to the sea, the place presents a graceful contrast of neatness. Curtains and potted geraniums are in the lower windows, and one of them, in addition, is graced with a beautiful picture. This is a lithograph in full color, suitable for framing, of Robert The Bruce, brandishing a mighty claymore with his left hand and a quart bottle of Duggan's Dew of Kirkintilloch with his right.

It was the lithograph, and not the sign, which caught Mr. Glencannon's eye that day, as relaxing in leisure, he strolled down the street from the yards.

The S.S. *Inchcliffe Castle*, of which he was Chief Engineer, was resting on keel- and bilge-blocks in drydock, there to undergo a much needed refitting. For the nonce, Mr. Glencannon was free to rove as he listed.

"Foosh," he commented, pausing to admire the portrait of the Highland chieftain. "A' braw bit o' art, indeed! 'Tis life-like, lusty and speerited — aye, and altogeether deesairving o' my patronage." Whereupon he pushed open the white-painted door and found himself in a bar parlor neat as a pin, the beer-pump scoured till its brass was as purest gold, and the ranks of glasses on the shelves polished to scintillant crystal. The barmaid was the very personification of scrubbed starched and laundered spruceness, from her spotless linen cuffs to her soap ruddied countenance.

"Gude morning, Muss," said Mr. Glencannon, touching his cap visor. "I'll thank ye for a dollop o' Duggans. Nice weather we're having." And then, as she reached for pitcher and water glass, "Ah, dinna trouble yersel', Muss, dinna trouble yersel' — I'm no' sae extravagant as to dilute my whusky either before or after taking."

"'Before or arfter tyking' . . . lawks!" she giggled. "Just farncy! Oh, ayn't you the comical joker, though?"

"Weel, Muss," said Mr. Glencannon, unfolding to her approbation like a morning glory to the dawn, "I'm widely known as a mon who combines deep weesdom wi' a keen sense o' humor. For instance, another droll way I sometimes put it is to say that if water'll sink a ship, what'll it do to a mon?"

"Oh . . . tee hee," said the barmaid, after an interval of profound pondering. "I tyke it you mean that water sinks ships and drowns men — is that it?"

"Yes, but wait!" chuckled Mr. Glencannon, wrinkling his eyes at the corners and preparing to launch a final and devastating shaft of wit, "Ye've often heard o' drunken men and sound ships, but did ye ever hear o' a sunken mon or a drowned ship? — Haw, Muss, haww! — D'ye get the point? Ye see, I mak' the joke simply by changing the d's and s's."

The humor and ingenuity of this sally appealed so strongly to the barmaid that she screamed with laughter. But at the very crescendo of her outburst, there came a voice from the distances beyond.

"'Ortense!" it said admonishingly. "Remember you're a lydy and that this 'ere is a respectable 'ouse."

In the awkward silence which followed, Mr. Glencannon filled his glass again and glanced apprehensively toward the door.

The Snyke in the Grass 3

"I'm no' sae extravagant as to dilute my whusky either before or after taking."

"It's Aunty," whispered Miss Hortense, busying herself with the bar towel. "She'll not stand for no skylarking with the gempmen, Aunty won't!"

Mr. Glencannon, whose head at that moment happened to be tilted back, found his eyes focused upon a framed document which hung on the wall behind the bar. It was an Excise License, by which permission to sell brewed, fermented and distilled liquors was granted to one Myrtle Bootle, spinster, at 27 West India Road, Poplar-on-Thames, London, E. Though his glass was empty, Mr. Glencannon still held it to his lips. He read the document again, and gave vent to a gusty sigh. His aesthetic soul was touched, for never, never had he encountered a name so lovely, so liquidly lilting, as Myrtle Bootle.

"Myrtle Bootle," he repeated aloud, as though reciting a sonnet. "Bootle . . . Myrtle . . . Myrtle Bootle. . . ."

"Yus," explained Miss Hortense, "My Aunt Myrtle — 'er as owns this pub. 'Ere she comes now."

A purposeful step sounded in the hall. The door opened, and in swept a woman at once ample, majestic, and formidable. Mr. Glencannon, in his admiration, at first likened her to H.M.S. *Iron Duke*; but then, hastily estimating her tonnage, and taking in the full effect of her black satin dress and her necklace of red coral, he revised his decision in favor of the *Aquitania*.

"Good arfternoon, Sir," she said coldly. "Is everything as it should be, 'Ortense dear?" and she fixed barmaid with a piercing gaze.

"Ah, noo, noo, o' course it is!" Mr. Glencannon interceded. "It was only that yere intelligent little niece was so gude as to laugh at some o' my jests and japeries. My name is Glencannon, Muddum. I'm Chief o' the *Inchcliffe Castle*, which is over the way in yon drydock."

"S'trewth, Aunty, it's syme's the gempman says," Hortense confirmed him. "Oh, but 'e's a comic one for fair 'e is!"

"Is 'e indeed?" inquired Miss Bootle, melting a trifle. "Well, in that c'yse I'm very glad to 'ave you as a guest of the 'ouse, Mr. Glencannon. This 'ere's a new plyce, and we welcome tryde, but I do try so 'ard to m'ynt'yne respectability. Arfter orl, it's the decent pubs like this which is the cornerstone o' the British h'Empire, so to s'y, so let's keep 'em so, says I."

"Aye, a vurra comeendable seentiment," agreed Mr. Glencannon, who had been hanging on her words. "Will ye no' sit doon at yon table, Muss Bootle, and honor me by accepting a lemon sqush?"

Miss Bootle was about to decline, but so courtly was Mr. Glencannon's bow as he pulled back the chair that she changed her mind and seated herself.

"A lemming squash would be very refreshink," she said. "Mix it wif splarsh instead of water, 'Ortense dear, and fetch over Mister Glencannon's bottle so's all will be 'andy and convenient." Then, lowering her voice that her niece might not hear, "Do you know," she said, "It's a pleasure, Mister Glencannon, to myke the acq'yntance of a cultured and cultiw'yted gempman like you, arfter orl the waterside riff-rarff that the 'ouse is forced to c'yter to?"

"Ah noo, Muss Bootle, ye're vurra kind," said Mr. Glencannon, blushing.

Myrtle Bootle was blushing, too.

Somewhere out beyond the docks, a passing tugboat hooted a signal — two long blasts and a short one. The barmaid glanced quickly at her aunt, but Miss Bootle seemed not to have heard it. The tugboat blew again, this time petulantly. Then, discouraged, it went snorting on its way down stream.

II

In the smoke-filled depths of the drydock, a gang of men were wielding scaling hammers against the *Inchcliffe Castle's* rusty plates, and a pneumatic rivet gun was singing its staccato song above the general din. It was Bedlam thrice multiplied, with Ypres and Jutland thrown in.

"What's this I hear about Mr. Glencannon?" asked Captain Ball, lighting a cigar and settling himself on the edge of his bunk. "Mister Swales tells' me he's keeping company with a woman or something."

"Mr. Glencannon is? W'y, the ugly Scotch behemoth!" exclaimed Mr. Montgomery, the *Castle's* first officer. "I 'adn't 'eard about it, Sir. 'Oo is she, anyw'y?"

"I don't know, exactly, and that's the trouble," frowned Captain Ball. "They say she's in some pub on West India Road. From what I hear, we're likely to lose him, next trip or the trip after."

"Three cheers for that!" exclaimed Mr. Montgomery, with deep feeling.

"Oh, now, see here!" protested Captain Ball. "I know that you and him are antagonostic, so to say, but you'll have to admit that he's the best engineer 'twixt hell and the Hooghli River. The ship can't spare him, Mister Montgomery. It's your plain juty to break this up and keep him from getting married. That's what I got you in here about."

"Orl right, Sir, orl right, if you s'y so, Sir," said Mr. Montgomery with a grimace. "But I carn't see ow it's any of my business."

Captain Ball raised his eyebrows. "Mister Mate," he said icily, "I've already told you where your juty lays."

"Well," sulked Mr. Montgomery, reaching for his cap. "I'll see wot I can do, Sir, but I mykes no promises."

When the door had closed behind him, he paused for a moment upon the deck. Gradually a purposeful light kindled in his eye, and in his pockets his hands doubled into fists.

"I'll fix 'im!" he muttered. "I'll fix 'im so 'e's fixed for life, and juty be blowed!" Crossing the gangplank to the dry-dock's edge, he headed for West India Road.

The Shipwright's Arms was empty save for a barmaid who wore starched cuffs and a strangely preoccupied mien. As she drew Mr. Montgomery's beer and scraped off the foam with the lather-stick, she emitted a thin, whispery sigh.

"A-ha!" said the Mate to himself. "The young lady's love-sick, that's wot!" And then, aloud, "Nice ply'ce you 'ave 'ere, 'aven't you, Miss — er — Miss . . . ?"

"Miss Bootle," said the barmaid absently, her eyes upon the opposite wall.

"Pleased to myke your acq'yntance, Miss Bootle. I'm Mister Montgomery of the *Inchcliffe Castle*."

At the name, the barmaid almost dropped a glass. "*Inchcliffe Castle?*" she repeated. "Oh, why yus, Mister Montgomery, I've 'eard Mister Glencannon speak of you."

"Oh, Mister Glencannon!" said Mr. Montgomery enthusiastically. "A very charming gempman. 'E's a rare spirit, and

"It's your plain juty to break this up and keep him from getting married."

the brightest man on our ship, Miss; indeed, 'e's probably the grytest engineer on the seven seas tod'y."

At this praise of Mr. Glencannon, Miss Hortense stopped polishing glasses and leaned eagerly on the bar. Mr. Montgomery, warming to his task, waxed eloquent. According to him, the engineer was a paragon of all the manly virtues, and even of those customarily reserved for saints. Miss Hortense drank it all in, though along toward the end, had Mr. Montgomery only observed it, she was swallowing hard. Also, what he mistook for the sparkle of lovelight in her eyes might well have been a rising tide of tears. But he paid for his drink and departed, flattering himself upon a job well done.

"There," he said. "Now I know 'oo she is. And she knows that 'e's the grytest man 'oo ever lived — though of course 'e's told 'er so 'imself. O, I'll 'elp 'er 'ook 'im, I will!"

Meanwhile, Miss Hortense had crossed the room and cautiously pushed open a wicket in the wall through which, upon occasion, drinks could be passed to the private parlor in the rear.

Through the crack she beheld Mr. Glencannon, seated in a red plush morris chair. Miss Myrtle Bootle was massaging his head with Macassar oil, a considerable quantity of which flowed down to lubricate his celluloid collar.

"'E's in 'er clutches," sniffled Miss Hortense, dabbing at the corner of her eye with the bar towel. "It's just the syme as Samson and Delilah. Orl she's arfter is more business for the 'ouse."

". . . Ah, yes, my hair's a wee bit thin on the top, I ken it weel," Mr. Glencannon was saying. "It got blown awa', if ye'll believe me, Muss Bootle, in the course o' the hurricane which deevasted the unhappy island o' Porto Rico in the year Nineteen Hoonderd an' Twunty Seeven. Ah, whoosh, but yon was a feerocious wind! . . ." He groped in his pocket for his pipe, and when he had found it, Miss Bootle playfully captured it, filled it for him, and then held the match until it was gurglingly aglow.

"Oh, you seafaring men do 'ave such thrilling h'experiences!" she said. "I do wish you'd tell orl your friends about our little plyce 'ere, Mister Glencannon, because we're so anxious to attract a good clarss of ship's-orfficer tryde."

"Ship's-orfficer tryde!" muttered Miss Hortense. "W'y, larst week I 'eard 'er telling that tug-boat captain that orl she c'ytered to was river and barge men. And 'im blowing 'is whistle to 'er every time he passes on the river, and 'er wy'ving 'er 'andkercheef to 'im from the upstairs window! . . ."

"I'll mak' a speecial point to tell a' my friends aboot yere vurra genteel establishment," said Mr. Glencannon. "Indeed, ye may deepend upon it. And noo, if ye'll permeet me, I'll endeevor to entertain ye with a little trick which has been accorded univairsal approbation wherever I've pairformed it. — Will ye ha' the goodness to hand me yon soup spoon from the table? — Ah, I'm obliged to ye, Muss Bootle."

With a preliminary flourish, he commenced whacking lustily upon the top of his head with the spoon bowl. He opened or closed his mouth at every beat, a hollow musical sound emerging with each percussion. Gradually the air of "Loch Lomond" took recognizable form, as though played upon a marimba sadly in need of tuning.

With the grand finale, which made up in volume what it lacked in verity, Miss Bootle burst into shrill paeans of praise, and produced from the cupboard a bottle and a glass.

"'Ear, 'ear!" she cried. "'Ave a spot o' this, Mister Musician! It's the Dew of Kirkintilloch, your special favorite. Lawks, lawks, lawks, wot talent! Is there anything that the man can't do!"

"Yus!" sobbed Miss Hortense, silently closing the wicket and burying her face in her apron. "'E can't 'eal my broken 'eart, 'e can't! W'y, only the d'y before yestidd'y, when Aunt Myrtle was in there wif the tug-boat captain, 'e pl'yed Blue Bells O' Scotland wif variations, thumpin' it out on the top of 'is 'ead wif the 'andle of my h'ice pick. 'E said it was only fer me, 'e did! And 'e promised that next time 'e'd show me a trick wif a 'orse 'air and

Through the opening she beheld Mr. Glencannon, seated in a red plush morris chair. Miss Myrtle Bootle was massaging his head with Macassar oil.

'is h'Adams h'apple. — Oh, the g'y deceiver — the 'andsome snyke in the grass!"

III

Work on the *Inchcliffe Castle* was nearing completion. Her officers, instead of going their separate and devious ways ashore each day, were now engaged from dawn till dark in inspection, supervision and direction of the finishing touches of the refit. Glencannon, grease from head to foot, was lording it over a gang of mechanics who were replacing gaskets, pouring bearings and packing stuffing-boxes in the engine room. Mr. Montgomery was in charge on deck, while Mr. Swales, the second officer, his dungarees red with anti-corrosive paint, held forth on the floor of the drydock beneath the *Inchcliffe Castle's* keel.

The night that the dock gates were opened and the *Inchcliffe Castle* was towed downstream to load, Mr. Swales waited upon the Mate in his cabin.

"I s'y, 'ave a look at these," he whispered hoarsely. "But w'yte, we'd better be careful, Sir — 'e might see us, 'e might."

"'Oo might?" asked Mr. Montgomery.

"Mister Glencannon might," said Mr. Swales. "And if 'e did, 'e'd ryse 'ell for fair. Just w'yte till you read 'em!"

Behind closed door and shrouded portholes, Mr. Montgomery examined the sheets of yellow paper which the Second placed before him. "Oh, 'pon my word!" he muttered. "Why, dash it all, Mister Swales, this 'ere beats anything I ever 'eard. Did you read this one?"

> "'I am Glencannon, a son of Neptune
> You are my lydy fair
> Though I roam the seas on juty
> My 'eart is always at 27 West India Road, Poplar,
> With my beautiful Bootle beauty.'"

"Yus, 'orrible, ayn't it?" Mr. Swales shuddered. "And did you notice, Sir, 'e's got 'em orl marked in advance with the nymes of our ports of call for the trip — Lisbon, Gibraltar,

With a preliminary flourish, he commenced whacking lustily upon the top of his head with the spoon bowl.

Genoa, Nyples — ready to post at every stop? But 'e must 'ave 'ad a chynge of 'eart, or 'e wouldn't 'ave thrown 'em aw'y. M'ybe 'is love 'as grown cold."

"M'ybe," growled Mr. Montgomery. "But it's up to us to see that she gets them, orl the syme. With these 'ere pomes fer h'evidence, she can tyke 'im to court for breach of promise, and then 'e'll be 'ooked fer fair. And . . . oh, Lord lumme, Mister Swales, just listen to this:

> "'Fair Lydy Bootle, I greet you from afar
> Glencannon's 'eart is lonely, this dark tempustrious night,
> I pray that you are well, and that the profits from the bar
> Continue satisfactory, also the bottle tryde
> And that the sun is shining bright.'

"There!" he said, thumping the table with his fist. "'Profits from the bar'! Profits is orl 'e's worrying about! 'E thinks she'll inherit that pub some day, so 'e's trying to 'ook 'er for 'er money. This one 'ere is a regular formal proposal . . .

> "'Soon will come the wedding d'y
> And the organ it will tootle
> If only "Yes" you'll s'y
> And consent to chynge your nyme to Glencannon
> Instead of Bootle.'

"— Oh, and underneath, it says, 'To be sung to the air of the Piobaireacbed Cuniha na Cloinne.' Well, I carn't s'y as I knows the tune."

"No, and you wouldn't want to sing it if you did," said Mr. Swales. "I've 'eard Mr. Glencannon fair strangle 'is bagpipes on it."

"Well, this potery by itself is enough to strangle a h'octupus," said Mr. Montgomery. "The point is, now, that we've got to keep the affair at w'ite 'eat, so's she'll be wy'ting for 'im with open arms when we get back. We'll 'ave to send 'er some more of them flowers right aw'y. And meanwhile," he rose and locked the papers in his dresser drawer, "Meanwhile, we'll s'yve these poems for our long-rynge artillery."

IV

Ten weeks had rolled by since the *Inchcliffe Castle* put to sea, and the bar-room of The Shipwright's Arms was filled with smoke and bad language. A full score of alcoholized Scotsmen were gathered at the tables, pounding upon them, scratching matches on their white marble surfaces, and using them as footrests.

"Ye lie, MacFeergus!" one of the Scots was shouting "'Twas no' the tail-shaft o' the *Ayleshire* that bruk, 'twas the crank-pin, and ye know it!"

Mr. MacFergus, piqued, lurched to his feet and took his hand out of his pocket. The hand was garnished with a set of brass-knuckles. "MacCrummon," he said "I fear ye're no gentleman, though I'll domned soon lairn ye how to be one!"

MacCrummon emitted the war cry of his clan, produced a monkey-wrench from his overalls, and stood ready for the attack. But the rest of the company intervened, the belligerents shook hands, and wept copiously upon each other's shoulders.

"Hoot!" shouted somebody. "'Tis time for a drink! Please, Muss, I dinna mean to cavil at the sairvice, but will ye gi' us fresh glasses? These is reekin' feelthy wi' tobacco ashes."

Miss Myrtle Bootle swept into the room and viewed the assemblage with disdain. "Orful, oh, orful, ayn't they, dearie?" she whispered to Miss Hortense. "Are any of them buying anything tod'y?"

"No," said the barmaid. "Not a drop. They brings their own whisky, they does, buying it at 'oles'yle prices by the c'yse, and then they expects the 'ouse to furnish glarsses."

"Humph," sniffed Miss Bootle. "A fine clarss of tryde that Glencannon ruffian brung us! Instead of being a 'igh-gr'yde waterman's pub, the ply'ce 'as turned into a boozing ken for cheap Scotch brawlers."

The loyal Miss Hortense was about to come to Mr. Glencannon's defense when the postman entered and placed two letters upon the bar — letters which bore Italian stamps and the postmark of Naples.

The barmaid flushed and hastily picked them up.

"'Ortense!" said Miss Bootle, ominously. "'And those letters 'ere!"

"Theye're for me, Aunty," said Miss Hortense, her voice trembling. "They're from a girl friend of mine 'oo . . ."

"'Ortense! They're addressed to me— 'Miss Myrtle Bootle.' . . ."

"Well, that one is," Miss Hortense conceded. "But one's for me. Yus, it's for me, and it's from Mister Glencannon, if you must know. From Mister Glencannon! 'E loves me, 'e loves me, 'e loves me so — there!" She stamped her foot and faced her aunt defiantly.

Miss Myrtle Bootle stared as though the girl had gone mad. "Oh, w'y, 'Ortense dearie, you're mistyken," she said pityingly. "It's me that Mister Glencannon pretends to be interested in, and 'e's been sending me pomes from every port, the impudent 'Ighland beast! W'y, ere 'Ortense — Look 'ere, see wot 'e's written to me." And she handed across the slip of paper which she had taken from the envelope.

Through her tears, Miss Hortense read

"Bootle, Bootle,. who loves a Bootle?
'I do,' said Certificated Chief Engineer Glencannon
'If you will wed me, I will be your lifelong vassal,'
Said the Chief Engineer of S. S. *Inchcliffe Castle*."

"Oh, 'orrors!" wailed the barmaid. 'E's been sending them to me, too. Let's see wot 'e 'as wrote me this time . . . Lawks, Aunty — w'y, the snyke in the grass! 'E's wrote us both the very syme thing!"

V

Before long it would be daylight; meanwhile the September sun was struggling its way up through the layers of fog and smoke which lay like a pall over sleeping London. Along the Thames the seagulls mewingly bestirred themselves for the day's duties of scavenging. Over in Limehouse Reach a liner's siren hooted, to be echoed by the throaty roar of an I. & C. freighter casting off from the company's wharf on the Isle of Dogs. Beyond the Millwall Docks a tug-boat churned upstream, her towline sagging back through the gloom to the bow of the *Inchcliffe Castle*, salt-crusted and freshly in from the sea.

Across the stern of the tug, in letters white and new, was painted her name. The name was "*Myrtle B.*"

"Well, tod'y's the d'y 'e gets it in 'is ruddy Scotch neck," chuckled Mr. Montgomery as he was joined upon the bridge by Mr. Swales. "Before long we'll be s'ying good riddance to 'im."

"Yus," agreed the Second Mate. "'E's planning to see 'er, right enough. 'E just now stopped me on my w'y up 'ere to show me a picture of the Juke of York wearing a pearl gr'y bowler. — Arsked me wot I thought of it, as one man of tyste to another."

"A pearl gr'y bowler, only farncy 'im in it!" said the Mate. "W'y, it would be more becoming on a walrus!"

Somewhat later in the morning, Mr. Glencannon retrieved his shore-trousers from beneath the mattress of his bunk, went over his fingernails with a bit of emery cloth, laundered his celluloid collar with a pencil eraser and a damp towel, and waxed the ends of his rather scraggly mustache into points like copper spikes.

"Oh, domn ye, Glencannon!" he exclaimed approvingly to the reflection in the washstand mirror. "Ye're a handsome beast when ye tak' the trouble to groom yoursel'! A-weel, I must be at my best today. Aye," and he nodded his head prophetically. "How deeferunt will be my condeetion and standing when I return to this vurra room tonicht!"

As a matter of fact, his condition upon his return was deplorable, and that he could stand at all was due solely to the friendly support of the *Inchcliffe Castle's* starboard rail. A full moon was bouncing up and down upon the rim of the *Castle's* funnel, and the masts were bowing politely to each other, like partners in the minuet. On Mr. Glencannon's left cheek were four scratches, deep, angry and parallel. Those upon his right cheek, while effective, were a trifle amateurish. But the egg-like bumps on the top of his head were palpably the handiwork of an expert — a tug-boat captain, for example.

"Meestery!" he said sepulchrally, gazing up at the bouncing moon. "Meestery, black meestery indeed! How them dommed pooms I wrote to Myrtle could ha' got to Hortense, too, is fair beyont me. Let's see, noo, let's rehairse the whole sorra business. . . .

"Feerst I composed the pooms in my room, whuch is here. Then I tuk the rough drafts and chucked them over the rail, whuch is still here. They fell into the water, whuch is there. But no!" he beat his brow in sudden inspiration. "The water's there the noo, but it was no' there the then! We was in drydock, so they fell into the bottom o' it."

He paused, chuckled, and politely acknowledged the bow of the main-mast. "Somebody picked them and sent them to Hortense, that's what they did!" he declared. — "Who was it? Ah, Glencannon, there lies the meestery. Ye've either got a mortal eenemy aboard this ship, or else, conseederin' how trade has fallen off in yon pub, ye've got a fromned gude — er, domned frude — no, er, a *domned gude friend.*"

Whereupon he tossed the remains of his pearl grey bowler into the Thames, ripped off his celluloid collar, touched a match to it, and lurched happily to bed.

The Ash Cat

"Ah, gentlemen — I mean to say, good morning!" greeted Captain Ball, beaming in for breakfast, but pausing at the porthole for a breath of the breeze which blew down from the Cyclades. "Great weather, gentlemen — great weather, you must admit it! Blue skies! Blue seas! Yes, they're both blue, if you get my point, though come to look at 'em a second time, they're a bit more purple — well, 'violet,' I s'pose Missis B. would call 'em. The sea, of course, is really a kind of a sea green, as you might say. Oh, it's days like this make a man glad he's alive!"

"Aye," said Mr. Glencannon tonelessly, "the parritch is loompy again."

Mr. Montgomery, the chief officer, snorted within his coffee cup. "Well, 'ammer it flat with the 'eel of yer spoon," he urged. "Good lawks, fer one 'oo calls 'imself a h'engineer, yer stryngely lacking in the ruddements of h'applied science if yer can't h'even cope with lumps in porridge!"

Mr. Glencannon was on the verge of a withering retort, but he changed his mind, shook his head, and slumped dispiritedly in his chair. His walrus mustache, heavily beaded with oatmeal and oleomargarine, was trembling at the fringes.

"Cope!" he repeated in a hollow voice. "Cope! Ah, aloss, captain and gentlemen, if ye but knew what I had to cope wi' i' the bosom o' my ain family! And loomps, did we say! Guid losh, gentlemen, tak' a look at this!"

He depressed his chin, and brushing aside the scraggly locks which artfully concealed the bald spot at the center of his crown, he disclosed a lump like the polished head of a two-inch rivet.

"There," he invited, "gaze upon it, gentlemen and by its omplitude judge the extent o' my chagrin. Gaze, I say, but dinna touch it, for it's sore as the boils o' Job i' Holy Writ!"

"Ah," said Captain Ball, considering the excrescence with the air of a diagnostician. "Ah — oh, yes, a lump. It wasn't Job; it was Lazarus — carbuncles. No, by George, it was Esau! Well, anyway, if that lump was on my head, d'you know what I'd conclude? Heh? Why, I'd conclude that somebody'd smote me, damme if I wouldn't!"

"I've a'ready concluded that somebody smote me," said Mr. Glencannon plaintively. "I' fact, I micht as weel swallow the shred o' pride that remains to me, and admeet that 'twas the theerd engineer. Yes, 'twas Duncan," he sighed. "My ain leetle nephew, my ain flesh and blood! Ne'er did I think when he was a bairn and I used to regale him wi' tales o' my prowess at sea — aye, and sometimes I'd e'en hold a penny oot o' his reach and let him feast his eyes upon it! — ne'er did I think that he'd one day return my tenderness by clouting me ower the head wi' a Stillson wrench!"

"Och, it must be beeter — beeter i'deed!" sympathized Mr. MacQuayle, the second engineer, thoughtfully running his finger across a swelling at the point of his chin. "Yere nephew Duncan is a high-speerited lad, o' that there is no doot!"

"Well, it's a good thing fer 'im that 'e is," declared Mr. Montgomery. "'E 'as a secret sorrow, if yer arsks my h'opinion — been jilted by some fluff in Glasgow, most likely. And besides,

"If that lump was on my head, I'd conclude somebody'd smote me."

Mr. Glencannon, yer orlw'ys picking on the kid. Why don't yer just ferget 'e's yer nephew fer a bit, and remember 'e's the most h'efficient third engineer we ever 'ad? 'E gets three-quarters of a knot more out of the ship orl through 'is watch than h'either of you two!"

"He does," admitted Mr. Glencannon. "He does i'deed. Oh, the lad's eefeecient, as ye say, but vurra much too much so. He reesorts to Spartan meethods, that's the trooble! Why, the stokehold wud be seething i' mutiny this vurra minute if he hadna' poonded the firemen to a heelpless, onreseesting poolp!"

"Well, now, see here," said Captain Ball. "I mean to say, wasn't it exactly such a chap you wanted when you signed him on in Glasgow? Wasn't it you yourself who was bellyaching about how we needed a third who could handle them tough oilers and ash cats — especially that Yankee, Jones, or Kempthorn, or whatever his name is?"

"Radway — aye, ye mean Radway, the Yonkee bruiser. Weel, sir —"

The ship's bell chimed and Mr. MacQuayle sprang to his feet.

"Pairdon me," he said, gulping the last of his coffee. "If I'm a minute late relieving the theerd, he's a'ways vurra annoyed."

Mr. MacQuayle's departure was followed by a tense, expectant silence. Presently, from the distant bowels of the ship, came voices raised in wrath. They were raised higher, higher, and higher. The company stirred uneasily. Suddenly there was a thump, and once more all was silent.

"Weel," mused Mr. Glencannon, "I fear that Muster MacQuayle was late again."

Heavy footfalls approached along the deck. Hastily the steward set a bowl of oatmeal at the vacant place. All heads were turned toward the door. It burst open and admitted a red-haired youth whose chunky contours and florid complexion caused him to look not unlike a side of raw prime beef. He stood glowering at the company with a pair of pale-blue eyes, and licking the skinned knuckle of a fist the size of a calking mallet.

"Ah, guid morning, Duncan m'lad, and how are ye this lovely, lovely day?" inquired Mr. Glencannon, with an avuncular smile too toothy to be quite convincing. "Ah, come, tak' off yer cap, lad. Tak' off yer cap when ye sit ye doon at table!"

"Wun't!" said Duncan, wrapping his hand around his spoon in the purposeful full-fingered manner of one who grasps a bludgeon. "Wun't, so there!"

"Oh, leave him be, do!" urged Mr. Montgomery, in an undertone. "Can't yer 'ear 'e's h'eating?"

Abruptly, the red youth cast down his spoon and ripped his napkin in two. "Dom parritch is loompy again!" he bawled. "Oh, ne'er hae I seen such a floating peegsty as this sorra tub!"

"Tush, Duncan, tush!" Mr. Glencannon scolded him. "Hommer the loomps flot wi' the heel o' yer spoon. Guid losh" — he glanced toward Mr. Montgomery for confirmation — "for one who ca's himself an engineer, ye're sodly locking i' the ruddiments o' applied science if ye canna' e'en cope wi' loomps i' parritch!"

"Oh, dinna worrit yersel' aboot what I can cope wi'!" growled Duncan, disclosing two front teeth like those of a squirrel. "I'll thank ye to mind yer ain business, Uncle Colin, though t'was a lucky day for you when I shipped aboord this ark to show ye how!"

Mr. Glencannon winced, sighed, and unfolded *The Presbyterian Churchman*. Mr. Montgomery chuckled and lighted his pipe. Captain Ball, feeling Duncan Glencannon's cold gaze upon him, arose, mumbled something to the effect that it might be stormy later, but in these latitudes you never could tell, and retreated toward the bridge.

The porridge consumed, lumps notwithstanding, Duncan sat back in scowling rumination. Absently, and without effort, he tied a double knot in the handle of a fork and pinched the sides of the loop together between his teeth.

"Why, strike me green," said Mr. Montgomery to himself. "'E 'as the strength of a pole-h'ox. If 'e was my nephew, which thank 'eavens 'e ayn't, I'd match 'im to fight Smelling or Carneria, and live at h'ease orff the bleddy profits."

There was a sound, "tsick," and Duncan's upper lip twitched with the rapidity of a winking eyelid. Simultaneously a cockroach which had been scurrying up the opposite bulkhead let go all holds and toppled backward to the carpet, like a Pathan hillman sniped from a cliff in the Khyber Pass.

Intrigued by the phenomenon, Mr. Montgomery peered first at the cockroach, which seemed moist and indignant, and then at Duncan. The youngster's face was as blankly sullen as ever as, steeped in reverie, he followed the gyrations of a fly around the lamp overhead. Again there was a "tsick," a flicker of the lip, and the fly went down in a tailspin.

"Lawks!" exclaimed Mr. Montgomery, in boundless admiration, "Orl Quiet on the Western Front, wot? Why, gor blyme if I ever seen the like! I wish yer'd spend a spare h'evening in my room, Mr. Duncan, practicing yer marksmanship on the crimson ramblers I've got in there!"

"Twud avail nowt," said Duncan, gloomily, and it was apparent that his mind was on other things. "If they're anything lik' the breed o' beetles that infests my ain mean cubicle, they're armored and water-pruff. 'Twas only last nicht that I captured the stallion o' the herd, harnessed him up, and made him run a new string i' the breeks o' my pyjamas."

Mr. Glencannon looked sternly at his nephew over the top of *The Presbyterian Churchman*. "Foosh, lad!" he admonished.

"Spare us the feegments o' yere callow imogination! Since when has a Glencannon tuk to wearing pyjamas?"

II

It was a bright, moonlit night, with a sea which heaved gently to the swell of a distant storm. Elbows on rail and chin in hands, Mr. Glencannon gazed down in melancholy thought at the black pools of shadow on the after well-deck. Occasional gusts of wind, whisking across the funnel, bore flurries of warm cinders which pattered unheeded against the back of his neck.

"Losh, what cud hae come ower him?" he mused. "He was docile as a shorn mutton till he found there were no letters waiting for him at Brindisi. But e'er since then —" Tenderly, reverently even, he slid his hand up under his cap and fingered several new lumps on his skull.

"'Tis a boffling problem!" he declared. "How i' the world to get reed o' him? Aye, for no motter, how I get reed o' him, the news o' it will gae the roonds o' the family i' Scotland and mak' me oot the blackest scoondrel that e'er drew breath wi' the scent o' whusky on it!"

A lone figure appeared upon the deck below — a man who bore a bucket in one hand and a cake of soap in the other. This person removed his shirt, spread it upon the tarpaulin cover of the hatch, and set about laundering it. Having soaped the garment thoroughly, he sloshed it with water and broke into song:

> *"Oh, my gal she's a big gal,*
> *My gal weighs a ton;*
> *You c'n betcher shoit*
> *She's a big-time skoit —"*

"She is, is she?" came a snarl from the darkness. "Weel, ye braying Yonkee scut, what d'ye mean by sneaking up here when it's yere watch below?"

A flashlight clicked to life, revealing the soot-smeared ash cat, Radway, and the irate third engineer. Their chins were very close together, jutting ominously.

"Whurra," whispered Mr. Glencannon, gripping the rail. "I'm aboot to wutness stark dromma!"

Radway met Duncan's gaze and seemed scornfully amused by it. Languidly he lifted a corner of his neck rag to wipe the coal dust from his face, in so doing disclosing tattooed upon his chest a beautiful scroll supported by two overstuffed cupids, and bearing the words:

KISS ME, GERALDINE; I'M A LOLLYPOP!

The name "Geraldine," however, had been canceled with a tattooed line, and Annie-Marie pricked in below it, outside the scroll. Annie-Marie was succeeded by Hildegarde; Hildegarde by Edna; Edna by Conchita; Conchita by three Chinese ladies, one Russian, and sundry whose names were limned in Arabic, Greek, and the quaint symbols of obscure exotic tongues.

The latest and sole uncanceled enamorata was registered in the abdominal region, due east of the umbilicus. Her name was written in romantic script, with many a flourish and curlicue. Its effect upon Duncan was terrific.

"Put on yere shirt!" he roared. "I dinna ken the exoct meaning o' this, but I'll no' permeet ye flaunting yere Yonkee amours aroond the ship while I'm aboord! Put on yere shirt before I clout ye, ye runagate!"

"Horse feathers!" said Radway calmly, but at the same time picking up his bucket and swinging it tentatively by the handle. "Horse feathers! As fer me bein' here on deck, there's pressure in all my boilers, as you'd of seen if you'd looked at the gauges. As fer me puttin' on my shoit, I'll put it on when it's dry and not before. As fer you takin' a sock at me with that wrench you got in yer hand, well, you better hadn't, buddy — you soint'nly better hadn't! Now, scram below, you bum Scotch joke, before I crown yer with this bucket."

Though Radway's voice was never raised and never did the smile leave his face, there was about him something that promised mauling and mayhem. Perhaps it was the manner in which he swung his bucket, or the canine curl assumed by his lip; in any case, Duncan retreated a pace.

"Radway," he said, his voice trembling and his shoulders hunched up to his ears — "Radway, I cud hae ye i' irons for mutiny ower this, but I willna. This is pairsonal betwixt us, ye gowk! I've loathed ye fra the vurra feerst minute I set eyes on ye i' Glesga. But, great swith, when my time comes to fix ye, I'll fix ye so ye'll stay fixed!"

"Horse feathers," said Radway again. He strolled across the deck and went about tying his shirt to a stay. Snorting in defeat, Duncan retired into the entrance of the alleyway.

Suddenly an idea came to Mr. Glencannon, and simultaneously a great peace descended upon him. "Whurra!" he chuckled. "Here is the end o' my troobles! Radway is the een-strument o' my deleeverance! . . . Ps-st, Radway! Stup up here — stup up here, lad! . . . How'd ye lik' to mak' ten poonds?"

III

Three miles ahead through the heat haze of the September

"When my time comes I'll fix ye so ye'll stay fixed!"

forenoon, Port Said lay baking on its sand spit — a strip of land so low that the cluster of buildings seemed to be floating in the sea. A grove of masts and funnels rose from the basins of the inner harbor, while outside, between the main channel and the shoal water within the jetties, two ragged ranks of tramps sweltered at their moorings.

Ordinarily, the Suez Canal Company so orders things that traffic flows steadily through its highly profitable ditch, but now, despite the imperious gesture of giant bronze De Lesseps, who, from his pedestal on the Western Mole, stood pointing a verdigris-coated finger toward the desert, the port was congested. This was strange.

One of the company's motor boats came lancing out of the Ismail Basin, and Mr. Montgomery, assuming that it bore the pilot who would guide the *Inchcliffe Castle* down to the Red Sea, shoved the telegraph over to "stop." The whurr-rum, whurr-rum of the engines gave way to silence broken only by the diminishing swish and tumble of the bow wave and the sibilant seething of the wake. She came to a standstill, swaying gently, and a gust of heat poured up out of her, as though she was heaving a sigh that her labors were ended.

"Op the bridge, there!" hailed the motorboat. "Are you stopping, to coal, or were you planning to go straight through?"

"Going straight through!" replied Captain Ball between cupped hands.

The gentleman in the boat consulted a notebook, scribbled something and glanced at his watch. "No, captain," he called, "I'm afraid you're not going straight through."

"Why ain't I going straight through?" demanded Captain Ball, leaning over the dodger, loosening his collar, and preparing for debate. "I mean to say, who says I ain't going straight through?"

"I do," replied the official, very cool in his whites and helmet. "Now just keep your hair on, captain; there's really no use elocuting. There's a Jap tramp down by the head and aground crossways in the narrow stretch this side of Timsah. She took a sheer and rammed one of our dredgers yesterday morning. We'll have her clear by tonight, but meanwhile we're all choked up both ways. So just follow me over to that end mooring, pass up your line and we'll make you fast. I'll thank you to have steam for our pilot at 1:45 A.M. tomorrow."

"Weel," remarked Mr. Glencannon, who had been listening to this colloquy, "'twill be hotter than heel lying here at anchor, and 'twull be hotter than heel's dry thrust bearings going through the ditch. Therefore, Muster MacQuayle, I shall arrange wi' Captain Ball aboot shore leave for some o' the freely pairspeering engineering deevision. And besides" — he lowered his voice and moved closer — "Besides, what better chonce cud we hae for letting Radway attend to Duncan?"

A blissful smile suffused the other's countenance. "Losh!" he sighed, half closing his eyes, "I ne'er dared hope it cud be monaged until we got to Aden. And noo — and noo, to think that we'll be quit o' the brick-topped deevil this vurra nicht! 'Tis too guid to be true, Muster Glencannon — too guid to be true!"

"Weel, we'll see!" said Mr. Glencannon, chuckling confidently. "Radway is a mon o' great reesoorce, wi' a grosping nature where money is consairned. He has e'en inseested that I pay him in advance."

"Aye, he's grosping, lik' a' the Yonkees," agreed Mr. MacQuayle righteously.

It was a long hot pull to the Ismail Basin, and Mr. Glencannon, in charge of the boat, observed that the members of his command appeared extremely thirsty. Duncan observed it, too, and when they had made fast to the wharf, he arose in the stern sheets and delivered a brief address. He touched upon the ugliness, slothfulness, and dishonesty of those present, especially of Radway. He warned them against insobriety and the sinful pitfalls of Port Said, although he realized that with their very advent the city was polluted beyond its previous foulest. He wound up with a promise to deal personally with any man failing to be on the wharf at sharp midnight and a reminder that a ten-inch spanner — Exhibit A — was at once hard, heavy and hurtful.

"Ye're harsh wi' the lads, Duncan — vurra harsh i'deed," his uncle chided him. "Why, there's some o' them, lik' Radway, for instance, that wud ornament any stokehold."

At the mention of Radway's name, Duncan bristled. "Ornament!" he repeated scornfully. "When ye talk lak' that, Uncle Colin, I ken better than ever that there's no foo' lik' an auld foo'. And noo I'll respectfully osk ye to gae alang aboot yere business and no' ruin my enjoyment o' Port Said wi' yere odious preesence."

He clambered out of the boat and proceeded along the Rue Sultan Osman, hands in pockets and shoulders moodily hunched. From time to time, as particularly rankling thoughts passed through his mind, he swung out his elbows and knocked Arabs into the gutter. At a discreet distance behind him walked the Yankee ash cat, Radway.

IV

Even under normal conditions Port Said is a city of boisterous nights, but now, due to the accident in the Canal, the place was jammed with a horde of thirsty celebrants who talked, shouted and sang in the manifold tongues of Babel, who drank an international variety of liquors such as could be duplicated only in a New York speakeasy, and who fought with characteristic folk weapons which ranged from bricks and booted feet to crooked daggers and silken strangling cords.

By nine o'clock there had been several minor riots. By ten, an impatient customer had set fire to Simon Arzt's department store. Thereafter, pistol bullets shattered a window of the Hotel de la Poste, a stabbing occurred across the street from the Greek Church, and three Lascar deck hands were thrown off a balcony in the Rue el Tegara. The police took to patrolling in pairs, their holster flaps unbuttoned.

Shortly before midnight there was a general movement toward the water front, and boat after boat put off into the harbor with its roistering cargo. The Canal was open now and a procession of ships was sliding through. Mr. Glencannon, strolling along the Quai Francis Joseph on his way to the landing, paused on the fringe of a crowd gathered around an Arab who was seated on a rug.

"*Hi-gulla-gulla-gulla!*" the Arab was crying. "Hi, gentlemans, do look! I make snake to dance. Very great trick, gentlemans; do for sixpence."

A little boy came through the crowd collecting money, so Mr. Glencannon felt that it was time to depart. Suddenly spying Duncan and Radway at opposite sides of the group, he changed his mind and remained.

"Deary me," he muttered, glancing at his watch, "it's quarter to tweelve. I dinna ken how Radway plans to do it, but he'll hae to do it soon. I wonder cud it be that Duncan suspects something and is behaving wary?"

"*Gulla-gulla-gulla!*" the Arab was repeating. "Do look, do look, do look!"

He made magic passes over the top of a basket on either side of which candles flickered in bright tin reflectors. Kneeling, he played a series of languourous discords upon a flute. At first there were no developments. Then sounds of life emerged from the depths of the basket. It joggled slightly. It rocked upon its base. The music became shrill, its tempo wild. Evidently, something was about to happen. A tense murmur rose from the crowd.

"Tsick" came a sound from somewhere, and, with a sizzle, the right-hand candle went out. The music stopped. Mumbling to himself, the conjuror rekindled the flame with a patent cigarette lighter, and then, the spell being broken, he repeated the opening strains of his tune. Again there was a rustling in the basket; again it joggled, rocked upon its base. Once more the music soared to crescendo. Soon, any second now —

"Tsick." The candle on the left blinked out as though snuffed by a bullet in a shooting gallery. Petulantly the Arab cast down his flute, spread his palms, and searched the sky for rain clouds.

"'Ere, you!" came a menacing voice from the audience. "Are we going to see yer ruddy snyke perform, or are we going to 'ave to tie it around yer ugly neck for yer?"

"*Hi-gulla-gulla-gulla!*" — the formula was delivered half-heartedly. "Just one minutes, gentlemans, and Mohammed make snake do very fine dance, wait see. *Gulla-gulla-hi-i—*"

This time there was no interruption. The snake — a sizable cobra — oozed up out of the basket, slid to the center of the rug, and reared half its length upright. Then, in time with the music, it swayed from side to side. On the third sway, however, there came the familiar faintly audible "tsick" The reptile ducked. Again — "tsick" — and it shook its head angrily. "Tsick." The cobra expanded its hood, and in the petulant manner of a prima donna whose efforts have gone unappreciated, writhed back into its basket, where it lay sulking.

An angry growl came from the crowd. There was a menacing surge toward the Arab.

"Now wait a minute, fellers" — it was Radway speaking. "Don't mussin' up the poor old nigger. It ain't his fault. It was this red-headed guy that crabbed the act, and you c'n just watch me take a sock at him."

"Aye, let's see ye!" Duncan accepted the challenge. "I'll show ye who's red-headed, ye blathering, tattooed, lolly-what-ye-m'call-it!"

There was a lively exchange of blows. The crowd, which had milled for an instant, opened up into a ring. Mr. Glencannon slipped away from the scene of strife and hurried across to the landing. It lacked five minutes of midnight, but all hands were waiting in the boat.

"Cast off!" he ordered. As they rounded the end of the basin, he heard police whistles, shouts, and the scurry of feet. Beneath the bright lights of the landing stage, he saw three policemen take up station as though intending to stay for the night.

"Weel," he chuckled, "even if he had a boat, he cud no' get past yon constables. I'm sorra for Radway, but he's airned his ten poonds."

V

Cut off from the Canal water front and with the police on their heels, Duncan and Radway fled side by side through the back streets of the town. Their feud was temporarily forgotten in a common anxiety to keep out of jail. When at length the sounds of pursuit had died away, they stood panting on the dark, deserted beach beyond the Western Mole.

"Weel, ye scut," said the engineer, "a heel o' a mess ye got the twa o' us into the noo! 'Tis after midnicht, and if either o' us shows his face at the boat landing, the police'll nab us sure. There's nowt for it but to swim oot to the ship."

"Swim?" repeated Radway. "Unh-uh, buddy; nope, not me! I can't swim a stroke. Let's walk along here a ways and see if we can't swipe a boat."

"No," said Duncan, putting his watch and money into his cap and stooping to unlace his shoes, "I'll no' chance being nabbed for boat stealing. I prefair to swim, but" — he leered vindictively — "I'll write and tell Winnie where I last saw ye!"

"Write who?" asked Radway.

"Winnie, that's who," said Duncan. "Yes, Winnie MacBeith, barmaid o' the Royal James, i' Wallace Road, Glesga. Aye, pairhops this will be a lesson to ye no' to gae aboot the world interfering wi' other people's love affairs!"

Radway considered him perplexedly. "Say, what're you talkin' about, anyhow?" he asked. "I don't know nobody in Glasgow excep' the police magistrate."

Duncan drew a quick breath. "D'ye mean it?" he asked eagerly, "D'ye mean it? But here" — he struck a match — "pull up yere shirt, mon — pull up yere shirt!" He held the flickering flame at the base of the tattooed column. "Minnie!" he exclaimed — "Minnie! Guid losh, it is no' Winnie after a'!"

"Yair, sure; Minnie Dillenbacher, a frail in San Diego," said Radway. "You must of read it wrong that other time on account of a wrinkle or something."

Duncan sat down in the sand and gave himself over to deep meditation. "Radway," he said at last, "ye've lifted a weight fra' my mind, and I foncy that, after a', it's no more than my Christian juty to get ye back to the ship. Therefore, I'll help ye steal a boat."

"You mean yer'll stick with me?" exclaimed Radway joyfully. "Well, well, well, 'at-a-kid! Oh, I knew you was a white man right along!"

"Tsick," said Duncan noncommittally.

A quarter of a mile farther down the shore they came upon a fishing boat, drawn up perhaps six feet above the water's edge, and unsecured save by a long line tied around a telegraph pole on the road above the beach. It was a sturdy tub and broad of beam, so heavy that the pair were unable to budge it. They peeled off their jackets, pushed, hauled, sweated and swore but all to no avail.

Suddenly Duncan ceased his efforts and pointed toward the water.

"Swith!" he said, "what a pair o' dullards we are! Why, look ye, Radway; another few minutes and the tide will rise and float it clear. Do ye just go back to yon teelegroph pole and cast off the line, and we'll sit us doon to wait."

VI

It was 1:43 A. M. Steam was blowing off through the *Inchcliffe Castle*'s main exhaust and the pilot was on the bridge.

Stepping into his carpet slippers, Mr. Glencannon made his way toward the engine room to exchange congratulations with Mr. MacQuayle, who would be standing the absent Duncan's watch. His heart was light, and as he started down the slippery iron ladder he hummed a little tune.

He heard the telegraph sound for "stand by," and he leaned over to wave at Mr. MacQuayle on the platform below. Mr. MacQuayle was not there.

"Duncan!" gasped Mr. Glencannon, grasping the handrail for support. "Duncan!"

"Aye, ye treacherous auld hoond!" said Duncan, who was dripping wet, but quite evidently pleased with himself. "As ye see, ye've lost the ten poonds which I owerheard ye paying Radway to mak' me lose the ship, and which he had the bad judgment to leave i' his coat when I sent him to ontie a rope. Weel — tsick — the moneys still i' the family, if that's any consolation to ye!"

The telegraph rang "slow ahead." and Duncan let steam into the cylinders.

"I prefair to swim, but" — *he leered vindictively* — *"I'll write and tell Winnie where I last saw ye!"*

"And — and what aboot Radway?" asked Mr. Glencannon, in a voice that was husky and strange. "Where is he?"

"Weel," chuckled Duncan, "the last I saw o' him as I swum aroond the end o' the breakwater, he was sitting i' a rowboat, waiting for the tide to rise."

"Waiting for the tide to rise!" repeated Mr. Glencannon. "Why, guid losh, lad, dinna ye ken that there's no such thing as tide in the Mediterranean Sea?"

"Sartainly I do," said Duncan, responding to the signal for half speed ahead. "And just aboot noo, yere friend Muster Ash Cat Radway will be making the deescovery for himsel'."

A Nosegay for Mr. Montgomery

Sir John Castle, chairman of the board of Clifford, Castle & Co., Ltd., shipowners, opened his eyes with an effort and gazed about him. His surroundings seemed vaguely familiar, and again they didn't, and yet again they did.

The room, he thought, might well be his own private office, provided of course, that it wasn't somebody else's. Possession was nine points of the law and all that, but the main point was, who possessed it?

"Who possesses what?" he asked himself aloud. "If you mean this headache, I possess it. But I don't mean the headache, old boy. I mean the office. But — but just exactly who are you anyway? He produced a gold-edged satin cardcase from his pocket and scattered its contents upon the floor. "Singular!" he muttered, scanning the little white oblongs. "So, I'm Sir John Castle, eh? Well, it's a small world, a small world! Just fancy my being here in my own office at this unearthly hour! Efficiency, what? Got to step things up, these days! . . . If you'll, just sit down there a minute, old fellow, I'll dictate a memorandum to you, Miss Melcher, and then we'll all nip out and snaffle a bit of an eye opener, what say, old bean? After that, tallyho for a Turkish bath!"

"I begs yer pardon, sir," came an admonishing voice from out the encircling gloom. "I ain't Miss Melcher at orl; I'm Missus O'Halloran, the char lydy, and I mykes bold to say that yer behyving like a bally idjit, with yer dress suit on and lipstick smeared orl over yer shirt front and that silly pink-pyper sunbonnet on yer 'ead and orl! Yus, an idjit, Sir John, and I don't 'esityte to tell yer so right to yer 'andsome disserpyted young fyce!"

Sir John Castle squinted painfully across something that was probably a desk and descried a black mountain looming beyond it. The mountain stood with its hands upon its hips, one of them clutching a broom and the other a dustpan.

"Ah, cheerio, Mrs. O'Halloran!" he greeted her. "What are you doing for tea this afterer — er — no, no, of course not! What I really want to ask you, Mrs. O'Halloran — what time is it?"

"It's 'arf-parst eight, and scarcely that," said Mrs. O'Halloran. "'Arf-parst eight in the morning — that is, in case there's any doubt abaht it. The morning of September the second."

"Ah," mused Sir John, "half-past eight in the morning! Extraordinary! 'Early to bed and early to rise,' what? Early worms and all that! I say, you know, I really must dictate a memorandum to Hazlitt about this! Something inspirational! Brimming over with constructive ideas to increase efficiency of business, understand? Must give off, see what I mean? Ready, Miss Melcher?"

"Now wyte!" said Mrs. O'Halloran. "Miss Melcher ain't 'ere and the orffice ain't even open yet, so I suppose you wandered in with yer pass key. But lawks knows I'm the larst lydy in the world to argue with a gempman in your condition, arfter the hexperiences I used to 'ave with my lyte 'usband, Gord rest 'is rotten soul! If yer'll just 'old on a minute, Sir

John, I'll wheel in Mr. 'Azlitt's helectric stenophone and connect it up for yer, and then yer can dictyte to yer 'eart's content, or even recite The Charge o' the Light Brigyde, fer orl I gives a 'ang!"

"Ah, capital!" said Sir John. "Most efficient woman. Mrs. O'Halloran!"

Thus it came about that an hour later, fussy old Mr. Virgil Hazlitt, the company's managing director, found upon his desk the following memorandum translated and typed by Miss Melcher from a curiously garbled record which she had found in the stenophone:

> From: Sir John Castle
> To: Mr. V. Hazlitt
> Subject: Efficiency
>
> In this period of depression we are compelled as never before to increase efficiency in all departments. Now, a Department, so-called, is merely a group of men, and the efficiency of the whole can be measured by that of its component individuals. Thus, the consumption of alcoholic beverages is to be deplored.
>
> I wish that you would send a form letter to the captains of all our twenty-three ships, directing them to announce that a 10 cent bonus, figured on a year's pay, will be awarded to that officer on board each vessel who, in the captain's judgement, shall have performed his duties most efficiently and set the best example of diligence and conduct to his associates throughout the remainder of the current year.
>
> I am certain that you will see the merit in the scheme, even as roughly outlined here, and will work out the details of its operation. Please send off the letter without delay.

Mr. Hazlitt put on a pair of spectacles in addition to the *pince nez* which already adorned his knifelike nose, and read the memorandum again.

"By gad, it's a good scheme — a capital scheme!" he muttered. "Why didn't I think of it myself? But — but how in the world did Sir John Castle ever happen to think of it? Sir John, Sir John of all people!"

Ever since the death of old Sir Philip Castle, twenty-three years before, Mr. Hazlitt had conducted the complex affairs of Clifford, Castle & Company, Ltd., practically unaided. To receive a constructive suggestion from the founder's sporting heir was like discovering a pearl in a pickled oyster. It was extraordinary. It was astounding. It was phenomenal.

"Well, well, well," he smiled, rubbing his scrawny blue-veined hands. "Can it be that the confounded young rake is finally taking an interest in things? Can it be that he himself is becoming efficient? Why, good heavens!" he glanced at his watch. "Here it is scarcely half-past nine, but he's been in and dictated this memorandum already! Excellent! Oh, excellent! . . . Miss Melcher! Ah, I say, Miss Melcher, just sit down and take a letter, to the captains of all the ships, addressed care our agents, first catchable port of call. Er — let's see now-ahem! . . ."

II

The noon meal was finished and Mr. Montgomery, first mate of the S.S. *Inchcliffe Castle*, rose from his place at the table, strolled to the porthole and dreamily considered the squat and squalid chimney pots of Limehouse which clustered like sooty gnomes in the lower wisps of the December fog. "Ah. London!" he mused aloud, fumbling for a toothpick in the pocket of his natty shore-going serge and, having found it, putting it pensively to use. "Dear old — Phit! — London! Ah, well, London Town is orlways 'ome, sweet — Tsik! — 'ome to me, fer 'ome is where the 'eart is! . . . I say, Captain Ball, with yer kind permission, I'll just nip ashore this afternoon and discharge a few of my social hobligations."

"Social obligations?" chortled Mr. Glencannon, the chief engineer. "Social obligations, did ye say? Swith, muster mate, the visiting hours in the London jails are from nine till eleven in the morning, so if ye're plonning to mak' a roond o' calls, I fear ye're a wee bit late!"

Mr. Montgomery turned and considered the speaker with a distaste which had in it something of patronage. "Oh, thank yer, Mr. Glencannon!" he retorted, patting the knot of his salmon-pink necktie. "Thank yer very kindly indeed! But really, I 'aven't no slightest hintention of looking up none of yer relatives, because I see quite enough of yer ruddy family right 'ere on board this ship!" Nodding to Captain Ball with the satisfied smirk of a man who has turned the laugh upon a heckler, he thrust the toothpick into the band of his bowler at a fashionable angle and took his departure shorewards.

"A-weel," said Mr. Glencannon, gazing after him and shaking his head sadly, "yon parting shot o' his was really no' much o' a comeback, and I fear the mon's mind is slipping. Losh gentlemen, I can weel remeember the time when a barbed shaft o' wit such as I just noo launched at him wud hae druv him poorple with rage and made him froth at the mouth. I wonder —"

"Oh, by the bye, 'e's bought 'imself a teethbrush!" interrupted Mr. Swales. "A teethbrush with a pink celluloid 'andle, now wot the 'ell do yer know about that?"

"Yus, and 'e's bought 'imself a fresh pair of socks too," declared young Mr. Levy, the wireless operator. "Tell yer wot, gempmen; do yer know wot' I think? Do yer really want to know wot I think? Well, I think Mr. Montgomery is keeping company with a lydy, that's wot I think!"

Captain Ball adjusted his paunch against the edge of the table and smiled a benignant smile. "Er — kerhuff, kerhum," he said, "Well, I mean to say, I shouldn't wonder if Mr. Levy ain't right. Oh, I've been noticing the signs myself for the past month or two, kind of — like — well, I mean you take when a chap takes to shaving every day when he's at sea, see what I mean, and always cleaning out his finger nails very neat and careful — with his fork before he starts to eat at mealtimes — why, then, I mean to say, it's a pretty, safe sign to *shushy le femme*, as our French cousins so navally put it."

"Ah, noo, noo, sir!" protested Mr. Glencannon, blushing. "I fear ye're doing him an injustice when ye go as far as that! Mysel', I loathe the fellow, and I'll put my mark on him yet, but I wudna impugn his morals, e'en though he is a teetotaler. No, Captain Ball, I think ye're needlessly harsh. I believe Muster Levy is richt and that the puir, deluded gowk has sumply fallen la love."

"Well — ker-huff — what do you mean to say you thought I meant to say?" demanded Captain Ball testily. "All I mean to say is that Mr. Montgomery is in love and I wish him luck. Yes, gentlemen, I hope he marries her, whoever she is, that's precisely what I hope! He's a good, steady chap with a sterling character, Mr. Montgomery is, and happily married, he'll set an even finer example than usual to some other people, I might mention aboard this here ship!" He glared at Mr. Glencannon, but the engineer's gaze was directed toward the ceiling.

"Aye, captain," he agreed, nodding at the lamp, "motrimony is a vurra laudable activity for all o' us who gae doon to the sea in ships, and it has always been a source o' bitter chagrin to me that I've ne'er found a lady o' the fair sex that I cud conscientiously say was worthy o' me. But o' coorse there's others more fortunate lik' Carstairs, o' the *Hardcliffe Castle*, who has a wife in Auckland one in Oslo, and another in Milford Haven. Aye, and the time I met him — in Samarang, it was — he said 'Congrotulate me, Glencannon, I'm aboot to become a benedict!'"

"Ah, there you have it exackly!" said Captain Ball, puffing out his cheeks and preparing to take his departure. "That's why I say I hope from the very heart of — er — no, wait — from the very bottom of my heart that Mr. Montgomery will press his suit — er — no, no, what I mean is, I trust he'll woo and win her, if you gather my meaning! Yes" — he paused at the door and stood brushing the crumbs from the upper slope of his abdominal drumlin — "yes, like I said before, he'd serve as an even more shining example to some of the rest of you I could happen to name!"

This time his remark was so accurately directed that Mr. Glencannon could not ignore its personal application, but before he could summon words with which to refute it, Captain Ball had stepped out on deck.

"Oh, why, dearie me, and did ye hear that?" he appealed to the company. "Only foncy that scut o' a Montgomery sairving as an exomple to a mon lik' me, which is plainly another way o' saying that Captain Ball intends to recommend him for that 10 percent bonus! Ho, domme, gentlemen, I dinna care if he marries all the merry widows o' Windsor, I'll no' soobmit tamely to a humiliation lik' this! Why, 'tis bad enough to hae to be shipmates with the sniveling, sonctimonious, sneaking teetotaler!" And warming to his subject, Mr. Glencannon recounted the history of his feud with the mate, accompanying his hymn of hate with impassioned gestures.

The dissertation wound on and on. At first the audience nodded politely, then they yawned, and finally, one by one, they tiptoed from the room. Mr. Glencannon, in the midst of a demonstration of how he would one day grasp Mr. Montgomery by the gullet, wring him out like a rag, hurl the cadaver to the deck and there jump upon it with both feet at once, paused dramatically to discover that, save for Jessup, the steward, he was addressing the empty air.

"Beg pardon, sir," said Jessup, diffidently flicking his dish towel, "I'll just clear orff the tyble, sir, so's yer'll 'ave more helbow room to thrash about in."

Mr. Glencannon grunted, relaxed, and settled into a chair. From his pocket he jerked a copy of *The Presbyterian Churchman* spread it out before him and scowled unseeingly at its contents. "Munstrous!" he muttered. "Him as an exomple! Munstrous!"

After a time his wrathful musings were interrupted by a knock at the door, and there entered a boy from the owners' offices bearing the ship's mail. "Ah, thonk ye, lad, thonk ye!" said Mr. Glencannon. "Ye can leave it richt here with me. I'd give ye a saxpunce, my brave little mon, but I left all my siller in my other unifurm, so I'll merely bid ye a vurra guid day. . . . H'm" — he turned to the mail — "here's three for Captain Ball — bills by the look o' them — and a couple for Hughes, and this week's *Churchman* for mysel', and *The Sporting Mirror and Turf News* for Muster Levy, and — Oh, ho!" He picked up a waxsealed, oblong packet addressed to Mr. Montgomery. "What in the heel d'ye suppose he's gone and bocht himsel' the noo? It comes from the Apollo Corporation, Limited, whoe'er the Apollo Corporation, Limited may be. Well" — he glanced around him stealthily, slipped the package into his pocket and made for the door — "there'll be no harm in taking a bit o' a look."

In the privacy of his room he very carefully sliced loose the seals with a razor blade, opened one end of the wrapping, and drew forth a little wooden box labeled:

THE APOLLO BEAUTYSLEEP NASAL MOLD
(RADIOACTIVE)

Inside was a circular illustrated with photographic profiles of ladies and gentlemen equipped with noses of every conceivable form, ranging from the slim, high-pressure jet to the blunt, heavy-duty nozzle. Some were duck-billed, others were drawn out to a point like a curlew, a few were snouted even as the boar which roams the wildwood, while one — his caption read "Mr. X. a prominent business man of Liverpool," — appeared to be a cross between a Mexican parrot and a Bactrian camel. All in all, the countenances were such as one sees in old Flemish prints of the demoniac revels of Walpurgis Night and they were ideally calculated to sour vinegar. According to the circular, however, each and every one of these deplorable proboscides had been transformed into an object of breath-taking beauty by the Apollo Beautysleep Nasal Mold — which, said the manufacturers, had been constructed "according to meticulous micrometric measurements taken from the nose of the actual world-famous Grecian statue of the Apollo Belvedere. The Apollo Beautysleep Nasal Mold is not to be confused with numerous inferior imitations being offered by unscrupulous manufacturers. Only the genuine Apollo contains the patented Inhalo-Pad, impregnated with a secret radioactive compound which, when inhaled by the wearer, softens the internal tissues of the nose and permits them to be gently but firmly molded into perfect classical contours."

"Ah, guid losh!" gasped Mr. Glencannon, expectorating at the porthole and missing it by the scantiest of margins, "to what ossinine lengths will his vanity lead the lout!" From the box he produced a cuplike aluminum contrivance with straps, somewhat resembling a Rugby-football nose guard. The lower portion of this gadget — the region which would cover the nostrils — was pierced with holes like a tea strainer and lined with pink gauze padding, presumably impregnated with the radioactive, tissue-softening compound.

Mr. Glencannon adjusted the device upon his countenance and considered his reflection in the washstand mirror. "Haw," he said, his voice sounding strange and distant, like that of a music-hall ventriloquist when he shuts the dummy in the trunk. "Ye look lik' a deep-sea diver whose mother was frightened by a tinsmith! But come, tak' it off, Glencannon, before it mars yere manly beauty, and arrange it so yon jockoss o' a Montgomery will stick his nose into more than he's bargained for!"

With pliers, then, he bent in the sides of the mold until only by dint of the greatest effort was he able to force it over his nose. Once there, the discomfort was intense. He pried it off and rubbed the throbbing organ to restore the circulation. "Ah, whoosheroo!" he gloated. "I foncy that will teach him to leave God's hondiwork alone! But noo there still remains this lovely pink gauze lining to attend to. M'm — let's see — let's see!" Suddenly inspiration seized him. "Asafetida!" he exclaimed. "The vurra thing! I'll tell Captain Ball that I'm needing a bit o' quinine oot o' the medicine chest, and I'll filch the asafetida bottle while I'm getting it!"

Now, asafetida is a powder with an odor which is most disheartening. It smells vaguely like a number of things, none

"But come, tak' it off, Glencannon, before it mars yere manly beauty!"

of them pleasant, but chiefly it smells like itself, which is not in the least vague and is most unpleasant of all. In olden times it was highly esteemed for driving malignant demons from victims of the plague, the theory being that no devil with a shred of self-respect would remain in the same canton with a single pennyweight of it. That the theory was no idle one is attested by its success in stemming the dread Black Pest in Palermo, in A. D. 1241, and in Naples, some sixty years later. To this day, olfactory evidence of its ancient use is noticeable when passing through the streets of these charming cities.

Thus it was that Mr. Glencannon held his breath as he sprinkled a copious measure of the powder between the layers of the radioactive Inhalo-Pad (Patented), and that he strangled as he tucked circular and Nasal Mold back into the box.

"Ah, losh, what a garden of roses!" he gasped, arranging the wrapping and heating the bottoms of the gobs of sealing wax in the flame of a match. "I misdoot that after a nicht or two o' that, his nose will develop muscles lik' the thews o' an ox!"

Gratefully gulping the chill river air, he made his way forward and deposited the packet upon the saloon sideboard with the rest of the mail. Then he returned to his room, uncorked a bottle of Duggan's Dew of Kirkintilloch and poured himself a brimming tumbler. "Weel, here's confusion to Muster Montgomery's nose!" he toasted. "Though my ain is flushed with monny an honest quart, I'd no' exchange it for the pallid badge o' a smug teetotaler! Ah, the treacherous, two-faced sneak! Go reporting to the captain aboot my haeing a bottle in the engine room, and tattling tales o' the skeermish I had with the constabulary at Cape Town, wud he? Oh, we'll see who sets an exomple o' efficiency, good conduct and deeligence aboord this domn ship yet!"

III

When Mr. Montgomery returned aboard that evening, the rest of the officers were half through supper. The mate was wearing a chrysanthemum in his buttonhole and a supercilious smile upon his face. "Oh, don't mind me!" he said gaily. "I 'ad a bit of a late tea, d'yer see, and so I ain't 'ungry now. Lawks!" His eye kindled with fond reminiscence. "First we 'ad some toasted strumpets with butter and plum jam, then we 'ad some little kind of sandwitchers with bloater paste in 'em, then we 'ad some 'ot kippered 'errings — delicious, they was — and fruit cake orl 'eaped up with wipped cream. Oh, my word, that's wot I'd call a proper 'igh tea!"

"What did they gi' ye to drink?" inquired Mr. Glencannon.

"Drink? Hmph, tea of course! Wot the 'ell do yer spose they serves at genteel arfternoon social gatherings?"

"Whisky," said Mr. Glencannon placidly. "Whisky by preeference, although brondy, rum, gin, vodka, slivovitz, arrack and marc are conseedered almost equally correct. Aye, and I've e'en droonk the methilyted spirits oot o' the tea lamp, in a pinch!"

"Oh, yus?" Mr. Montgomery snorted righteously. "Well, just let me tell yer, yer web-footed Scotch sot, yer ruddy well couldn't go swilling any of them there 'ell broths around the company I was in this arfternoon, yer wouldn't! I was tea guest of Mr. 'n' Missus 'Erbert 'Opkins and their daughter 'Arriet, of 'Opkins Temperance 'Otel, on the Preston Road in Poplar. We're all fellow members of the International League of Militant Teetotalers, and yer can bet yer boots there's none of yer narsty snyke juice served in their plyce!"

"Hear, hear!" applauded Captain Ball. 'Oh, that's what I call commendable company for a ship's officer to spend an afternoon ashore in! No drinking and boistering around, like I am sorry to say some of you gentlemen do, Mr. Glencannon. No, nothing of that sort, but instead a nice, refined high tea, like it was in the buzzom of your own family with kippered herrings and all, if you follow me. Ah, let me tell you, Mr. Montgomery and gentlemen, there's no happiness like that of a sailor ashore sitting snug with his own hearthstone and his wife on his lap and maybe a mastiff and a kid or two and a nice high-powered electric piano whanging away at the bass notes of The Battle of Prague, all comfy and cozy! Er — ker — huff — see what I mean?"

"Yus, sir," said Mr. Montgomery, simpering callowly. "I get yer meaning exackly." He busied himself with his helping of hash, and, as he forked it up, Mr. Glencannon studied his nasal appendage critically. There was, he observed, quite a lot of it; it was located in approximately the right place, but its contours were indefinite and pudding-like, as though the mortal day in which it was modeled was still half baked and soggy. It was not a nose to write home about; in fact, the more he considered it, the less could Mr. Glencannon blame its owner for having written the Apollo Corporation, Ltd.

At length the mate finished his meal, rose and strolled to the sideboard. He spied his package, flushed and stuffed it into his pocket. "Good night, orl!" he bade them, and hastened away to his room.

Now, despite the fact that Mr. Montgomery had gone to bed at an early hour, his appearance and condition next morning were scarcely those of a man who had passed a night in restful slumber. Covertly scanning him across the breakfast table, Mr. Glencannon saw that his face was drawn, his eyes puffy and his nose a blotchy mauve, as though it had been frozen and was just beginning to thaw. The mate attacked his porridge sullenly, trying to piece together in his mind the nightmares which had tormented him. Once, he remembered, he had dreamed that the ship was sinking and that a watertight collision door had slammed shut on his nose; again he had fallen into the Ganges River just below the Benares burning ghats, and had awakened strangling for air as the vile, polluted waters closed over him. But — he shuddered at the thought of it! — though the waters had been but the figments of a dream, their reek had remained in his nostrils even in wakefulness. His nose throbbed painfully as it twitched in reminiscence — and it still was filled with the disheartening odor which had haunted him throughout the livelong night.

When Jessup served the eggs, Mr. Montgomery cracked one open, sat for an instant with spoon poised, shuddered and pushed away his plate. He slumped back, frowning to himself, breathing through his mouth and gingerly massaging his nose. From time to time he ventured an experimental whiff through the nostrils, but the results were uniformly discouraging. He shifted uneasily and coughed behind his hand.

"I say, Mr. Glencannon," he said, "you're a scientific bloke, so per'aps you can tell me something. Did yer ever 'ear of radium turning rancid?"

"Radium turning roncid?" repeated Mr. Glencannon with authoritative austerity. "Oh, to be sure I have! Radium is roncid by nature, Muster Montgomery — in fact, that's the way they mak' it. Ye see, after the two component elements, the ray and the dium, are stirred together, they cover them up in a vat and let them set until they curdle. Weel, after they've feermented and bubbled and stewed and putrefied for ten or eleeven weeks, they naturally start to decompose. Then a crew o' men in goss mosks come in and — But I'll spare ye the revolting details! Ah, whoosh, Muster Montgomery, did ye ne'er smell a radium factory operating at full blast?"

"Yus — er — well, anyway, that's wot I wanted to know," said the mate, feeling reassured and disappointed at the same time. He closed his eyes, steeled himself to the ordeal, and resolutely took a long breath through his nostrils. Then, suddenly, he rose, and muttering "Pardon me," made his way out of the saloon.

"Haw! " Mr. Glencannon exulted to himself. "'Twud seem that the leaven is beginning to work!"

That noon, as on the previous day, Mr. Montgomery appeared in his shore clothes, but this time his spirits were low, his appetite nil, and his nose even sorer than it had been in the morning. With the return of circulation, livid ruts had appeared along the sides where the edges of the Apollo Beautysleep Nasal Mold had left their mark, and the nostrils were still filled with the overpowering scent of rancid radium.

He scowled at the boiled beef, forced himself to swallow a mouthful, and then gave it up as a bad job.

"Ha-ha!" Captain Ball chided him. "No appetite, hey, mister mate? Well the lovesick swain he feeds on love, better his fare than beefsteak of,' or however the poet laureate has sung it!"

Mr. Montgomery grinned a sickly grin, and his nose flushed to the roseate hue of an autumn sunset in the Strait of Gibraltar. "'Well, sir," he explained, "I'm hinvited to another of them there 'igh teas agyn, so I'm syving a bit of room in my stommick fer orl the cakes and bloaters and 'errings and — er — er" — suddenly his eyes became glassy, his brow moist and his voice trailed off into an agonized whisper — "and fer orl the

— the w-w-wipped cream. Er — excuse me!" And he staggered from the room.

"Oh, now, by jemmy, I just call that too touching!" exclaimed Captain Ball delightedly. "'How he doth languish in love's sweet anguish,' see what I mean? Ah, gentlemen, there comes a time when every man who's worth his salt goes through the same experience, and he comes out of it worth more of it for going through with it. Once you get a steady, sober-going chap like Mr. Montgomery joined in married wedlock, and you'll see him forge forth forcibly to the fore like never before, if you'll f-f-forgive me the alliteration, which was partly on account of these damn f-f-false teeth. Well, it won't be long now! Yes, and from the look of things, gentlemen, Mr. Montgomery'll have that 10 per cent bonus to help him set up housekeeping."

Mr. Glencannon said nothing, but he rolled a fishy eye.

IV

The week wore on; soon the *Inchcliffe Castle* would be putting to sea. Each morning found Mr. Montgomery feeling lower and looking it. But as Captain Ball had said, the mate was a sticker, a man of dogged determination; he had set his mind on remodeling his nose, and now that he could see it actually beginning to soften, he tightened the straps of the Apollo Mold, gritted his teeth and suffered through night after sleepless night. His appetite was completely gone, his nerves were raw and ragged, and always, always his nostrils were packed with that awful odor which deadened his olfactory sense to every other smell. At first he found it curious that nobody else seemed to scent it, but gradually, to his dismay, he observed that his fellows were looking at him askance and moving out of his lee whenever he approached. Worst of all was the effect upon Miss Harriet Hopkins and her worthy parents.

At the beginning, of course, they were extremely polite. They murmured something about a dead mouse in the wainscoting, opened the windows, observed that the neighbors were cooking cabbage, and closed the windows again. But as he sat there on the red-plush parlor sofa balancing his teacup on his knee and forcing himself to eat, Mr. Montgomery could see that the tide of suspicion was rising steadily against him. More than once, he caught Mr. Hopkins glancing sidewise at his nose. Finally, one evening when he was taking his leave of Miss Harriet, she spurned his tender embrace and moved across the vestibule out of his aura.

"You mustn't, Chauncey," she said, giving an involuntary shudder as the hall light shone full on his nose. "No, not till we're — we're really truly hengaged."

"Why, wot's the matter?" he demanded petulantly. "Good lawks, 'Arriet, I've arsked yer twenty times orlready, but now I arsks yer agyne. Will yer marry me or won't yer?"

Her lips were tight pressed. Instead of answering, she ran into the house and slammed the door. It was with sinking heart that Mr. Montgomery realized she had been holding her breath.

"'Ell!" he growled as he stamped down the street. "So that's the considerytion a poor chap gets fer trying to myke 'imself hattractive! Yus, and it was orl on account of 'er telling me that she adored a nose like Ronald Colman's, that night I took 'er to the cinema, and 'inting that my nose didn't suit 'er fastidious tyste and, orl. Well, now I'm going to stop trying — yus, I'll chuck that blarsted hinstrument of torture into the ruddy Thames as soon as ever I get back aboard the ship. Mybe I can henjoy a decent night's sleep and a breath of fresh air fer a chynge!"

But though he carried out the first part of this program with such violence that the Apollo Nasal Mold plunked into the oily waters at the middle of Blackwall Reach, and though he did manage to sleep for a fitful hour or two, so dense were the fumes of radium that fresh air was even scarcer than in the Black Hole of Calcutta. "Blyme, I'm habsolutely himpregnated with the narsty stuff!" he moaned. "But I spose it'll wear orff by morning."

But it didn't wear off by morning. At breakfast Mr. Glencannon noticed it first. "Ah, frichtful, frichtful!" he muttered, hastily lighting his pipe. Captain Ball sniffed the air tentatively and bawled for Jessup. "See here, my man," he said severely, fanning himself with his napkin, "it's that frowsty in here you couldn't cut it with a knife. Has something gone wrong in the galley or something, or what?"

"Why, no, sir," said Jessup. "But — m-m-m — yus, good 'eavens — phew, it is a bit 'igh in 'ere at that! Oh, I'll tell yer wot, sir; it must be that there factory over in Greenwich where they mykes jellies and soups and delicacies fer invalids out of 'orse 'oofs and orl like that, sir."

"M'm'ph, well, maybe," said Captain Ball, "but it smells a damn sight nearer than Greenwich to me. You don't mean to say you can't smell it, too, Mr. Montgomery?"

"No, sir," said the mate. "I — I don't smell a thing."

"You don't? Eh, you don't? Well, if you don't smell something as rotten as Denmark around here, there's something wrong with your nose! Er — kerhuff, ker-hem — just what is wrong with your nose anyway, Mr. Montgomery? Oh, my word, it's in a shocking state, come to look at it! Where from did it get all them mottles?"

"From bottles," interjected Mr. Glencannon. "Oh, I ken these teetotalers, with their secret vices and their —"

"Bottles?" screamed Mr. Montgomery, finally overwrought. "Bottles?" He seized the water decanter by the neck and lurched to his feet. "I'll give yer bottles, yer guzzling Glasgow walrus! "I'll —"

The decanter crashed against the bulkhead behind Mr. Glencannon. Mr. Levy and Mr. Swales seized the mate by the arms and hustled him struggling from the room.

"Oh, why — ker-huff — er — I mean to say!" puffed Captain Ball. "Why, what's got into the man of a sudden? Suddenly shouting and screaming and screeching like a banshee-shreece-shreep — oh, damn these teeth! — er — and chucking the water bottle at you — there, that's what I mean to say, Mr. Glencannon!"

The engineer sighed and blew a noxious cloud toward the ceilmg. "Captain Ball," he said, measuring his words, "it ill becomes a dissolute specimen lik' mysel' to creeticize a mon whom y've so often held up as a shining exomple to the rest o' us, but I'll osk ye to think ower what I just noo said aboot secret vices! Some days ago I told ye that e'en though I loathed him, e'en though I'd put my mark on him yet, I wudna impugn his morals. Weel" — he lowered his voice and shuddered — "weel, I see that I was too choritable! Beware o' him, captain, beware o' him! He's a slave o' dark and secret and unholy practices the vurra thocht o' whuch mak's my bluid run cauld!"

"Bottles?" screamed Mr. Montgomery, finally overwrought. "Bottles? I'll give yer bottles!"

Wagging his head ominously, he went out on deck. Shortly thereafter he saw Mr. Montgomery, jaw protruded and shoulders hunched, heading purposefully for Preston Road, Poplar.

"A-weel," he chuckled, "from the frontic look o' the brute, motters are aboot to come to a climox!"

They did come to a climax in the private parlor of Hopkins' Temperance Hotel. Mr. Montgomery burst in unannounced and stood there wild-eyed and panting.

"Why, Chauncey Montgomery!" exclaimed Miss Harriet, recoiling from him. "'Ow 'orrible you do look! And — and wite a minute, while I open the window. There! Phew, but it's stuffy in 'ere!"

"Yus," rasped Mr. Montgomery, "it is stuffy in 'ere, and yer needn't go pretending like yer don't know why! It's me, it's me, it's me, that's wot it is, and I can see by the look in yer eye that yer despise me fer it! Well, 'Arriet" — he raised his voice — "it's orl yer fault that I got sniffing them ruddy chemicals up my nose. Yus, orl yer fault, and if yer going to throw me down now because I've ruined myself for yer, I calls it a bally rotten shyme!"

Miss Harriet bristled: "See 'ere, you just better keep a civil tongue in yer 'ead, Mr. Montgomery! Wot do yer mean, yer loathsome beast, coming into a lydy's own parlor and — Stop! Stop!" she screamed. "Don't come near me! No! No! Not another step!"

"'Ere, 'ere, now, wot's the meaning of this?" demanded a truculent voice. Mr. Montgomery turned to behold Mr. Hopkins and his wife standing in the door. "Was this person annoying you, 'Arriet dear?"

"Annoying me!" sobbed the daughter. "Lawks, pa, the 'orrid brute was hinsulting me! 'E says as 'ow it's orl my fault 'e's ruined 'imself with chemicals in his nose and —"

"Ah-h-h, so that's it!" exclaimed Mr. Hopkins, rolling up his sleeves. "Dope! A dope fiend! Well, I might have guessed it! . . . Ma, just you blow the police whistle out the window while I attend to this 'ere narsty specimen!"

V

Some hours elapsed before Mr. Montgomery was able to take much interest in the proceedings, but at length he was aware that somebody — yes, the police surgeon; he recognized him now — was addressing him.

"— so, naturally, we thought the powder was dope. However, if you want to carry asafetida around in your pockets and in your hatband, it's your own business, and not against the law. Why, good heavens, Mr. Montgomery, the sergeant reports that the search party even found a lot of it in your pillow on your ship! But now, if you'll just go easy with us about the false arrest and all, I'll guarantee to fix up this smashed nose of yours so it'll look like Ronald Colman's. Yes, Mr. Montgomery, I'll give you a nose like Apollo's!"

"To 'ell with it!" snapped Mr. Montgomery "If 'Arriet's father 'as mashed it flat, orl the better reminder it'll be to steer clear of women in the future. Oh, I've learned my lesson, doctor — about women and other things!"

Late that afternoon Sir John Castle arrived at the company's office and sent at once for Mr. Hazlitt.

"See here," he said. "What's all this in the evening papers about our man Montgomery and a dope-smuggling plot and a raid on the *Inchcliffe Castle?*"

Mr. Hazlitt spread his thin pale hands. "I don't know, exactly, Sir John," he said. "It appears it was all a mistake, and the charges have been withdrawn. I've been in touch with Ball, of, course, and he says the whole thing is mysterious — most mysterious!"

"Rather!" said Sir John. "And what's more, it's jolly rotten publicity for the line. Isn't Montgomery the fellow Ball was going to recommend for the efficiency bonus?"

"Yes," said Mr. Hazlitt. "But after today's — ah — unfortunate incident, he's changed his mind. Even though the charges were withdrawn — well, where there's smoke there's fire! And so Ball's recommended Glencannon."

Ah, fine!" approved Sir John. "A thoroughly efficient chap, Glencannon!"

The Pearl of Panama

In the region around Leadenhall Street and St. Mary Axe which is the administrative center of London's shipping world, there is no man more highly respected than Virgil Hazlitt and none of whom his fellow men know less. Forty-three years ago he joined Clifford, Castle & Co., Ltd., as junior clerk; today he is the firm's General Manager and the outstanding genius of the British Mercantile Marine. Myopic, bald and crabbed, Mr. Hazlitt remains a spry and serviceable relic of the heyday of the Empire, when Victoria was queen, sail was giving way to steam and Mr. Kipling (or maybe it wasn't) was able to remark that the sun never set on the British flag. Thanks to Mr. Hazlitt's methods of management Clifford & Castle's cargo fleet has increased from four vessels to twenty-three; the firm has seldom passed a dividend, and even in present slack times when hundreds of thousands of tons are layed up rusting in the estuaries, the C. & C. ships are one and all at sea with cargoes which Mr. Hazlitt, in his unaccountable way, has contrived to book at a profit. According to his baffled competitors, old Virgil Hazlitt is in league with the devil.

Now all of the foregoing is public knowledge which anyone may glean from the liftman at the Baltic Exchange or the be-medalled hero of Zeebrugge Mole who whistles you a taxi at the portal of Lloyd's. But of Mr. Hazlitt's private life, of Hazlitt the man, of Hazlitt the human being, the inquirer will be hard put to it to uncover a single revealing fact. Cavillers declare, quite bluntly, that he isn't human at all, which means that he isn't as they are; and this, in turn, means that he isn't a mixer. For he has few friends in business, and none outside it; he shuns those luncheons, conferences and other gabby mediums of contact so dear to the gregarious herd, and instead of making speeches about business over banquet tables he transacts it quietly over his desk. He works day and night; he never delegates to another a job which he can do himself; and he can do everything.

Mr. Hazlitt's knowledge of ships and shipping is encyclopedic and his memory is prodigious. He can tell you out of his head, for example, that the *Durhamcliffe Castle* (Eastbound through the Gulf of St. Lawrence with a grain cargo and at the moment, according to the "D"-flag on his ships' position map, just off the tip of Anticosti Island) is burning 17.5 tons of coal per day whereas ten months ago she was burning only 15.2; and he knows that this is due to the condition of her boilers. Things like this he remembers. The only thing he cannot remember is where he puts his eyeglasses, and until he hired the mountainous Mrs. O'Halloran as charwoman in the company's offices, it was not uncommon for fourteen clerks to be searching for them at once. Mrs. O'Halloran is unerringly able to discover his glasses on his nose, a faculty which Mr. Hazlitt considers nothing less than genius.

It is probable that Mrs. O'Halloran knows as much about Mr. Hazlitt as any living person. But there was a time last Spring when the old gentleman's behavior became very strange indeed. His routine was upset. He seemed preoccupied. His habitual testiness was varied by moments of unprecedented geniality. Not only was Mrs. O'Halloran puzzled; she was intensely worried.

"Yus, dearie, I don't 'arf like the look of it," she screamed from her window through the misty May twilight of Catsmeat Yard to Mrs. Jessup, who was skinning an eel on the doorstep of No. 6. "The squinty old weasel's not 'imself; 'e was worse today than 'e was yesterday, and lor-lumme if I know wot to myke of it."

"But do yer really think 'e's going orff 'is chump?" demanded Mrs. Jessup, whose husband was steward of the *Inchcliffe Castle*. "Good 'eavens, Veronica dear, if old 'Azlitt goes barmy, I 'ate to think wot will 'appen to Clifford & Castle's and orl our menfolk at sea!" The eel wriggled violently so Mrs. Jessup tied a knot in it and jerked it tight.

"Just hexackly wot is the matter with 'im, Missus O'Halloran?" came Mrs. Gonigle's voice from the second floor of No. 6. "Now that my louse of a 'usband 'as finally got promoted donkeyman of the *Ormcliffe*, it'd be rotten luck hindeed if something was to 'appen to 'Azlitt and the 'ole ruddy line go to smarsh!"

Mrs. O'Halloran nodded grimly, observing as she did so that wives of C. & C. deckhands and firemen were bulging from windows on all four sides of the yard.

"'E's neglecting 'is work, that's wot 'e's doing," she went on, raising her voice for the benefit of the new auditors. "Oh, now, mind yer, 'e still does work enough fer six, but that's only 'arf enough fer 'im. Sumping — sumping 'as come over 'im — I can't explyne just wot it is, but I feels it — yus, I feels it!" She smote her forehead with one hand and with the other reached back and turned down the gas stove, upon which a beef heart was commencing to sizzle. "Why, at four o'clock this very arfternoon, instead of dictating his regular narsty weekly form letter to the Captains of orl the ships, rysing 'ell with 'em about this and that, 'e puts on 'is 'at and goes out fer a walk. Yus, girls, out fer a walk, right in the middle of business hours!"

"Oh, blyme!" exclaimed Mrs. Gonigle in dismay.

"It's bad, bad, bad," sighed Mrs. Jessup who, the half-skinned eel still showing signs of life, was flogging it lustily against the doorstep.

"Lawks, it's a tradegy!" chimed in Mrs. Flynn, of No, 4, taking a quick one from a bottle of gin which she shoved back under her apron. "But tell us, Missus O'Halloran, dearie — hexackly wot mykes you think 'e's losing 'is mind?"

Mrs. O'Halloran lit a cigarette and puffed at it thoughtfully before replying. "Welp, as close as I can figure it out there's sumping wrong with 'is 'ead. I don't know whether 'is brains is curdled or wot, but it must be. Every few minutes 'e stops wotever 'e's doing and sits back and rubs the top of 'is crown. — Got 'is bald spot polished like me own brarss doorknob, till even a bleddy 'ouse-fly couldn't get a foot'old on it. And besides that, 'e's orlways complaining about the cold, cold draught."

"The cold, cold draught from where, dearie?"

"The cold, cold draught from where, you arsks — and that's wot I arsks too! 'Ere we are, sweating and sweltering in the month of May with only sixteen foggy days so far; but though 'is windows tight shut and a shilling's worth of coals is blyzing in 'is grate, 'e still keeps fussing about 'is 'ead being in the cold, cold draught. Now frankly, lydies, wot the flyming 'ell do yer myke of that?"

"Well," declared Mrs. Jessup despondently, "it means 'is brains is frowsty, no doubt about it. 'E's got chillblains on 'em and they're starting to ferment, as one might say. Oh, I'm very much afryde that it's only a matter of days before they trice 'im up in a straight-waistcoat and tyke 'im orff yammering to the mad'ouse!"

"Yus," sighed Mrs. Tousey, of No. 3, "and then wot'll 'appen to Clifford & Castle's, our 'usband's jobs, and us?"

"Starvytion and the Dole, that's wot'll 'appen!" opined Mrs. Jessup, tramping back and forth upon the eel, to make it tender. "In these 'ere putrid times, jobs is scarcer than scarcer. Oh dear, oh dear, why couldn't the mean old dotard pick a decent time to go orff 'is chump while he was about it?"

"Indeed, why couldn't 'e?" demanded Mrs. O'Halloran, hurling her cigarette butt at a skeletal tom-cat which was prospecting in the garbage pail below. "Well, all we can do is 'ope fer the 'best, 'oping that it won't be the worst! — Soak 'im in winnigar fer at least three minutes, Missus Jessup, dear, or else 'e'll go wiggling orl over the bleddy stove. Don't fry 'im, dearie, stew 'im, stew 'im, and may the good Lord 'ave mercy on us orl!"

2

Mr. Hazlitt snapped open his watch and squinted at it. "A quarter to four!" he muttered. "By gad, I've got to hurry!" He layed aside the tonnage graph upon which he had been drawing lines like silhouettes of icebergs and pushed the buzzer button on his desk. "Sit down, Miss Melcher," he said when his stenographer appeared. "I just want to dictate — er, to dictate a — Mrs. O'Halloran! Mrs. O'Halloran! I do wish you'd be more careful about my glasses! I had them a minute ago, and — well, well, so I have, so I have! — But now that you're here, Mrs. O'Halloran, just take a look at that window." He shuddered and rubbed his bald spot. "There's a draught, a cold draught coming from some place. . . ."

Mrs. O'Halloran stood squarely, or rather, roundly, before his desk and placed her hands on her hips. "Now see 'ere, Mr. 'Azlitt," she said with finality, "this 'ere mykes five times today yer've complyned about the cold draught, and there ain't none. The trouble is with yer own bald 'ead, Sir, and I says it meaning no disrespeck to you. Wot you need is a bit of a wig, Sir — a two-pea is wot they call 'em — to keep yer brains warm. Yer can buy yerself a nice yellow one with curls on it, or even . . ."

"A wig?" Mr. Hazlitt tensed. "A *toupee?* For Me? Why, how old do you think I am, Mrs. O'Halloran?"

"Eighty-seven," said the charwoman, without hesitation.

"Rot! I'm only sixty-three!" Mr. Hazlitt would have given further vent to his indignation on this score had he not been so elated on another. For secretly, through many long weeks, he had hoped, yearned, dreamed of hearing this very suggestion. He wanted a *toupee* more than he had ever wanted anything in his life, but he lacked the courage to buy one on his own initiative. People would call him a fop, a burned-out dandy, a vain old fool. But if the idea were to come from somebody else — if he were able to say "Ah yes — my friends kept after me! — Health reasons, don't you see?" — well, in that case it would be different! Hence his elaborate complaints about draughts, his rubbing of his bald spot, his constant angling all through the office for the suggestion, which Mrs. O'Halloran (hosanna to her!) had volunteered.

"This 'ere mykes five times today yer've complyned about the cold draft, and there ain't none."

"H'm, a wig," he repeated, tapping his finger tips together in simulation of deep thought. "Why, upon my word, such a thing never occurred to me! But then, why not, why not? What do you think about it, Miss Melcher?"

"I agree with Mrs. O'Halloran, Sir," simpered Miss Melcher, whose legs were not too bad and who knew it. "It is a very *chic* idea."

"Really? Mm, I must think it over. — Ha, a *toupee*, to be sure! Well, now, Miss Melcher," he consulted his watch again and cleared his throat briskly, "take a letter to Mr. Campbell, Chief Engineer, S. S. *Inchcliffe Castle*, care Gaskell & Waterman's Shipyards, Sunderland; a-hem: My dear Mr. Campbell, semicolon; I have your memorandum report of the 18th ult. *in re* engine room repairs now in progress under your supervision. This progress is not satisfactory. Furthermore, Item Six, Specification Three, relating to thrust block bearings, is an outrageous . . ."

Miss Melcher crossed her legs from East to West and coughed discreetly. "I beg your pardon, Mr. Hazlitt, but the *Inchcliffe* isn't at Sunderland, she's on the way home from Yokohama. According to the map she's just passed through the Panama Canal. Perhaps you're thinking of the *Normancliffe*. But the thrust block job is really in the *Swalecliffe*, which layed up at Clydebank day before yesterday in Hammond's Yards."

"Eh?" Mr. Hazlitt looked at her in blank disbelief. "Eh?" he whirled in his swivel chair and faced a large-scale wall-map of the world from which jutted twenty-three little paper flags each marking the position of one of the company's vessels. Yes, Miss Melcher was right — there was the *Inchcliffe's* flag at Colon, the *Normancliffe's* at Sunderland, and the *Swalecliffe's* in the Clyde, exactly as he himself had located them that morning. He removed his glasses and pressed his hands against his eyes. "Dear me!" he said, expelling a tired sigh, "I — I fancy I've been trying to handle too much detail. I think I'll step out for a little walk, Miss Melcher; you can write that letter to Mr. Campbell."

"Yes, Sir," said Miss Melcher. "His name is Mr. Sanderson."

Mr. Hazlitt made a helpless gesture with his sleek top hat and headed for the door.

Once on the sidewalk of St. Mary Axe he heaved his shoulders as though striving to cast off a heavy burden and turned Southward. "Well, tomorrow you'll have your *toupee!* Oh, Hazlitt, you gay dog, you!" He started a chuckle but as he saw the clock on the bank the chuckle turned into a groan. "Four-ten already! You're too late, Hazlitt! By gad, what a rotten slave's life you do lead yourself! Too much detail, m'boy — you're swamped, swamped, swamped by detail!"

3

It was June; the S. S. *Inchcliffe Castle*, battered, rusty and salt-streaked, lay in Limehouse Commercial Docks discharging that portion of her Japanese cargo which was consigned to London. Leaving the day after the morrow she would traipse across to Antwerp to unload the remainder and then return for a thorough and much-needed refit. She had been away for five months, and plainly though her exterior showed the ravages of the voyage her internals were even more travel worn. This afternoon her Chief Engineer, Mr. Glencannon, was in his room conferring with a certain Mr. McTooth about the repairs. Mr. McTooth, a former shipmate of Mr. Glencannon's, now represented the Vulcan & Atlas Marine Engine and Boiler Works, of Greenock, and had come to estimate on the job.

"Weel, now, look ye here, Colin," he said, producing from his brief case pencils, paper, a slide rule and a corkscrew, "working oot this estimate in the ordinurra way wud be a vurra complicated motter, but I see no reason why you and I canna co-operate to sumplify it. After all, Colin, the only thing whuch consairns us is that my bid shud be a shade lower than the others. Am I richt?"

"No, Andrew, ye are wrong," said Mr. Glencannon, a dour, stocky gentleman with a ruddy face and a walrus mustache. "Yere bid must be the lowest, it is true; but the most important thing . . ." he extended his hand, rubbing finger and thumb together as though feeling a banknote, ". . . the most important thing is my little rake-off, and if ye want this job, dinna ye dom weel lose sicht o' the fact!"

"Oh, why Colin lad!" Mr. McTooth drew himself up righteously. "Ye forget who ye're talking to! An old-estoblished and provairbially-ethical firm lik' the Vulcan & Atlas Marine Engine and Boiler Works wud be the last in the world to try and do ye oot o' yere fair and just perquisites. Why, I'm surprised at ye for e'en suggesting it!"

"I want ten per cent," said Mr. Glencannon, bluntly.

Mr. McTooth gasped. "Ten per cent? Oh, losh, mon, be reasonable! After all, I must figure things so the shop mak's a few bawbees o' profit oot o' it!"

"I dinna care a fig what profit ye mak', as lang as I mak' my ten per cent," shrugged Mr. Glencannon. "If twull help ye any to look ower the secret and confidential bids whuch yere competitors have soobmitted, here they are."

"Ah, noo ye're talking!" said Mr. McTooth, producing a quart of Duggan's Dew of Kirkintilloch from his brief case. "Do ye open that, lad, and let us lubbricate oursels against the dry mothemotical labors we have ahead o' us. H'm," he took up the estimate of his principal competitor. "Here's Hutchinson & Derby. Why guid heavens, Colin, they're high — high! Just offhand, noo, I'd say they were a guid twunty-five per cent above what we could do it for, if we were to scamp things a bit."

"Weel, scamp things a bit," said Mr. Glencannon placidly. "— Then just add twunty per cent instead 'o ten to yere estimate for me, and ye'll still be five per cent lower than they are."

Mr. McTooth considered the matter. "But can ye get it past auld scrooge Hazlitt? Remember, Colin, he's no doot got some figures o' his ain, by this time!"

"Haw, can I?" scoffed Mr. Glencannon. "I've mulcted the dom auld ram oot o' hoonderds o' poonds ere this, and I foncy I've no forgotten the knack. O' coorse," he downed another slug of Duggan's and wrinkled his eyes shrewdly, "o' coorse, Hazlitt's a vurra canny fish, as weel ye ken, and it isn't every mon who can flummox him. If at the last minute I find it expedient to change yere figures aroond a bit, can I depend on ye to stond by them?"

"Aye, o' coorse ye can! Use yere ain discretion!" said Mr. McTooth. "I'll just draught the whole thing oot in the rough for ye so ye can tak' it up informally with him when ye see him tomorrow. Losh, but wudn't ye think the stingy auld brute wud appoint a reegular Engineer Superintendent to look after such matters, instead o' sticking his nose into everything himsel'!"

"Aye, wudn't ye!" agreed Mr. Glencannon. "Weel, this time again his parsimony will cost him dear!"

"Yere bid must be the lowest, it is true; the most important thing is my little rake-off."

Mr. McTooth took his leave but left the bottle; with it and the sheaf of estimates Mr. Glencannon went forward to the saloon, spread the papers on the table and set about preparing himself for his interview with Mr. Hazlitt on the morrow. Writing in his notebook he was halfway through a digest of the various bids which was a masterpiece of distortion, falsehood, fraud, piracy, barratry and camouflage when he was interrupted by a cough. Looking up, he saw the steward.

"Aye, Jessup, what is it?" he asked.

Jessup wiped his chin with his dishrag and glanced cautiously behind him into the alleyway.

"I've got some news fer yer, Sir," he said. "— Confidential news from the horffice."

"Oh, aye?" said Mr. Glencannon. "Are we all aboot to be layed off, or what?"

"No, Sir," Jessup shook his head. "This 'ere is good news, as far as you're concerned. Yer see, Sir, from wot Veronica O'Halloran tells my missus, old man 'Azlitt 'asn't been 'imself lately. — Gorn slack' in 'is work, 'e 'as, and acting that strynge that there's many people thinks 'e's in 'is second child'ood. Bought 'imself a wig, no less, and 'as taken to dressing fancy! Well, within the past week or so 'e's been bellyaching about 'aving too much detyle to hattend to, and Sir John Castle and some of the other directors 'ave been telling 'im as 'ow 'e ought to 'ave a Hengineer Superintendent to relieve 'im of some of it. At first he pertended like 'e didn't care fer the idea, but pretty soon 'e says yus, there might be sumping to it, but 'oo could 'e happoint to fill the job? Then," Jessup lowered his voice, "then, Sir, there's some of the gempmen mentions Mr. MacLean, of the *Bournecliffe Castle*, others favors Mr. Ogilvie, of the *'Ardcliffe*, and some of 'em speaks up fer you."

"— For me?" Mr. Glencannon's hand trembled as he lifted his glass, and so did his voice as he asked, "For me? Losh, Jessup, dinna keep me in suspense! How — how did they decide it, mon?"

Jessup flicked his dishrag. "It 'asn't been decided yet," he replied. "They've left it to Mr. 'Azlitt to choose from among the senior hengineer horfficers of the line. It'll be a nice cushy shore job right 'ere in London at 'andsome pay, and — well, Sir, a word to the wise is sufficient!"

"Ye're dom richt it is!" agreed Mr. Glencannon. "A thoosand thanks to ye, Jessup, for giving me the tip! But all the same, great swith, I bitterly resent their mentioning me in the same breath — er," he fumbled in his pocket for a clove, "— in the same breath with droonken whusky-guzzling louts lik' Malcolm MacLean and Alec Ogilvie! — No, Jessup, no! What Clifford & Castle's need is a mon lik' mysel' — a mon o' vost experience and stairling chorocter — steady, abstemious, efficient and incorruptible! For seventeen years I've sairved in the putrid engine rooms o' this line, and today —" his face flushed and he beat his tumbler belligerently on the table, "— and today neither you nor I nor any other mon can look me in the eye and say that I have stolen a single soliturra farthing that was no my just due!"

"No, Sir," said Jessup, retreating in confusion down the alleyway. "I — I was just telling yer, that was orl, Sir!"

For a moment Mr. Glencannon sat snorting with righteous indignation; then, seizing the bottle, he poured himself a mighty hooker to steady his nerves. Lifting the tumbler to his lips, he was astounded to find it empty, and simultaneously he became aware of a warmly-tingling irritation in his sub-abdominal region.

"Ah, foosh!" he snarled, "what deevil's hondy work is this?" Holding up the tumbler against the light, he saw that it was a mere bottomless tube; its base, reduced to splinters, was glistening on the table amongst the estimates.

"Ho, so that's their toctics, is it?" he fumed, writhing in his chair and endeavoring to shake the stinging liquid from the forward slack of his trousers. "— Weel, ye fulthy hounds! (Aye, I mean you, Malcolm MacLean, and you, Alec Ogilvie!) I'll — I'll show ye who's the best mon yet!"

4

At three o'clock the following afternoon Mr. Glencannon, bearing with him a large paper bag somewhat as the Greeks bore gifts, was shown into Mr. Hazlitt's oak-panelled sanctum. He was astounded at the change which had come over the General Manager. There was the wig, sure enough — a lifelike confection of iron gray, tastefully parted on the side. Instead of his gold *pince nez* Mr. Hazlitt was wearing rimless glasses of the kind called invisible; his stand-up collar and black cravat had given way to a soft blue shirt with tie to match, and he had discarded his black tail coat, striped gray trousers and patent leather shoes for tweeds and brown suede oxfords.

"Ah, Glencannon!" He extended his hand and smiled the first smile the Engineer had ever seen on his face. "Sit down, sit down Glencannon — the armchair there — that's it! Well, I hear the good old *Inchcliffe's* engines gave you a bit of trouble on the home passage. But now, ha, ha, I fancy a lay-up of a month or six weeks will put everything to rights, what?"

"A month or six weeks?" repeated Mr. Glencannon, swinging into action without delay. "Ah noo, noo, Sir, I fear ye've been talking to some o' the shipyard people! — Noturally, the langer they can string oot a job the better they lik' it. But obviously, Sir, it's no' to the interests o' Clifford & Castle to have a ship layed up for any such period!"

"Eh?" whinnied Mr. Hazlitt incredulously. "Do you mean the job can be done quicker?"

"I do," said Mr. Glencannon positively. By using my pairsonal influence I can guarantee to have it finished in a fortnight, or three weeks at the vurra most."

Mr. Hazlitt sat back, produced a gold-tipped cigarette from a brand new platinum case, and very deliberately lighted it. For the first time in all history an Engineer had suggested that a refitting job could be done in less time than the yards had, estimated. The situation was not only unprecedented, it was astounding!

"Well," he nodded, trying not to cough as the smoke tickled his unaccustomed tonsils, "I must say I like your spirit, Glencannon. — Pleasant as it is for a ship's engineer to have a bit of extra time ashore, ah-hem!, it plays hob with her earnings. And now as to the costs of the job; er, I myself have consulted one or two firms and have jotted down a few figures which I believe ought to cover things nicely. Here, I'll just read the totals off to you."

He read, and as he came to the end of his list, "Well?" he asked, and in his voice was a challenge and in his eye a victorious twinkle, "how does that sound to you? Just about rock bottom, eh, Glencannon? No margin for — ah — for anything in, the way of cumshaw, baksheesh, graft and so on, what?"

Mr. Glencannon turned upon Mr. Hazlitt a gaze like that of a faithful collie whose honesty has been wrongly impugned but who is nonetheless determined to protect his master from harm.

"Why, Muster Hazlitt!" he said. "I — I hardly know what to say! The figures ye've just quoted are no' merely high, they're rideeculously, lavishly extrovagant! They're practically the same as those quoted me by Hutchinson & Derby's thieving reepresentative day before yesterday, and at least forty per cent higher than I can get the job done for elsewhere."

"Forty per cent higher!" Mr. Hazlitt gasped. "Oh, now, see here, Glencannon, that's incredible! I'm prepared to concede that these figures of mine may be subject to some slight revision, but . . . forty per cent, oh, my dear fellow!"

Mr. Glencannon felt that the psychological moment had arrived. He leaned forward and pounded his fist upon the desk. "Muster Hazlitt!" he thundered, "it's time for a show-doon in the engineering monogement o' this company! For monny and monny's the year I've been painfully aware that we were paying too much — aye, vurra much too much! — for all the boiler and engine work we've had done. The repair shops are crooked one and all — because under our present system, they have to be! Unless they grease the palm o' the ship's engineer, they canna get the job! But for mysel' —" he rose from his chair and beat his breast dramatically "— for mysel', I'm — thoroughly sick o' it! I canna bite the hond that feeds me — no, not I, Sir! So here are the figures o' an ethical firm, the Vulcan & Atlas Works o' Greenock — the fair and square, the true, the honest figures, and — and —" he made a helpless but heroic gesture "— I'm — I'm here to sairve ye, Sir!"

There was silence while Mr. Hazlitt studied the estimate. "Extraordinary!" he said at length, tweaking a hair out of his right nostril and contemplating it studiously. "Extraordinary! But, well, if you and they agree it can be done for this price, it's good enough for me! Mr. Glencannon, in behalf of Clifford, Castle & Company, Limited, I want to congratulate and to thank you!"

Mr. Glencannon bowed. "I've merely done my juty, Sir," he murmured, "though I'm pairsonally deeply grateful for yere kind praise. Oh, and by the way, Muster Hazlitt —" he reached for his paper parcel and layed it deferentially upon the desk, "I've taken the liberty o' bringing ye a little trifle whuch I picked up in Cristobal and whuch I hope ye'll accept with my compliments."

"A present for me? Oh, I say, Glencannon! Why by George, it's a Panama hat! — A beauty!"

"Aye, a Panama hat — a vurritable pearl o' Panama!" agreed Mr. Glencannon. "Ye'll note that the weave is practically as fine as fine linen, or e'en finer, Sir. Aloss, such craftsmanship is rare, nooadays — almost a lost art! That's why such hats commond a pretty penny, e'en when ye buy them on the Isthmus where I bocht this one."

Mr. Hazlitt was delighted. Also he was somewhat embarrassed. It was the first time in his forty odd years with the company that anyone had given him anything, and he was at a loss for words. He rose, went to the mirror in the clothesrack and set the hat on his head. It fitted him perfectly. There was a rakish sweep to the brim, and all in all he felt that it made him look years younger. Nothing, nothing could have pleased him more.

"Glencannon," he said, "I can't begin to tell you how grateful I am!"

Mr. Glencannon made a deprecating gesture. "It's merely a most inadequate expression o' the odmiration I've always had for ye, Sir," he said. "There's monny an Engineer in the line's employ that thinks ye're a sneak, a sniveller, a weasel, a scoondrel and a Chinese stinkpot — in addition, o' coorse, to being an auld fool. They mak' no bones aboot saying so. But I — "his voice broke "— but I feel different, Sir!"

Mr. Hazlitt winced, resumed his place at the desk and shuffled his papers. Then he leaned back, whistling softly and gazing at the ceiling. The Engineer could see that he was deep in thought. At length he nodded as though arrived at a decision.

"Yes!" he said, half to himself, "Yes! Glencannon, this has been a most enlightening interview. You've opened my eyes to a lot of things, and I won't forget it! You're sailing for Antwerp tomorrow; — well, perhaps before you go you'll hear something that will interest you! Goodbye, Glencannon and — thanks!"

When the Engineer had gone, Mr. Hazlitt heaved a long, comfortable sigh. "Well, that's decided it!" he said. "No doubt about it, Hazlitt, Glencannon's the man for the job. — With him running things, you'll have time to — to play a little. Lord knows you've got it coming to you, Hazlitt; you've never played in your life, and you haven't many years left!" He looked at his watch. "Well, come on!" he ordered himself gruffly. "Now's the day and now's the hour!" Taking a final glance at his hat in the mirror and finding it good, he left the office.

As usual, he headed Southward. Two blocks, three blocks he walked. He was tense with excitement. At length he halted on the corner opposite a tea-room labelled "Ye Cake and Candle Shoppe." Yes, there she was at her table in the window.

"Now Hazlitt, buck up!" he muttered. "Stop trembling! You've got to go right in and speak to her, today — after all these months you've got to go in, you've got to, got to! Ah, look, she sees you! She's smiling! It'll be easy, it'll be easy . . ." With elaborate jauntiness he produced his platinum case, took out a cigarette and flipped his lighter.

POOF!

There was a blinding flash. Mr. Hazlitt's Panama hat vanished in a cloud of smoke and a stench of burned celluloid. Stunned, he put his hand to his head, and realized in horror that the hair of his wig had vanished with it.

He was vaguely aware that a crowd had gathered. "— Now see 'ere!" the voice of the law was saying, "Yer can't shoot off fireworks in the street, Mister, so move along before I tyke yer in charge!"

Mr. Hazlitt turned toward the tea-room window. She was still there. She was choking on a muffin.

In a taxi and on the verge of collapse, Mr. Hazlitt removed the smoking debris from his head and examined it. Of the wig, nothing remained but the webbed fabric foundation. Of the hat, the only thing left was the leather sweatband. Dully he turned it inside out. On it were words stamped in gold.

"'Genuine Panama,'" he read. "'Genuine Pan . . . no, 'Pam' — 'Genuine Pamana.' And here, below, it says 'Made in Japan'!"

5

The S. S. *Inchcliffe Castle* was about to sail for Antwerp. Captain Ball and the pilot were on the bridge, the mates were at their respective stations on forecastle and poop while down below Mr. Glencannon was keeping one eye on the gauges and the other on the engine room ladder.

"There's still time!" he muttered confidently. "Haw, haw! — Ah, losh, when I think o' how yon bondit o' a McTooth will feel when he hears he's got to do the job at a loss! But o' coorse with me as Clifford and Castle's Engineer Superintendent, giving oot the repair contracts for the whole dom line, he'll no dare raise a beef aboot it!"

The main exhaust blew off like a pent-up tornado. The telegraph flanged and the pointer went to STAND BY. The Third Engineer came down the ladder with an oblong package addressed to Mr. Glencannon.

With unsteady fingers the Chief tore off the paper, disclosing a handsome box of cigars and an envelope. "Losh!" he gloated, "here's the guid news, no doot aboot it! Ye're on yere last trip, to sea, Glencannon; 'twull no be lang the noo before ye say fareweel for guid and all to this fulthy swill barge and to the maggoty life o' an engineer at sea!"

He took a cigar, bit the end off it and lighted it in the flame of a duck lamp. "Noo let's see, let's see!" he opened the envelope and shook out the letter.

It read:

My dear Glencannon:

For some time past the Directors have been urging me to appoint an Engineer Superintendent to relieve me of the detail which our established method of operation has always placed upon me. I was persuaded that they were right and was about to make such an appointment when the able and efficient way in which you handled the matter of those repairs estimates demonstrated how unnecessary a Superintendent would be. You showed what can be done, and now I shall insist upon all our other engineers following your example. Furthermore, I have now eliminated certain distracting matters which were recently claiming too much of my time and hence I will be able to give the work my general supervision as in the past. Many thanks to you for saving me from an extremely foolish step.

Sincerely,
Virgil Hazlitt.

Beneath the signature was scrawled, "I believe you'll agree with me that the well-known theory 'There's no fool like an old fool' is pretty well exploded!"

Mr. Glencannon, chewing his cigar, was still scowlingly wondering what it all meant when BANG!, there was a shattering detonation and the cigar's incandescent fragments went rocketting into the utmost corners of the *Inchcliffe Castle's* engine room.

Three Lovesick Swains of Gibraltar

Late one summer afternoon the S.S. *Inchcliffe Castle* rounded Europa Point into Gibraltar harbor and let go her mud hook just off the coal wharves at the base of the Rock. A fly swarm of bumboats headed for her, their owners bending sweatily to the oar, screaming invective at one another and beseeching the crew of the *Inchcliffe*, gathered along the rails, to "looka-looka-looka, gentlemins; vair fine goods, vair chip price." The merchandise in question consisted of rotten fruit, pink soap, tin razor blades and nickel-plated junk at exorbitant prices, as well as the usual bottled corrosives bearing forged labels of the world's great vineyards and distilleries for which Jack Tar — whose name, signed on the ship's articles, is likely to be Olaf Olafson, Gus Schmidt or merely X — will cheerfully trade his eyeteeth.

Mr. Colin Glencannon, the *Inchcliffe's* chief engineer, emerged upon deck and peered over the side at the cargo of the shallop bumping the plates immediately below him. "'Duggan's Dew o' Kirkintilloch," he murmured wistfully. "Yon is the dear familiar label, but I fear 'tis merely counterfeit, pasted on a bottle o' dago hell broth distilled from the dondruff o' the octopus and sweetened with the venom o' the cobra. Weel, I'll have to nurse my thirst till I go ashore to congratulate Cousin Dooglas on his engagement. But then — but then —"

His anticipatory musings were interrupted by a renewed burst of shouting from the bumboats as into their bobbing midst there plowed a new arrival. This craft, propelled by a terrified Spaniard, was so heavily laden aft that its bow rose clear of the water. The reason for this was a passenger of colossal proportions, clad in the brave bright uniform of the Argyll and Dumbarton Highlanders, who sat sprawled in the stern sheets in a basket of Malaga grapes. This giant was sobbing garbled fragments of a song about a heart bowed down by weight of woe, and beating time with a bottle. Suddenly spying Mr. Glencannon, he lurched half erect, bellowed "Cousin Colin!" in a tragic basso, and then collapsed back into the grapes with a mighty squashing sound.

"Cousin Dooglas!" Mr. Glencannon winced as he returned the greeting. "I got yere post card aboot yere great happiness just before we left Naples! But come aboord, dear lad, and teel me what in the world's the motter with ye!"

After some slight unpleasantness with the boatman, who demanded payment for a quart of whisky and a stick of shaving soap which he claimed his passenger had eaten under the impression that it was nougat, Mr. Glencannon succeeded in assisting his kinsman over the side. The boatman headed back, whining plaintively through a broken nose.

"Swith, Cousin Colin," sighed the Highlander, leaning against a stanchion and wringing grapejuice from the tail of his kilt, "I come to ye sore beset and in a muck o' trouble. But flood is blicker than thud is flicker fl —" A great sob shook him and he wilted upon Mr. Glencannon's shoulder.

"Noo, noo, control yersel', Dooglas; ye've imbibed too much o' yon bumboat bilge," the engineer admonished. "As ye say, the ties o' blood are strong, and if ye're in trouble o' any sort — 'cept o' coorse, finoncial — I'll do my best to help ye oot. If ye'll just kindly stond off my foot wi' yere domn great hobnailed boots, ye unburden yere soul to sumpathetic ears."

This giant was sobbing garbled fragments of a song about a heart bowed down by weight of woe, and beating time with a bottle.

Cousin Douglas took three steps backwards, two sideways, and brought up abruptly against the rail. He expelled a long breath and several soap bubbles. "Cousin Colin," he blurted, "the mact o' the fatter of fact is, her domn father has slandered me to her. Though I'm sure she still loves me, she's — she's thrun me doon!"

Mr. Glencannon pursed his lips beneath his walrus mustache and nodded judicially. "Weel, I'd already deduced that something had slipped, but do ye pull yersel' together and give me all the details. Who is she, for exomple?"

"Her name," said Cousin Douglas, "is Clematis Mahoney, and she's the daughter o' Sergeant Major Marty Mahoney, o' the Sixty-Seventh Royal Garrison Artillerillerill — er — wait, wait, I can hondle it! — illery. Here" — he groped in his breast pocket "here ris ser snopshot."

Mr. Glencannon considered the photograph critically. "Vurra attroctive, vurra attroctive," he murmured. "What are these things in the foreground?"

"Teeth," said Cousin Douglas, peering over his shoulder. "Pairhops I shud hae explained it to ye. That other part, there, is the drain pipe o' the veronda."

"Ah, precisely!" nodded Mr. Glencannon. "The camera doesn't lie. And as lang as it doesn't, there remains no doot that the owner o' this uniformed and chevroned arm whuch she's holding — the rest o' whom ye've so carefully scissored off the picture — is a corporal in the Royal Garrison Artillery. A corporal and" — he nudged the other slyly — "yere rival! Am I richt, Cousin Dooglas — am I richt?"

The Highlander scowled, and the effect was that of a thundercloud's shadow falling upon a shoulder of raw prime beef.

"Aye!" he said. "Richt ye are! A corporal, a newly promoted corporal — a domn conceited young smarty by the name o' Alf Chatterton. And here am me — my — I, twunty years in the King's sairvice, with the Mons Star, throrty-five furreign-sairvice ribbons, a hoonderd 'n' foorty-three battle clasps and eighty-two wound stripes. Er — weel, at least I've been recommended for them — that is, I shud have been!"

"Exockly!" Mr. Glencannon nodded. "Ye've everything in yere favor, so I fail to see why ye've let this other lad cut ye oot. And besides, as ye say, he's only a vurra junior corporal, while you, Dooglas, are a vurra senior sergeant."

A sob escaped Cousin Douglas. Hesitantly he extended his arm and nodded toward the sleeve. There, where sergeants stripes should have been, Mr. Glencannon saw only a few ends of snipped-off threads.

"Dooglas!" he gasped. "Dooglas! Dye mean to say —"

"I mean to say I'm nowt but a private, as ye see!" bellowed the giant. "I've — I've been rejewced to the ronks! Yon squirt o' a Chatterton is noo my superior officer, and when I meet him in The French Poodle tonicht, I'll smosh his nosty smirkin mug for him!"

"Oh, deary me," said Mr. Glencannon. "But why did they rejewce ye, Dooglas?"

"For being drunk," explained the Highlander. "Aye, I got drunk because I was hoppy, I lost my stripes because I was drunk, I lost my girl because I lost my stripes, and noo I'm drunk again because I lost my girl. Cousin Colin, I want ye to go to see her parents — to intercede for me — to help me win her back!"

Mr. Glencannon glanced again at the photograph of Miss Clematis Mahoney and shuddered. "Weel, fronkly, Dooglas, I canna help but feel that in some ways ye're luckier than ye realize. How lang had ye been keeping company with her?"

"For months and months! Aye, I loved her e'en before she'd got the letter."

"Got whuch letter, Dooglas?"

"The letter from the solicitors in Liverpool, aboot her aunt eating the tinned salmon. The tin was rusty, the salmon was musty, and noo her number's up. Sairves her richt, the auld skinflint! Why, I had a foortune o' ower two thoosand poonds, I'd no' eat tinned salmon or e'en tinned angels. I'd —"

"Two thoosand poonds!" gasped Mr. Glencannon. "Two thoosand poonds! Ye mean she's aboot to inherit her aunt's money? Great swith, ye lummox, why did ye no' say so before? Come, Dooglas, come; we must get ashore at once! . . . Bumboat ahoy-y!"

II

Arrived at the Commercial Wharf, Cousin Douglas commenced mumbling that he needed sleep, so Mr. Glencannon led him into The French Poodle, an establishment on the Ramps much frequented by noncoms of the Garrison Artillery, and assisted him to arrange himself on a settee in the corner of the bar parlor. The Highlander lapsed into slumber at once. Mr. Glencannon was about to take his departure when he saw a bottle protruding from the other's sporran. Capturing it, he drew the cork and sniffed the contents. "Braugh!" he shuddered. "More o' that bumboat bilge wi' the Duggan's label! He must have stolen' it on the trip in." Prudently shoving the bottle under the bench, he went on his way.

Hurrying across the town and through the Gardens, he came at length to a little street called Balaklava Row. On the lamppost at the corner was a sign:

MARRIED QUARTERS
67TH REGT. R.G.A.
NO LOITERING

Mr. Glencannon had observed this sign in the course of previous visits to Gibraltar; its insinuations had always rankled him, but today he nodded at it cheerily.

"Richt ye are!" he chuckled. "There'll be 'no loitering,' because there's no time for it. After all, I'll be sailing day after tomorrow, and I must mak' hay while the sun shines. Noo let me see, let me see; No. 3 is the address, and ower the way it is."

No. 3 Balaklava Row was one of a double rank of red-brick cottages so exactly alike in their ugliness that they could only have been built by military engineers, and in Victoria's reign at that. Each was surrounded by a border of grass and a whitewashed fence which seemed to choke it like the Sunday collar of a stevedore. In the garden of No. 3 a young lady was beating a strip of carpet. The carpet was sending great clouds of dust up into the summer twilight, but through them Mr. Glencannon recognized the damsel of the snapshot. He was dismayed to note that, as usual, the camera had not lied.

Bolstering his courage with thoughts of the two thousand pounds, he leaned over the fence and doffed his cap politely. "Guid afternoon," he said. "I believe I have the pleasure o' addressing Muss Clematis Mahoney?"

The young lady paused in her labors and surveyed him with evident distaste. "The pleasure is orl yours," she replied.

"Haw, capital, capital!" the engineer applauded, stepping through the gateway. "Wit and beauty seldom go hond in hond, but when they do — weel, 'tis a pity for the hond to wield a rug beater! Pairmit me, Muss Mahoney!" He was about to seize the rattan when, with a mighty full-arm saber swing, she whacked it stingingly across his coattails.

"Stand yer ground!" she snapped. "Keep yer 'ands orff! I'll teach yer that no narsty civilian can myke free with a 'igh-ranking non-commissioned horfficer's daughter!"

"Aye, pairdon, pairdon!" Mr. Glencannon apologized, hastily retreating with his hands pressed behind him,. "There, see? I dinna mean ye harm! Oh, quite the contrary! My name is Glencannon, muss, and I —"

At the name, Miss Mahoney emitted a piercing scream and launched into a fit of hysterics.

From the house came a rumble and clatter like that of a battery of field guns unlimbering for action, and down the veranda steps hurtled a lady who might well have posed as model for the Rock of Gibraltar itself. In one hand she clutched an unsheathed bayonet and in the other a raw mutton chop.

"Yus, Clematis, wot is it, dearie?" she demanded, thrusting her bulk between her daughter and Mr. Glencannon, and scowling down upon him. "'Oo is this 'ere walrus and wot's 'e been up to hey?" She brandished the chop threateningly, realized what it was, and dropped it into her apron pocket. "Well?" she demanded, presenting the bayonet to his throat. "'Oo are ye, mister? Speak hup!"

Mr. Glencannon swallowed his Adam's apple out of the range of the bayonet point and assumed his most charming and magnetic smile.

"Oh, why, Mussis Mahoney," he said, "I'm surprised ye're no expecting me! As soon as I heard the news, in Naples I sent ye a cablegram. Oh, guid heavens!" He trembled with sudden apprehension. "Ye dinna mean to teel me ye didna — get it? Ye dinna mean to say I'm — I'm too late?"

Mrs. Mahoney lowered her bayonet. "Cablegram?" she repeated. "Why, I never got no cablegram in orl my life! 'Oo are yer, that's wot I want to know?"

"My name is Glencannon, moddum," he answered, bowing his head in shame. "Tis an auld name, an honest name and I shud be prood to bear it despite him! But" — he dashed the tears from his eyes — "he — he has drogged it in the dust! Ah, he's the black sheep o' the family, Cousin Dooglas Glencannon is! When he wrote me in Naples that Muss Clematis had succoomped to his blondishments and consented to be his bride, I saw where my juty lay. At frichtful expense I sent ye a cablegram o' warning. At e'en more frichtful expense I've come here the noo in pairson to confairm it."

Slowly a look of understanding dawned upon Mrs. Sergeant Major Mahoney's large face. "Oh!" she said apologetically. "Oh, why, you poor man! Now I hunderstand yer, Mr. Glencannon!" The bayonet slipped from her fingers, and though the engineer leaped sideways as the point of it grazed his foot, she caught his arm and dragged him toward the house. "Come in, come in!" she urged cordially. "Oh, 'ow can I ever apolergize fer the way Clematis 'as treated yer? ... No, you stay houtside, Clematis! Stop yer crying and beat them carpits! Yer've done enough 'arm fer today!"

Once in the parlor, Mrs. Mahoney tossed the mutton chop into a polished-brass howitzer-cartridge case which had the scene of the Nativity painted on the side of it, and waved Mr. Glencannon to a violet plush armchair. "Yus, yus, I see it orl now," she said. "Yer wanted to bryke up the match between Douglas Glencannon and my daughter! Well, I can't never tell yer 'ow gryteful I am to yer fer yer kindness, Mr. Glencannon; even though we orlready broke the 'ole thing orff as soon as 'e lost 'is sergeant's stripes fer drunkenness. Yus, we told 'im never to dock on our door agyne!"

"Ah, thonk heavens!" breathed Mr. Glencannon. "Ye've saved yer daughter from the clutches o' a wastrel, a rakehell and a foortune hunter o' the deepest sty!"

"Well, well, well, is 'e really as bad as that?" she gasped. "I was saying only yesterday that if 'e could get 'is stripes back, I wouldn't mind 'im calling on 'er agyne. But in view of what yer say — ugh, no! The only trouble is, I'm afryde 'e's broke 'er 'eart."

Mr. Glencannon dismissed her fear with a wave of the hand. "A brukken heart will heal," he said, "but a ravished foortune, never!"

"True!" agreed Mrs. Mahoney. "But she 'asn't really got Aunt Jezebel's money yet, because it tykes tinned salmon a long time to work. In fack, I arsked the medical sergeant about it only yesterday, and 'e says 'as 'ow in Egypt' and Iraq 'e's seen it tyke as long as two months. But then, of course, 'e's talking about ordinary gov'ment rations."

"Two months!" said Mr. Glencannon. "Ah, my dear Mussis Mahoney, ye've snotched yere daughter from the clutches o' a foortune hunter in the vurra nick o' time. I mysel' am heir presumptive to a conseederable foortune and have lang been a prey to adventuresses and vompires seeking to snoffle it. I know how they operate. For ye see" — he coughed diffidently — "in addition to my present comfortable means, I expect ere lang to inherit the vast wealth o' my uncle, Muster Jock Glencannon, Esquire, o' Milngavie, one o' the most eminent misers in Scotland."

"Indeed?" and Mrs. Mahoney pricked up her ears. "Well, I seen as soon as I set eyes on yer that yer were a man o' substance, Mr. Glencannon. Er" — she leaned forward slightly — "do yer 'appen to be married, if I might myke so bold as to arsk?"

Three Lovesick Swains of Gibraltar 77

"No, moddum, I'm a lonely botchelor," he sighed, but it was obvious that the news pleased her. "I'm a wanderer, a globe trotter, forever traveling from one great copital to another, in my yacht, the *Inchcliffe Castle*, seeking by means o' study and culture to fill the void in my heart whuch ought to be occupied by a wife, a home, a loudspeaker and a litter o' streectly legitimate offsprings. And — oh, yes, Mussis Mahoney, I almost forgot to mention to ye that I'm a hoonderd per cent teetotaler, shunning alcohol in all its forms."

"Well, good lawks, yer a regular paragon of orl the virtues, I must say!"

"Aye, and I'm generous to a fault," said Mr. Glencannon modestly.

Mrs. Mahoney sat back and beamed upon him with appraisal and approval.

"Mr. Glencannon," she said at length, "yer've showed yerself to be a true friend of the family. I can see 'ow a gent of 'yer experience and character can be a gryte 'elp to Sergeant Major Mahoney and I regarding about planning Clematis's future. She's a charming slip of a girl, like yer've olready seen, and we wants 'er to marry well. Just now — er" — she hesitated — "there's a young man my 'usband brought around 'ere 'oo's just been permoted corporal — Alf Chatteron, 'is nyme is — wot's paying 'er court. But just between us, Mr. Glencannon, 'e's only a calf fer orl 'is conceit, and 'e ain't myde much progress as far as Clematis 'erself is concerned."

"Aweel, fronkly," said Mr. Glencannon, "I'm vurra glod to hear it. In the feerst place, moddum, I feel that yere daughter shud mak' a more advantageous motch than is possible in the army. In the seecond place" — he blushed and shuffled his feet in callow embarrassment — "in the seecond place, I — I — Ah, foosh, Mussis Mahoney, I canna say what I want to say!"

"Oh, go on, do!" she urged him.

"No," he said, firmly, "No! I really must leave ye the noo and look up my runagate cousin. And besides, 'twud no' be genteel o' me to speak what's on my mind after such short acquaintance. Pairhops tomorrow —"

"Yus, tomorrow, by orl means!" gushed Mrs. Mahoney. "Come and tyke a dish o' tea with us, do! I'll 'ave Clematis byke a kyke. Oh, she's fair wonderful at cooking, that girl is. The sergeant major's orff juty tomorrow arfternoon and I want you to give 'im yer views about Clematis not marrying a soldier. Yer see" — a troubled look crossed her face — "well, frankly, my 'usband is very strong fer a military marriage, and now yer cousin is out of the running 'e's very strong fer Corporal Chatterton."

"I'll be delichted to discuss it with him, and have no doot I can mak' him see the licht o' reason." Mr. Glencannon rose to take his leave. "Haw, wud ye believe it, Mussis Mahoney, ye really mak' me feel lik' a member o' the family?"

III

As Mr. Glencannon cut back through the town toward The French Poodle, he was more than a little pleased with himself. "Progress!" he chuckled. "Progress! Cousin Dooglas is clearly eliminated and noo nobody remains but this scut o' a Corporal Alf Chatterton. By hook or by crook, I must fix him so he'll lose his corporal's stripes. 'By crook,' preeferably — aye, the crook o' his elbow!"

He found Cousin Douglas still wrapped in slumber, tossing fitfully and muttering to himself. "I dinna care if ye're the Archbishop o' Dundee," he was saying, "ye've stolen my umbrella"

Mr. Glencannon peered apprehensively beneath the bench, but the bumboat whisky was still there. He settled himself at the table, ordered a drink and looked around the smoke-filled room. It was now nearly ten o'clock and the place was doing a rushing business; a double rank of artillerymen and Highlanders were standing it the bar, an electric piano was hurling forth large quantities of galloping melody, and in the center of the floor, numerous gentlemen in the uniforms of His Majesty's forces were treading a hobnailed measure with dark-eyed daughters of La Linea de la Concepcion. The engineer was just about to call the waitress and inquire if Alf Chatterton was present when the street door opened to admit a group of new arrivals. One of them, a raw and ruddy young artillery corporal, spied Cousin Douglas, sneered superciliously, and strode across the room.

"Well, strike me if yer ain't blotto agyne!" he addressed the sleeping Highlander. "Yus, ye're blind to the wide!" Then, turning, he winked at Mr. Glencannon. "Pal of yours?"

"Hardly," replied Mr. Glencannon with an indifferent shrug. "He hoppens to be my cousin but ye must odmit it's through no fault o' mine."

Cousin Douglas stirred uneasily. "Ye can stop dog fights with an umbrella too," he mumbled. "Stick it betwixt 'em and snop it open."

"Lawks, 'ear 'im!" chuckled the corporal. "Would yer believe it, it's the third time 'e's been tiddely this week! If it wasn't fer 'is twenty years' service, they wouldn't 'ave stopped with tyking 'is stripes. No, sir, they'd 'ave chucked 'im into the clink."

Mr. Glencannon nodded sadly. "Aye," he agreed. "There's no doot he desairves it. I beg yere pairdon, young mon, but do ye hoppen to be Corporal Alf Chatterton, by any chance?"

"I do, but there's no chance about it," replied the other grandly. "They permoted me to be corporal because I'd ought to be corporal, and that's just why I am a corporal. Yus, sir, Corporal Alpheus Chatterton, at yer service!" He clicked his heels and saluted smartly.

". . . Eight steel ribs and a bit o' a black rag are all ye need to mak' an umbrella," came the sepulchral voice from the bench.

"Ah, foosh, corporal, pay no attention to him!" Mr. Glencannon dismissed the interruption, at the same time wringing the other's hand. "Sit doon, sit doon, lad! After all the guid things I've heard aboot ye today, it's a pleasure indeed to mak' yer'e pairsonal acquaintance!"

Corporal Chatterton's bulging chest bulged still farther as he settled into the proffered chair. "Well, I'm orlways glad to 'ear good things about myself," he admitted blandly. "Just 'oo did yer 'ear the latest reports from — my horfficers or only from my pals?"

"From neither," replied Mr. Glencannon. "From neither — and from better than either! This afternoon, ye see, I had the difficult tosk o' calling upon Mussis Sergeant Major Mahoney, to apologize to her for the way yon droonken oaf has behaved toward her charming and talented little daughter. While I was there, the guid Mussis Mahoney confided to me the great hoppiness whuch is shortly to be yours and — and — weel, I hope ye'll honor me the noo by drinking a drop o' whusky to the bride, Corporal Chatterton."

". . . The Joponese, however, mak' them oot o' split bomboo and paper," said Cousin Douglas.

"Whisky?" repeated Corporal Chatterton. "Well, rather! A man on private's pay don't often get a bite at anything better than beer, and of course I won't draw my first noncom's screw till next Friday a fortnight. Yus, indeed, sir, I'd relish a spot of whisky no end!"

"Pairfict!" said Mr. Glencannon, reaching under the bench and dragging forth the bottle of bumboat bilge. Ye're aboot to mak' the acquaintance o' whusky in its most deleectable form. Noo, this bottle o' Duggan's Dew o' Kirkintilloch" — he placed it reverently at the center of the table — "is one o' the last remaining 'o a cherished private stock whuch has been in the Glencannon family for ceenturies. We keep the priceless auld stuff under lock and key until one o' the clan is aboot to wed. Then — Then — Weel, corporal" — there was a catch in his voice — "ye can imagine my feelings, after having brocht this ceremonial bottle half way around the world, to lairn aboot our family's shame."

"When the wind blaws it inside oot, sumply turn aroond, let it blaw it back again!" soliloquized the sleeper on the bench.

"There, ye see?" Mr. Glencannon appealed, at the same time flagging the waitress. "Losh, Corporal Chatterton, may none of yere babies be dipsomoniacs! . . . F-s-s! . . . Here, muss! Please fetch a corkscrew, two glosses and a bottle o' arrack. . . . I'll leave ye to drink the whusky by yersel', corporal. For sentiment reasons, whuch I know ye'll appreciate, I — ugh — no, I cudna touch a drap o' it!"

"Well, yer sentiments does yer proud," said Corporal Chatterton, eyeing the brimming glass which the waitress had poured for him. "'Ere's to the blushing bride and the 'andsome bridegroom! Hupf! Hapf!" He unfastened his collar hooks and wiped his eyes. "Why, d'yer know, this stuff is a bit of orl right! It tystes something like hornets boiled in boot polish in a slop pail."

Mr. Glencannon smiled as he gulped his arrack. "Aye, that's because it's ower four ceenturies auld," he explained unctuously. "Four hoonderd years — think o' it! When that whusky was laid doon, the Rock o' Gibraltar was only a pebble, the giant thesaurus was roaming the earth, and men and women were riding aboot on velocipedes." He poured himself another jolt of arrack.

"Well, it certainly 'as one 'ell of a muzzle velocity," agreed Corporal Chatterton. "In fack, I wish I 'ad time to myke this bottle larst. But at midnight" — he glanced at his bright new chromium wrist watch —" at midnight sharp, I've got to tyke my men up on the Rock, so I 'aven't any time to wyste. We've target practice at sunrise in the morning."

"Her Mojesty the Queen invariably carries one," said Cousin Douglas, saluting in his sleep.

"Target proctice? Ho, I envy ye!" said Mr. Glencannon. "I mysel' am a famous shot with firearms o' all descriptions, including, bross knuckles. When I was a boy, I used to think nothing o' shooting the eye oot o' a tomcat at five hoonderd yards with a .22 pustol."

"Twenty-two pistol!" scoffed Corporal Chatterton, replenishing his glass. "Oh, 'oo the 'ell wants to bother with a .22 Pistol? We — er — I — why, tomorrow morning, I'm going to fire a fourteen-inch rifle!"

Mr. Glencannon's shoulders shook with patronizing mirth. "A foorteen-inch rifle!" he scoffed, measuring the distance between his hands. "Haw, guid losh, corporal; d'ye mean to teel me that His Mojesty's troops are rejewced to playing with miniature popguns whuch e'en the Boy Scoots would scorn with derision? A foorteen-inch rifle, to be sure! Oh, haw, haw, haw! Noo I understand why ye're so cautious aboot drinking that whusky. Whusky is a mon's drink!"

"Oh, yus?" retorted Corporal Chatterton truculently. "Well, just to show yer that I'm a man [gluck] there goes a whole ruddy tumblerful, see? And just to show yer agyne, I'll drink a [gluck] another! And as fer that fourteen-inch rifle yer giggling about, let me tell yer that fourteen inches ain't the length of it, it's the bore! Yus, a fourteen-inch bore — n'ow wot do yer think of that?"

"Swith, the Royal Garrison Artillery can boast the biggest bore in the world!" replied Mr. Glencannon heartily. "Come, have another drink, corporal, and tell me more aboot this mommoth popgun o' yours."

"Don't call it a popgun!" cried Corporal Chatterton, pounding his fist on the table. "It's a cannon, a cannon — a Mark XI Vickers fortress rifle, the very larst-word in 'eavy hartillery! It's a thirteen-point-six, to be hexact, or three 'undred and fifty millimeters. It's sixty feet, three inches long from muzzle to breech, and it'll throw a four 'undred 'n' fifty pound Mark XIV shell thirty-one thousand yards, or happroximately eighteen miles. Up there on the Rock, we —"

". . . His Royal Highness, the Juke of York, carries a silk one whuch has an electric floshlicht cunningly concealed in the hondle," announced Cousin Douglas oracularly.

"Oh, shut up, do!" snapped Corporal Chatterton. "Up there on the Rock we've got twenty of them guns in emplacements between O'Hara's Tower, which is thirteen hundred and sixty-three feet above sea level, and Rockgun Battery, which is thirteen hundred and fifty-six. I'd like to see the ruddy Dago navy try to get through the Strait when I'm on the job!"

"Haw, so shud I!" said Mr. Glencannon. "Come, let's drink to yere vurra guid aim!"

Corporal Chatterton needed no urging; in fact, he followed the drink with another. But though he was now outside the greater part of the quart, it seemed to have little effect on him.

Mr. Glencannon, who had done nobly with the arrack, observed the corporal's apparent sobriety with amusement. "Losh!" he chuckled to himself. "He's got the vurra worst kind o' a jag — the kind with revairse English on it, when ye're so drunk ye're sober! But just wait till he gets ootside and the fresh air hits him! Aye, and wait till he reports for juty at the barracks!"

"It's quarter to twelve," the corporal announced briskly. "I'll just swill the 'rest of this 'ere whisky, and then I must shove orff. Well, cheeri-ho, Mr. Glencannon! Many thanks fer yer 'orspitality, and if yer'll tyke my tip, yer'll walk yer ruddy cousin around a bit before 'e tries to get back to quarters. If yer don't, 'e'll get fourteen days in the clink."

"Thonk ye, I will," said Mr. Glencannon, suddenly realizing that his own faculties were becoming somewhat arrackized and that a walk might prove beneficial to himself. "Weel, Corporal Chatterton, in love and in target proctice, may ye have all the success ye desairve! Guid nicht, my brave lad."

"In Siam, the golden umbrella is the inswignia o' royalty," declared Cousin Douglas.

"Weel, shove it doon yere throat and open it, then!" retorted Mr. Glencannon, shaking him violently. "Come, it's time to wak' up, ye great drunken booby, ye!"

Cousin Douglas opened his eyes and then sat bolt upright. "Colin!" he cried. "Did ye see her? Did ye see her mother?"

"No, they were both oot; I'll see them in the morning. Come on, Dooglas, get up; we're gaeing for a bit o' a stroll."

"Stroll?" repeated the Highlander. "Foosh, Cousin Colin, what are ye leaning against the wall for? Why, I do believe ye're in in yere cups! Weel, dinna worrit, lad. I'll see ye safely back aboard yere ship." He snatched up the arrack bottle, gulped what little remained in it, grasped the table by a leg and tossed it over the heads of the surrounding drinkers.

"Ah, Dooglas, Dooglas!" Mr. Glencannon chided him. "Are ye no' yet sober enough to realize that a donce floor is no place for furniture?" Lurching between the startled couples, he picked up the table and hurled it back into the corner.

Not without difficulty, then, they assisted each other into the night and headed for the water front. "Funny," muttered Cousin Douglas, gazing up at the stars, "I thocht it was raining. Then I thocht I was Kitchener. Then I knew I was sober. Weel, I must have been dreaming. On the other hond I may have been drunk. But domn if I can find the other hond.... Whoa, steady. Canna ye stond up straight?"

"'Tis ye that's teetering, no' me." Mr. Glencannon protested thickly.

"Weel, somebody's teetering" said Cousin Douglas, "but at this time o' nicht, I dinna suppose there's any way o' finding oot who wrote it."

"Is there no British Consulate in this sorra town?" demanded Mr. Glencannon, scratching his pipestem against a lamppost and throwing away the match. "It seems to me that in 1926, when I was here, I was there. They guarontee it to give ye thirty-five shaves per blade."

"Exockly!" agreed Cousin Douglas, helping himself to a sixpence from the cup of a blind Moorish beggar. "The following nicht they sairched his bag and found eleven packs o' marked cards."

"Weel. it's Foscism, Communism, Socialism — call it what ye will!" Mr. Glencannon's countenance opened in a cavernous yawn: "Whoo-a-ah! Guid losh, Dooglas, control yersel'! Dinna ye ken that yawning is contagious?"

"Yo-a-whoo! Um! M'm!" The Highlander stretched and nodded sleepily. "But why did ye sign it withoot reading it?"

"A vurra guid suggestion," said Mr. Glencannon. "Let us lie doon in the shade o' this signboard by the water's edge and enjoy the customarra noontime siesta." Cousin Douglas unstrapped his wrist watch, wound it, and tossed it over the signboard into the inky water. "Wak' me airly, airly, mother, for I'm to be queen o' the May," he mumbled, settling down beside Mr. Glencannon.

IV

Mr. Glencannon was awakened by the roar of express trains rushing by behind the sign board. Ordinarily he would not have minded them, but this morning he had a splitting, or arrack, headache and he found their clatter definitely annoying. For a while he lay without opening his eyes, trying to piece together the events of the preceding day. At length, through the mental association of express trains and honeymoons, he remembered Clematis Mahoney, and her inheritance of two thousand pounds.

He sprang up. "Be still, my heart, be still!" he murmured ecstatically.

The sun, he noted, was half an hour high and the water of the Strait, deserted save for a government tug steaming slowly along a mile or two away, was a brilliant pink. Cousin Douglas, his Glengarry cap pulled over his face as though it were a feed bag was emitting snores like the soughing of the wind in a graveyard cypress.

"Puir lad!" mused Mr. Glencannon, contemplating him. "I misdoot he'll be in a muckle o' trouble again for absence withoot leave. Weel — haw! — yon prig o' a Corporal

Chatterton will keep him company in the clink for showing up drunk at target proctice. . . . Corporal Chatterton! Private Chatterton, I shud say, because no doot they'll rejewce the drunken swine to the ronks and —"

He paused to listen. while another express train sped past. "Strange, strange!" he muttered, strolling along the heavy timber at the wharf edge. "There wasn't any railroad in Gibraltar yesterday, so they must have built it owernicht. Weel, we live in a progressive commercial age! Odvertising, there's the secret! I dinna doot, for exomple, that the front o' this hoarding bears a poster O' Duggan's Dew o' Kirkintilloch, identical with those that they've plastered all ower the British Isles. Ah, the Dew o' Kirkintilloch!" He smacked his lips. "How snoogly a dollop o' Duggan's Dew wud do me the noo! Weel, I —" Suddenly his voice became a cross between a croak and a shriek. "Dooglas!" he ordered. "Quick! Come aroond here!"

Cousin Douglas rose, blinking, and stumbled around the end of the signboard. He found his relative staring stupidly toward the town. Toward it, yes, but the town wasn't there! Instead was a vast expanse of water, with the sunbathed peaks of Andalusia and the summit of the Rock just showing above the distant horizon.

"Oh, losh!" he gasped. "Why, domn it, Colin, we're oot in mid-ocean on a roft! There must have been an earthquake during the nicht; the wharf bruk loose and —"

He was interrupted by the roar of another approaching train — a fast train, a heavy train, which sounded as though it were crossing a trestle.

"Duck!" he screamed. "Lie doon!"

The invisible express thundered overhead. Instantly, out of the sea beyond the raft, leaped a towering white geyser which climbed up and up. For aching minutes it hung suspended; then it collapsed upon itself in a patch of steaming spume. Faintly from across the water rolled a muffled "Boom!"

"Colin! The fourteen-inch rifles!" Douglas gasped. "It's target proctice — and we're — we're on the target!"

Mr. Glencannon's blood turned to cold jellied consomme. He rolled up his eyes toward heaven, observing, as he did so, that the fencelike structure which he had mistaken for a signboard was in reality a white-painted oblong of wooden slats. Large sections of it had been crudely and recently repaired.

"S-s-shr-r-o-o-o-oof!" another projectile came ripping through the air. "Pl-l-osh-h-h!" it hurtled into the water a scant fifty yards from the raft. The solid wooden hull dithered in the swell, and as countless gallons of chill sea water crashed down upon him, Mr. Glencannon emitted a piercing scream.

Then there was a rush, a deafening roar, a shattering crash. A thirty-foot section of the target soared into the air and vanished in a seething maelstrom which swept over the raft and stood it on its beam ends. Gasping for breath, Mr. Glencannon felt that a pile driver had hit him in the diaphragm.

"Ah, Dooglas, ye lout!" he was finally able to snarl. "If I only had my bross knuckles, I'd mak' ye think that shell had struck ye square! Ye call yersel' a soldier? Foosh, why did ye no' have sense enough to see it was a target last nicht?"

"Oh, aye?" countered Douglas hotly. "Ye call yersel' a sailor? Blosh! Ye cudna e'en distinguish this roft from the wharf it was tied up to."

"Ho, so it's my fault, is it?" Mr. Glencannon seized a splintered timber and started for his cousin. "Weel, ye stuppid sot, ye, I'll soon show ye whose fault it is!"

When the speedboat from the target tender arrived to ascertain the damage done by the direct hit, its crew was horrified to find two limp forms sprawled side by side upon the narrow raft.

V

Col. Sir Basil Burton-Melville, O.C. 67th Regiment, R.G.A., acting provost marshal of the Crown Colony of Gibraltar, scowled across his desk at the two battered prisoners.

"Well, my man!" he snapped at Mr. Glencannon. "What did you think you were doing out there on that target? Have you any idea of the fate you escaped?"

Mr. Glencannon drew himself up with vast dignity. "Sairtainly I have, as ye'll lairn to yere cost!" he retorted. "I escaped being murdered by yere domn Vickers Mark XI fortress rifles, throwing a four-hoonderd and fufty poond Mark XIV shell approximately thirty-one thoosand yards. I know that ye've got twenty such guns up there on the Rock betwixt O'Hara's Tower and the Rockgun Battery, and I know furthermore, that I intend to drog ye into the law courts and sue ye for domages for yere cruminal neegligence in shooting them at me. Foosh, 'tis an ootrageous state o' affairs when —"

"Wait!" barked Colonel Burton-Melville. He sat back, frowned and placed his finger tips together. "H'm! It seems to me you know a good bit more about our artillery than you've any business to know, my fine fellow!"

"Aye, sir, he's a spy!" blurted Cousin Douglas. "He's a distant reelative o' mine — a sort o' cousin — and I've lang been suspicious o' him. Last nicht I shadowed him doon to the water front and saw him sneak aboord the roft. I snuck aboord too and hid on the other side o' the target. I thocht I'd denoonce him when they started towing us oot to sea before daylicht. Then I thocht it wud be better to wait and catch him red-handed, actually obsairving the fire. No doot he plonned to jump owerboord and get picked up by a boat. I —"

"Well, by gad, that was plucky of you, I must say!" the colonel nodded approvingly. "As an infantryman, you, of course, didn't know that they try to straddle the target, not to hit it — although they often do hit it accidentally, as they did this morning. Oh, I'll see that you get your stripes back for this. Yes, by gad, you can consider it all settled! I'll recommend you for the D.C.M. for bravery too! But as for you" — he turned accusingly upon the engineer — "where did you get all your information about the Rock armament? Speak up!"

"From yere ain lout o' a Corporal Chatterton," said Mr. Glencannon. "I didna give a hoot aboot yere guns, but he inseested on teeling me."

"Corporal Chatterton, eh!" fumed Colonel Burton-Melville. "Well, he'll be rear-rank Private Chatterton and cooling his heels in clink, when I get through with him! Blab military information to civilians, will he? . . . Send for him at once, Mahoney!"

"I just 'ad a phone call from the Rockgun Battery that they've put Corporal Chatterton under arrest, sir," reported the sergeant major. "'E was acting orlright when 'e went into the emplacement, but then it happears 'e was suddenly tyken drunk,

"If I only had my bross knuckles, I'd mak' ye think that shell had struck ye square."

sir — in fact, it was 'is fault that they laid that gun wrong and smarshed up the target. The charge is intoxication, insubordination and removing 'is breeches on 'Is Majesty's fortified property to the prejudice of military discipline, sir."

"So! I'll attend to his case later. Now you!" The colonel leaned across his desk and shook his fist in Mr. Glencannon's face. "You get out of Gibraltar in two hours' time, or I'll put you under arrest! Spy? Spy? You're not a spy; you're just a damned nuisance! . . . Sergeant Glencannon, show your precious cousin to the door and boot him through it! . . . Boot him I said! Boot him, sergeant! . . . Harder! Harder! . . . Ha, that's the way!"

The Wailing Lady of Limehouse

Shortly before dawn on a misty morning some years ago, a British tramp ship called the *Sherwood Forester* rounded the North Foreland at the mouth of the Thames Estuary and settled into the home stretch of her long trek from the Far East. What with one thing and another, including quarantine at Singapore, condenser trouble in the Red Sea, bearing trouble since Port Said and dirty weather in the Bay, it had been an arduous passage; and now that it was all but over, those of her people who were on deck gazed away at the friendly glow above the city of Margate and at the winking beacons along the coast of Kent and permitted their thoughts to stray ahead to the luxuries awaiting them in London, each man according to his lights. The crew were thinking of a good old binge, three days blind and then stony broke; Captain Whitstead was pleasantly occupied in thinking what he would say to those swine, the owners; Mr. Hale, the First Mate, was polishing the scathing valedictory he would shortly address to that curmudgeon of a

Captain Whitstead; while the Second Mate, Mr. Cowley, rehearsed the farewell remarks with which he would blister the scoundrelly Mr. Hale. Thus, for once and at long last, comparative contentment reigned upon the ship, even extending to the slumbering members of the watch below.

In his room on the starboard side of the alleyway aft, Mr. Frazer McFidd, the Chief Engineer, lay blissfully dreaming that he and the lady of his heart were standing hand in hand in the summer sunset before a snug little inland cottage, watching the Second Engineer burning at the stake in the center of a flowerbed. In his room directly opposite, the Second Engineer, Mr. Colin Glencannon, dreamt no less blissfully, of leading his bride up the aisle of Glasgow Cathedral while Mr. McFidd lay out into five distinct, gory and still-palpitating fragments beneath the wheels of a tramcar which for some reason had entered the cathedral nave through the transept.

The peculiar, the significant circumstance about these two dreams, a circumstance fraught with dire potentialities, was that both of them featured the same leading lady.

Early on an evening some months previously, shortly after Mr. Glencannon had signed as Second on the *Sherwood Forester* and before he and his Chief had come to look upon each other with repugnance, they repaired ashore to a pub hard by the Regent's Canal Dock in the Limehouse district of London and there quaffed deeply. At closing time they were still quaffing and minded to continue, but the harassed publican produced a police whistle and a sand-filled sock from under the bar and threatened to blow the one and wield the other if his guests tarried longer. Retreating into the night and pausing only to kindle a bonfire against the pub's front door, these good companions set forth along the Commercial Road in quest of surcease for their all-consuming ennui. They had progressed no farther than the head of Three Colt Lane when they beheld a young lady engaged in putting up the shutters of a fried-fish shop and weeping softly to herself.

Now weeping ladies, old and young, are by no means rare in the causeways of Limehouse, especially on a Saturday night. But this young lady was pretty, after a pinkly, buxom fashion, and so the two toilers of the sea paused, leaned against each other for support and viewed her with sympathetic interest.

"Oh, come, come, lass!" said Mr. Glencannon consolingly, with a spontaneous gesture offering her a cigar. "Do ye dry yere tears and cease yere bellyaching. What in the heel is the motter with ye, anyway?"

"Aye, what's amuss, lass?" inquired Mr. McFidd somewhat thickly, swaying away from Mr. Glencannon and bringing up against a lamppost. "If some foul droonken beast has been insoolting ye, lass, ye've only to point oot the foul droonken beast oot to us! Why, Muster Glencannon and I will tromple him so flat that he'll be able to use himsel' for his ain bedsheet, the foul droonken beast!"

"Aye, he will if he can monnage to scrape himsel' off the pavement, the foul droonken beast!" rasped Mr. Glencannon, slipping a knuckle duster over his fingers and polishing the spikes of it against the breast of his jacket. "Speak up, noo, lass, and let the mayhem proceed!"

Instead of speaking, the young lady set down the section of shutter which currently occupied her, buried her face in her apron and emitted a series of earpiercing wails. A crowd collected. The situation was embarrassing. Mr. McFidd produced a ten-inch Stillson wrench from his hip pocket, balanced it ominously in his hand and glowered into the assembly. The crowd melted away.

Meanwhile Mr. Glencannon was giving attention to the immediate surroundings. The fried-fish shop was, he saw, more properly a booth, a newly white-painted wooden structure built against the brick wall of a seamen's lodging house. In contrast with the sordidness prevailing throughout the neighborhood the booth had a cheery, supersanitary gleam about it which reminded him of the refrigerated storage chamber of the Liverpool morgue. Across the front of it was a sign: "Laura's Fish & Chip Shop."

"'Laura,'" he read aloud, turning to the wailing lady. "So Laura's yere name, is it? Weel, Muss Laura, if it's the sorra state o' trade yere worriting aboot, stop yere bawling at once! Muster McFidd and I will stup into yere neat little establishment here and eat ye oot o' house and hame. Why, bless ye, lass, we'll stoomach every last fish and chip ye've got in stock!"

"Aye, we will in vurra deed!" agreed Mr. McFidd stoutly. "A guid auld seafood guzzle is exockly what my puir parched system craves. Open up yere shop again, Muss, and when we've choked doon all the fish that's edible we'll start afresh on the heads, the fins and the unspeakable etceteras."

"B-but there ain't no fish in stock, th-th-that's just the trouble!" wailed Miss Laura, emerging from her apron. "The b-b-bleddy fishmonger promised me a week's credit to 'elp me get started, and now 'e's let me down! 'Ere it is my first Satiddy night in business and orl the pubs just out and everybody 'ollering fer a dish of fried plaice or a nice bit of piping 'ot boiled heel, and 'ere am I without so much as rotten sprat in me hice chest!"

She looked from one to the other with appealing eyes, and in that instant, though neither of them was aware of it, their respective destinies swung apart like outwardbound ships at the mouth of a river.

"Ho!" said Mr. Glencannon. "So 'tis a fishmonger has done ye dirt, is it? Weel, Muss, if ye'll just give us his name and address, Muster McFidd and I and mysel' will tak' great pleesure in pointing oot to him that credit is the vurra lifeblood o' trade, pairhops e'en spilling a bit o' his ain to prove it. . . . Won't we, Muster Mac?"

Mr. McFidd gripped his Stillson, compressed his lips and nodded grimly. He was all prepared to time a savage bellow simultaneously and concealingly with a long-impending hiccup, but though tensed and on the *qui vive* the hiccup beat him to it. "Yic!" he said, irrelevantly but with a certain dignity. "That is — er — yic!"

"Well," said Miss Laura, dabbing at her eyes, "I 'opes yer can convince the 'ard-'earted blighter better than I, and I must say it's very 'andsome of yer even to try. 'Is nyme is Woolstocking, 'Enery Woolstocking, and yer'll find 'im at the fourth barrow on the left just arfter yer turn into the market in Ropemakers Fields, down there at the bottom of the lane."

"Richt ye are!" said Mr. McFidd. "We'll be back in just a jiff — ic — iffy, so go inside, licht yere stove and prepare for a rooshing business. Come alang, Colin — you and I are going f-f-FICK! — fishICK! — er — angling!"

There were neither ropemakers nor fields in the squalid thoroughfare called Ropemakers Fields, but along both sides of it stood rows of pushcarts with naphtha flares, the flickering light of which danced on the silver scales of stark, stiff fish in thousands. On the slime-coated cobblestones a regiment of cats was feasting, while the dank night air above was filled with a medley of smells and the clarion cries of the costers: "'Ere yer are, gents — 'ere's the best place to buy the best plaice! And if yer 'aven't 'ad my 'addock, why, yer've simply never 'addock!"

"Losh!" snorted Mr. Glencannon. "Did yer e'er listen to such nauseating puns? Is yon the smirking swundler she told us aboot?"

"I dinna ken," replied Mr. McFidd, at the same time screwing open the jagged-toothed jaws of his Stillson wrench that they might inflict a double dent in a single application. "To tell ye the truth, Colin, I'm feeling a wee bit fuddled and I canna recall whether she said the third barrow in April or the seecond Wednesday on the left."

"'Erring? 'Erring? Yer won't be erring if yer buy my 'erring!" declaimed the importunate punster, stridently. "Eel? Fresh conger eel? Well, gempmen, this 'ere conger eel is rally fresh — yus, it's congereely fresh!"

"Oh, dom! Did ye hear that?" demanded Mr. Glencannon, shuddering.

"Aye, and I Stillson do!" said Mr. McFidd, leaning across the punster's pushcart and felling him with a blow.

For some minutes, then, great tumult arose in Ropemakers Fields and the mean streets surrounding. It was audible even to the lady who had been the unwitting cause of it, as in her booth at the head of Three Colt Lane she stirred the batter in the bowl, tilted the sputtering margarine across the pan and exhorted her impatient customers to "just 'old 'ard fer 'arf a mo', gents — yer nice fresh fish will arrive 'ere any minute!"

Arrive it did and in bountiful measure. Staggering under the weight of his burden Mr. McFidd appeared bearing in his arms a tunny fish the size of a small canoe. Just behind him, a Laocoön in Limehouse, Mr. Glencannon wrestled grimly among the thrashing coils of a live conger eel full seven feet long. From his

Mr. McFidd appeared bearing in his arms a tunny fish the size of a small canoe. Mr. Glencannon wrestled grimly among the thrashing coils of a live conger eel.

pockets and the front of his jacket protruded the tails of sundry bream, plaice and herring.

"Well, Muss, we've brought ye yere fish!" announced Mr. McFidd somewhat superfluously, maneuvering the tunny endwise through the doorway.

"Aye, and there's plenty more where this came from," added Mr. Glencannon, finally succeeding in landing his knuckle duster on the conger's elusive chin. "We've established yere credit beyant question or quibble and if there's aught else ye want, from a shrimp to a shark, ye've only to say the word!"

Impetuously Miss Laura leaned across the counter and kissed them, smack, smack! "Lawks!" she exclaimed, a catch in her voice. "It's — it's a fair treat indeed to meet up with a pair o' 'igh-clarss chivalorous coves like you!" And again she burst into tears.

'Twas thus the romance started.

II

For some reason, beginning with that fateful Saturday night, the affairs of Laura's Fish & Chip Shop flourished apace.

Messrs. McFidd and Glencannon spent many hours and large sums of money at her spotless counter; gallantly they consumed entire shoals of fish; but invariably numerous other customers were present. Thus, though rejoicing in the turn of her fortunes, it was impossible for the lovesick swains to tell her what was in their hearts, even when they went there separately.

So far, barring an almost imperceptible coolness which had come between them, their rivalry was friendly. Gorged with fish they would return aboard the *Sherwood Forester,* discuss their passion and compare notes of their respective progress, although the progress was nothing to brag about. For a day or two, Mr. McFidd would feel himself the favored suitor; then, for a while, her smiles would be all for Mr. Glencannon. Nothing was definite. And always, always, time was growing shorter. Finally:

"Noo, look ye, Colin," said Mr. McFidd, the very morning before sailing day, "tomorrow we're leaving for the Orient; we'll awa' five months at the least and before we go we've got to have a showdown with her."

"Aye, that we have," agreed Mr. Glencannon. "We've filled oursel's with fish till we bristle lik' hedgehogs with the bones and I give ye my wurrd that my razor is so full o' knicks I can use it for a comb. Ugh! The vurra thocht o' a fish mak's my gorge rise and my puir pooncture stoomach palpitate lik' a busted bagpipe bladder. But still, despicht it all, neither o' us kens his stottus."

"Exockly, and besides, I'm all bruk oot with hives," said Mr. McFidd, reaching over his shoulder and scratching his back with his Stillson. "Therefore I suggest that we gae ashore richt the noo, catch her while the shop is empty and teel her fronkly that she's got to tak' her choice."

Mr. Glencannon put on his cap. "Lead on, McFidd!" he said simply.

Arrived at the booth at the head of Three Colt Lane, they found Miss Laura daintily engaged in eviscerating a mullet. "Well, lorlulmme, if you two ain't the early birds today!" she greeted them, dislodging a handful of tangled mechanism and tossing it, kerslither, into a bucket. "'Ow about a nice bit o' this 'ere mullet fer yer farewell breakfuss, wotcher say, boys? First I'll fillet it fer yer, then I'll roll it in batter, then I'll . . ."

"Er-weel," broke in Mr. McFidd, turning green around the edges. "Er, weel, fronkly, no."

"Ho, what's this? No fish this morning, Muster Mac?" Mr. Glencannon chided in feigned astonishment. "Weel, in that case, I, too, will relooctantly deny mysel' the, p-p-pairdon me, the pleesure!"

Without further beating around the bush they stated the object of their visit. Miss Laura dissolved in tears. But her suitors had long since observed that she could outweep even the oft-sung lachrymose heroine of "Ben Bolt," weeping with delight when they gave her a smile, weeping with chagrin when they didn't and weeping for no apparent reason at any time at all, until it seemed, in sooth, that she kept her tears on draught, like beer in a pub. Between sobs and sniffles, then, she begged them not to force a choice upon her. Confessing a great tenderness toward them both, she still was unable to say which was the nearer, dearer. Tomorrow they would be gone — (loud wails) — and while they were away at the far side of the world, playing fast and loose with Japanese rickshaw girls and the shameless ukulele dancers of Ohio, she would be searching her heart and praying for guidance. But upon their return they would find her waiting; yes, waiting with her answer. . . .

At this point her wailing soared to such a soul-piercing pitch that Messrs. McFidd and Glencannon with difficulty suppressed an urge to tilt back their heads and howl like dogs at a violin. Even had they known what to say, Miss Laura couldn't have heard them say it; and so having kissed her, each man to a salty cheek, they turned away and left her weeping into the mullet.

III

Next day as the S.S. *Sherwood Forester* slid through Gallions Reach on her way down to the sea, the two senior officers of her engineering staff were moody and morose. What might have been a bond of sympathy between them seemed rather to be developing into a bone of contention, each man in his disappointment considering the other an obnoxious obstacle between him and happiness. After the first few days they no longer spoke of the matter. By the time they had reached Gibraltar they were speaking only in monosyllables on any subject. After that, except on duty, they didn't speak at all. As time wore on, Mr. Glencannon found himself becoming more and more annoyed by the manner in which certain tufts of hair bristled from Mr. McFidd's ears. Mr. McFidd, a notably careless eater, was lashed to a sullen fury by what he deemed Mr. Glencannon's snobbishness in polishing his fork with his pocket handkerchief and drinking his tea from the saucer. And these were to be but minor items in the logbook of this five months' voyage of hate — a hate which was, we have already seen, festering even in their dreams as on that misty morning the *Sherwood Forester*, London bound, turned into the placid home waters of the Estuary.

Mr. Glencannon smiled in his sleep as he heard the cathedral bell toll a single note of rejoicing for his wedding and for the death of Mr. McFidd. The great edifice, he saw, was packed, and he estimated the gate receipts at somewhere between six and eight millions of pounds. He was about to turn to Laura and offer her a mullet when he perceived with dismay that his rival had succeeded in reassembling his component parts and was emerging from under the tramcar with upraised Stillson. Instinctively Mr. Glencannon's hand moved toward his pocket for his brass knuckles when he realized — ah, horrors! — that he had neglected to wear trousers. He turned to flee, but too late. With a savage cry Mr. McFidd sprang, swung the Stillson and —

"Almost eight bells, sir! Almost eight bells, sir! Quarter-to bell's gone orlready, sir!"

"All richt, all richt, canna ye see I'm awake?" Mr. Glencannon grunted at the man in the doorway. He yawned, stretched, stepped into his carpet slippers and donned his boiler suit. Then, having bolted the door, he produced from the locker a bulky bundle wrapped in Shanghai newspapers and carefully enveloped it in an old oilskin coat.

Now, this was the year when many ladies of fashion and almost all grand pianos were wearing Spanish shawls, which are really not Spanish at all but Chinese. In consequence of their popularity, they were fetching fancy prices in London. Mr. Glencannon's bundle contained an even dozen of them — one for Miss Laura, the rest for sale and all of a splendor to challenge Zuloaga's brush or Hergesheimer's pen. Mindful of the well-known nosiness of His Majesty's customs inspectors, Mr. Glencannon deemed it imprudent to arrive at London with these shawls in his room and therefore planned to secrete them elsewhere for a few days until he could smuggle them ashore one by one.

Descending the ladders into the heat and thunderous turmoil of the engine room, he picked up a duck lamp and made for the entrance of the shaft tunnel. It still lacked four minutes to eight bells and young Mr. Ferguson, the Third Engineer whom he would shortly relieve, did not notice him pass.

The shaft tunnel of the *Sherwood Forester* was a steel housing something like a sewer main, extending the hundred-odd feet between the after bulkhead of the engine room to the tube glands in the very stern of the ship. Scarcely five feet high, one had perforce to stoop when walking in it. Along its port side the great propeller shaft turned in the bearings, underfoot the plates were slick with oil, while overhead, oppressively, one sensed the tons of cargo stowed on the tunnel's roof in the afterholds. All in all it was a fearsome burrow and no promenade for anyone subject to claustrophobia.

As by the duck lamp's flame he made his way along it, Mr. Glencannon hummed a merry madrigal in time with the rhythm of the engines and chuckled to himself. "Eleven shawls at fufty quid apiece mak' five, hoonderd and fufty poonds — a tidy nest egg to set up housekeeping on! The twelfth shawl she can wear for her wedding dress and . . ."

From the depths of the tunnel a flashlight darted its beam. "What the heel are ye snoopling aroond back here for?" rasped the voice of Mr. McFidd.

"What the heel do ye think?" Mr. Glencannon countered blusteringly, dropping his bundle and stepping in front of it. "I'm aboot to tak ower the watch, so it's plainly my juty to tak' a look at these rotten auld bearings. From the sound and the feel and the hot-metal smell o' them, I shud say we'd be lucky to —"

"What have ye got in yon boondle?" demanded Mr. McFidd.

"What have ye got in yon tins?" and Mr. Glencannon pointed accusingly at a dozen bright cylinders which Mr. McFidd was striving to conceal beneath a square of jute sacking. "Aye, what have ye got in those tins besides Chinese oopium ye dope smoogler! Come hame to Laura with dirty money, wud ye? Ah, foosh and shame to ye, Muster McFidd! Why, ye nosty, veenomous boglie, ye're no' fit to —"

WHANG! Something struck him on the side of the head and it wasn't Mr. McFidd's Stillson. CRASH! In the echo of a fearful thunderclap like the crack of doom, Mr. Glencannon felt himself being swept through the tunnel on the bosom of a madly rushing cataract. Mr. McFidd and the bundle of shawls were running him a close second.

IV

When Mr. Glencannon opened his eyes, he found himself in a little white room with an unmistakable hospital smell about it. Beside his bed sat a mountainous gentleman in shirt sleeves, reading a newspaper and twisting the points of a waxed mustache. Mr. Glencannon could not see below this person's waistline; but from the handcuffs, chain nippers, keys and other odds and ends depending from his belt, he felt reasonably safe in assuming him to be a policeman.

"Guid morning," said Mr. Glencannon, politely.

"Good evening," replied the policeman, pontifically.

"Where am I?" inquired Mr. Glencannon.

"Royal Mariners' 'Orspital, London," said the policeman in a brusque official manner. "Besides that, yer under arrest."

"What are ye snoopling back here for?" rasped the voice of Mr. McFidd.

"Under arrest!" exclaimed Mr. Glencannon, starting up indignantly but subsiding as a twinge of migraine drilled through his skull. "Under arrest? Ho, dom, what for?"

"Fer smuggling Chinese hopium," said the policeman. "Oh, my word, yer won't 'arf catch it, you won't! I was just now reading about it in this 'ere newspyper 'ere, and twenty years from now, when they let yer out, why, just remember that I —"

"R-read it to me," urged Mr. Glencannon weakly.

"Hunh, as if yer didn't jolly well know orlready!" sneered the policeman, grimly. "Now just lie quiet, Mister, while I goes out and hinforms the horderly yer've finally woke up. Then I'll 'ave to telerphone the magistryte's clark so's 'e can come over 'ere and tyke yer formal stytement!"

When he had gone, Mr. Glencannon reached for the paper on the chair. His head was still throbbing, but he read:

SHIP SAVED BY ENGINEER'S HEROISM
OPIUM PLOT BARED IN THAMES DRAMA
'MERELY DOING JOB,' SAYS MCFIDD

Early this morning while the S.S. *Sherwood, Forester*, 3325 Tons, Burwell, Chaney, Ltd., owners, was off Whitstable, her Chief Engineer, Mr. Frazer McFidd, entered the shaft tunnel in search of opium which he had reason to suspect was being smuggled by one of his subordinates, C. Glencannon. He found not only twelve tins of opium but Glencannon himself, in the act of secreting a package of shawls, silks and other valuable contraband. Grappling with the smuggler, McFidd had just succeeded in subduing him when the vessel's tail shaft broke in such manner as to cause a serious leak at the after end of the tunnel. More serious still, a fragment of metal, possibly the cap of a bearing, was thrown through the tunnel roof thus giving the water free ingress to the vessel's hold. With rare presence of mind McFidd thrust Glencannon's bundle of contraband into this puncture, dragged the, unconscious smuggler out of the tunnel and closed the watertight door at its entrance. At the time of this adventure McFidd disclosed nothing of Glencannon's criminal part in it nor of his own heroism. It was not until the *Sherwood Forester* was drydocked at Sheerness, where the opium was discovered in the tunnel and the shawls in the hole in the roof, that McFidd, in matter-of-fact tones, volunteered the whole stirring story of how he had saved the ship. "I was merely doing my job," he concluded modestly. Glencannon, still unconscious from the blow dealt him by McFidd and suffering from the effects of oil and water swallowed when in the flooded tunnel, was put under arrest and brought to London in a police ambulance.

The paper fell from Mr. Glencannon's fingers and slid rustling to the floor. "Losh!" he gasped, covering his eyes. "'Tis almost too much for my puir, cracked head! But, noo, let's see, let's see! In the feerst place, the chunk o' metal whuch went through the roof o' the tunnel must have clouted me on the head on the way, in the seecond place, the water whuch was rooshing in from the leak in the stern glands must have foorced my boondle o' shawls up into the hole in the roof and plooged it, lik' a washrog in a bathtub drain. And in the theerd place" — his aching head drooped wearily — "in the theerd place . . . Ah, what will Laura say?"

V

On the morning of the second day following, the charges against Mr. Glencannon were withdrawn and he was released with a warning. Repairing to the owners' offices to draw the wages due him, he was paid and given the sack. Hastening then to the corner of the Commercial Road and Three Colt Lane, he found Laura's Fish & Chip Shop with its shutters up and a card on the door reading: "Closed until Fryday."

By this time he was stunned by the succession of calamities which had befallen, but as he stood gazing dully at the card he sensed that he was in for still another. Turning to a blowzy lady who was sweeping the steps of the seamen's lodging house, "I beg yere pairdon, moddum, he said, "but can ye teel me why the fish shop is closed?"

"Yus," replied the lady, leaning on her broom. "It's because Laura got married yestiddy and 'as went orff on 'er 'oneymoon to Brighton, that's why. At 'igh noon, it was, at the Lime'ouse Registry Horffice and there never was a bride look prettier, although she did bawl and beller sumping fearful, that I must say. Arfter the orgies, the 'appy couple went direckly to . . ."

Mr. Glencannon, his knees trembling, swayed back against the booth. "Teel me," he managed to ask, though knowing full well, "teel me who was the groom?"

"The groom? Yer mean 'er 'usband? Oh, lor-love yer, 'e ain't no groom, 'e's a ship's hengineer! Why, e's the fymous cove which orl the pypers 'ave been printin about lytely! 'Ere, wyte, I'll show yer!" Crossing the sidewalk to a garbage pail, she fished out several parcels done up in newspapers and scanned the wrappings. "Yus, 'ere, it's this one," she said. "I knew it was me third-floor cuspidors.

"Read it yerself, Mister — I 'aven't got my glarsses."

Halfway down the parcel, Mr. Glencannon saw:

LLOYD'S TO HONOR HERO
Gold Watch for McFidd for Saving Ship, Cargo
WEDDING BELLS TODAY

Frazer McFidd, whose heroism on the S.S. *Sherwood Forester* Wednesday prevented the loss of the vessel and its cargo, was voted a Lloyd's Gold Watch by the Underwriter's Association at a special meeting yesterday. The Lloyd's Gold Watch is awarded for valor while saving insured property and is considered a high honor among the officers and men of the Mercantile Marine. Its value is £150. When notified of the distinction in store for him, McFidd only blushed modestly, but his fiancée, whom he will wed today, was completely overcome with pride and happiness.

"Yus," said the blowzy lady, "it happens that Laura's 'usband is no end of a 'ero. At the Wedding yestiddy, 'e — But 'ere, 'old 'ard, Mister! Why, wot's the matter — are yer drunk?"

"Not yet, Moddum," said Mr. Glencannon, lurching across the Commercial Road.

VI

Time, though a greater healer than the greatest specialist in Harley Street, worked only half a cure in the case of Mr. Glencannon. In two months his heart was whole again and he realized that he had wanted Laura less for herself than for the satisfaction of humiliating a rival. But even two years did nothing to heal the wound which McFidd's perfidy had inflicted and the very thought of the base betrayer rankled him like a thorn in his seat. And then one night in a smoke-filled barroom in Durban, Natal, he met the scoundrel face to face.

"Come ootside, McFidd," he croaked sepulchrally. "I've a word to say to ye!"

"Ah, and so it's you, Colin!" Mr. McFidd licked his lips as he tried to smile. "Ah, come, come, lad," he whined. "Ye — ye surely dinna mean to say ye'd hit a mon when he's doon!"

Taken aback by this answer, Mr. Glencannon observed that Mr. McFidd seemed to be very far down indeed. His clothes were shabby and he needed a shave; also, he gave off dense fumes of alcohol, although for some reason these were not perceptible to Mr. Glencannon.

"Ah, swith, Colin, dinna hold a groodge!" he went on wheedlingly. "I know I played ye foul but — weel, look at me the noo and judge for yersel' if I haven't attuned for it! Come, let's sit doon and have a friendly drink — although fronkly, auld mon, I canna offer to pay for it!"

After a moment's hesitation, Mr. Glencannon let the knuckle duster slip from his hand into his pocket, led the way to a table and beckoned the waiter. "McFidd," he said solemnly, "what in the world has hoppened to ye, mon?"

"Everything," said Mr. McFidd, striving to conceal his frayed cuffs. "Everything, Colin! As ye see, I'm nowt but a puir wreck rotting on the beach."

Mr. Glencannon drank deep. "And — and what about Laura?" he asked.

Mr. McFidd drank deeper and laughed bitterly before replying. "Laura? . . . Laura? Weel, Colin, ye dinna ken yere ain luck! Sparing ye the harrowing details, all she did was weep aboot this and weep aboot that till domned if I didn't sometimes think I'd married a showerbath. In the end it was too much for me, so I — I, weel, I sumply disappeared!"

"But why are ye so doon in yere luck, mon? Surely ye can find a berth aboord a ship — espeecially, er, being a Lloyd's Watch winner and all!"

"Oh, Colin, Colin, dinna roob it in aboot the Lloyd's Watch!" groaned Mr. McFidd. "As for getting a berth, the Board o' Trade has conceled my certificate. So unless I ship as donkeymon there's no' a hope. I've got a job promised me up on the Rand, running a stationary engine at the Premier Mine, but I haven't e'en got the price o' the fare from here to Cullinan."

Mr. Glencannon refilled the glasses. As he considered the pitiful ruin across from him he could not help reflecting that there, but for the grace of God, sat himself.

"Lloyd's Watch!" said Mr. McFidd in a faraway voice. He shook his head and took a drink. "Lloyd's Watch! . . . Lloyd's Watch, won by a mon named McFidd! Aye, they e'en engraved his name in it — 'Presented by the Society o' Lloyd's to Frazer McFidd, for Valor.' Weel, my name's Johnson, noo, or Smith, or Reilly or Cohen. Frazer McFidd is dead; yes, dead, I say, Glencannon, so e'en his watch doesna do me any guid!" He dragged out the gleaming timepiece and sneered at it.

Mr. Glencannon stirred uneasily. "Let me look at it, McFidd, will ye?"

Without a word the other pushed it across the table.

Now Mr. Glencannon did not need a watch; he already owned one which he valued highly — a massive silver key winder, Glasgow built, which gave off sounds like a stamping mill in the distance. It was a family heirloom which had come into his possession shortly after his twenty-first birthday, and though he had not paused amid the hue and cry to inquire the name of the family, the initial on the case was C. It had been a simple matter to alter the C to a G, thus establishing his ownership beyond question or cavil. Every six months, religiously, he would pry open the back door of this timepiece, swab down the machinery with paraffin oil and then pack it with a good grade of heavy cup grease; and so it had served him faithfully through the years. But he knew that the watches bestowed by Lloyd's were the finest in the world, and that they were worth one hundred and fifty pounds. And besides, he smelled a bargain.

He examined Mr. McFidd's watch critically. "Weel, I must say it doesna look lik' much," he announced, shoving it back.

Mr. McFidd shrugged his indifference. "It doesna mean much, either," he said, "— to me."

"How much wud ye sell it for?"

Mr. McFidd picked up the watch, grimaced at it and put it down again. "Colin," he said, "the domned thing is a Jonah. I wudna advise ye to buy it at any price. Aye, and in teeling ye that, I dinna ken where my next meal is coming from!"

"Ten quid?" suggested Mr. Glencannon.

"It cost a hoonderd and fufty," said Mr. McFidd.

"Fufteen?"

"Sold!" said Mr. McFidd. "But I promise ye, Colin, that if I didna need the money to get to Cullinan, I'd rather have thrun the beastly thing awa'."

Mr. Glencannon paid over the fifteen pounds and took delivery of his purchase. "Come, we'll have a drink on it," he invited. They drank. Shortly thereafter Mr. McFidd, his confidence somewhat restored by the fifteen pounds in his pocket, went forth into the African night.

"Haw!" gloated Mr. Glencannon when he had gone. "A hoonderd-and-fufty-poond ticker for one-tenth o' the oreeginal price! Aye, ye're in luck for fair, Glencannon! And beyant that, there's the still luckier circumstance that yon puir tromp McFidd, and no yersel', is married to the weeping Laura! Oh, haw, haw, Glencannon m'lad, ye surely canna complain!" The more he thought about things the luckier he felt, but by the time he had finished the bottle he was inclined to credit his good fortune not to luck but to cleverness.

"Aye, intellect, intellect, there's the onswer!" he muttered, heading down Point Road toward the harbor. He paused beneath a street lamp and consulted his new watch. It gave the time as eleven minutes past midnight. "Occuracy! Precision! Ah, ye little beauty!" he addressed it. "I wonder how lang it will be before I can sell ye at a hondsome profit? No' vurra lang, I'll wager!"

Perhaps five minutes later, though, a new thought struck him. "Sell it? Sell it? Why shud I sell it, when I dinna need the money? No! I'll sumply tak' it to a jeweler, have my ain name engraved instead o' McFidd's, and lo, there'll be one more meember in the Honorable Company o' Lloyd's Watch Heroes!" Pausing again, to examine the engraving, he was surprised to note that the hands now stood at twenty-one minutes to three. "Weel, *'teapot tempus in a fugit'!*" he quoted. "Aloss, that our allotted time on earth for chority and guid works shud be so short and fleeting!" In meditative mood, he looked at the watch again and saw that the hour and minute hands were moving in opposite directions and at considerable speed. At first he was inclined to attribute this phenomenon to his personal overstimulation; but even as he gazed, the racing hands collided at twenty-seven minutes to seven and there locked together. Simultaneously there came a click, a snarling buzz and then all was still.

"Oh, dearie me!" said Mr. Glencannon. "I fear that something is sodly amuss. Pairhops, though, it has merely run doon." He held the watch to his ear and shook it. It emitted sounds like a Zulu gourd rattle. He gave the winding button a tentative twist and the entire stem came off between his fingers!

"Weel, 'tis neglect, gross neglect!" he diagnosed the trouble. "That lout o' a McFidd treats a watch as shobbily as he treats his engines. But ne'er mind, ye little beauty — a guid watch once is a guid watch always, and feerst thing tomorrow papa'll have ye' repaired by the shrewdest watch tinker in Durban!"

Next morning, though, the slightly overnosed horologist whom Mr. Glencannon consulted broke into mocking laughter the moment the timepiece was put before him. "Vat, another vun?" he cackled, letting the little black spyglass tumble from his eye. "Vell, vell, vell, Mister, you're the sixth gent who's been in here with vun of these fake Lloyd's Vatches in the past month! I don't know vat this feller MacFidd's game is, but I do know that this piece of junk is vorth ten shillings hardly, if it's vorth that. It vas made in Japan, and . . ."

With a hoarse cry, Mr. Glencannon shoved the little brass beauty into his pocket and stumbled from the shop.

VII

One blistering April morning in the current year of supposititious grace, a ship named the *Inchcliffe Castle* lay at anchor in the harbor of Tamatave, on the eastern side of the island of Madagascar. She was waiting for a cargo and while her crew chipped paint and cursed the heat and the officers, her officers sat under the awning rigged across the poop, at intervals bestirring themselves to curse the heat and the crew.

On the horizon beyond the reefs, a smudge of smoke rose out of the cobalt Indian Ocean; then two stump masts climbed up, then a funnel, then a hull, and before long a tramp ship stood just outside the pass, seesawing in the long swell and hooting impatiently for the pilot.

In his deck chair aboard the *Inchcliffe Castle*, Mr. Glencannon, the four stripes of a Chief Engineer on the shoulder straps of his tropical whites but otherwise unchanged by the years, laid down a three months old copy of *The Presbyterian Churchman*, squinted off at the new arrival and stirred uneasily. "She's British, that's sure," he announced. "Ye can teel by the oogly bluff snout o' her. But besides that, she looks fameeliar — aye, strangely, distoorbingly fameeliar! Noo, I wonder, aye, I wonder, if she can be or can't be, and if she is or if she isn't?"

"Wot's that?" demanded the First Mate, acidly. "Yer wonder if she can or can't or was or couldn't wot? Blyme, Mister Glencannon, I really do think yer might be a bit more implicit!"

Mr. Glencannon shaded his eyes with *The Presbyterian Churchman*. "Why, I wonder if she is or isn't a ship I once sairved in years ago, Muster Montgomery — a ship that was the scene o' a great roomonce, a great trogedy, a —"

"Well, 'er nyme's the *Sherwood Forester*, if that's any 'elp to yer," announced Mr. Montgomery, peering through his binoculars. "But, lawks! Romance, did I 'ear yer say? Do yer mean to tell us yer was ever guilty of a romance, Mister Glencannon? Oh, haw, haw, haw and three tee-hees, as the mermaid said to the walrus!"

Mr. Glencannon favored him with a glance of extreme distaste. "Aye, roomonce," he said, half to himself. "I had a vurra tender roomonce while sairving in the auld *Forester* and if ye haw-haw-haw again, ye blathering jockoss, I'll fix ye so ye'll tee-hee-hee into yere ain ear. But alock and aloss for the days o' my youth! I was hopeful, ambitious, then! I dreamed o' becoming a Superintendant, a shipowner, a mullioneer — aye, I had visions o' being a gentleman, even! Instead o' whuch" — he turned appealingly to the company — "instead o' whuch, my middle years find me still slaving in a rotten tromp ship and still forced to consort with nosty offal lik' this mon Montgomery. A-weel" — he rose and moved toward the *Inchcliffe Castle's* ladder. "I obsairve that the *Forester* is aboot to moor at that next buoy yonder, and so I shall row mysel' o'wer to her and invoke meemories o' monny sweet and bitter hours. Pairhops some o' the auld crowd is still aboord her and will stond me a drink."

The only member of the original company left in the *Sherwood Forester* was Mr. Ferguson, the young Third Engineer whom Mr. Glencannon had been about to relieve on that long-ago morning in the Estuary. But now Mr. Ferguson was middle-aged and wearing four stripes of his own.

"Ach, Colin, Colin! Twelve years since we've met — just think o' it!" he sighed when the greetings were over. "Weel, plenty's the water that's flowed ower the dom and e'en more the whusky that's treekled past our tonsils in the interim! . . . And noo that ye hoppen to meention it, there's a bottle o' Duggan's Dew back there in my room that — Ah, but I see ye still remeember yere way aroond the ship!"

Whisky in circulation and pipes gurgling comfortably, the pair fell to reminiscing of old times. "And that black scoondrel McFidd," mused Mr. Glencannon, "the last time I saw him was in Durban, and he was doon on his lowest uppers for fair! I wonder whate'er hoppened to him?"

"McFidd? Oh, why McFidd's dead; I thocht surely ye'd heard!" said Mr. Ferguson. "He got drooned ower by Mozambique, five or sax years agone, guid riddance to him and rest his soul! But he was going under the name o' Johnson at the time and that's what's caused all the trooble."

"Trooble?" repeated Mr. Glencannon. "What trooble, Alan?"

Mr. Ferguson eyed him narrowly and sipped his drink before replying. "Why, the legal trooble aboot Mussis Laura McFidd. Losh, Colin, d'ye mean to say ye didna know? Ye, o' all men?"

Mr. Glencannon laughed the cynical laugh of a man of the world. "Alan," he said, with an airy wave of the hand, "noo it can be told! Laura was only a possing foncy with me and I dinna mind confiding to ye that I let McFidd win her withoot opposition. In foct, fronkly, I engineered the whole thing! I canna abide a weeping woman and I cud plainly foresee that married life with Laura wud be one lang vale o' tears. And sure enough, when I met McFidd that time in Durban, he told me she was still spilling brine lik' a battleship's condenser."

"But dinna ye ken why, Colin? Come, teel the truth, noo!"

"Weel," said Mr. Glencannon, "I can only give ye my scientific theory, which is that there was too much salt in her system, on account o' her being in the fish business. But Nature is a vurra wonderful reegulator, Alan, and so I foncy that tears were her notural ootlet. Laura was weeping the feerst time I saw her and I'll wager she still is."

"Richt ye are!" said Mr. Ferguson. "She wept all ower Lime'ouse when Mcfidd was alive and she's weeping all ower London today. And the reason — noo get this, Colin — she says the reason is because she married the wrong mon! She's been in love with with somebody else from the vurra ootset!"

"Aye?" Mr. Glencannon blushed to the roots of his walrus mustache and smiled sheepishly at the toes of his shoes. Then he sat back and toyed with his glass; and when he ceased toying, the glass was empty. "Weel, weel, weel!" he breathed. "So that's it, is it? Ah, I suspected it all alang! Weel, Alan, what ye teel me wud be vurra gratifying if it wasna so patheetic! Tsk, tsk, tsk, puir woman! To think that I bruk her heart when she was only a girl and that noo I dinna care a tinker's Saturday fig aboot her! And yet, if I shud go to her today, I suppose she'd marry me in a minute!"

"Oh, no!" said Mr. Ferguson. "Oh, no, indeed, she wudn't! She wudn't marry not even you! And that brings us richt back to the legal trooble I spoke aboot at the beginning. Withoot legal proof that McFidd is dead, she canna marry at all, d'ye see? Three or four swundlers have showed up from time to time, with eevidence they'd concocted themsel's, and tried to marry her, but dom if the fat auld girl was fooled by any o' them! She knows the whole bag o' tricks, does Laura McFidd! Aye, Colin, she must weigh all o' two hoonderdweight, but she's as canny a businesswoman as ye'll find in the United Kingdom!"

"Two hoonderdweight — losh, just imogine it!" and Mr. Glencannon shuddered as he did so. "Why d'ye suppose anybody wud want to marry her?"

"Weel," shrugged Mr. Ferguson, "being married to the owner of the Britannia Fish & Chip Chain Shops, Limited, with ower five hoonderd restaurants throughout the British Isles, means marrying an income o' something lik' a hoonderd thoosand poonds a year. Fat as she is, Laura McFidd, the London mullioneeress, wud mak' a vurra hondsome catch for a mon lik' — lik' — Oh, but what's the motter, Colin? Here, quick, drink this! I'm holding it steady for, ye! Swith, Colin, ye've a nosty touch o' the fever coming on, that's what ails ye! Here, drink another and I'll row ye back to yere ship!"

VIII

Ensconced in his chair aboard the *Inchcliffe Castle* and still prostrated from shock, Mr. Glencannon sat with eyes closed. "A hoonderd thoosand poonds a year!" he muttered. "A hoonderd thoosand poonds a year! And I cud marry her tomorrow if 'twere no' for that dom McFidd getting drooned by the name o' Johnson! Foosh — ah, foosh — the scoondrel still mocks me from beyant his watery grave!"

After a while he opened his eyes and by taking stock of the familiar surroundings tried to dismiss the matter from his mind. Mr. Montgomery, he observed, was trailing a stout fishing line over the bulwark of the after well deck. Even as he looked, the line jerked taut, the Mate shouted, and several firemen ran to his assistance.

Moving to the rail and gazing into the water, Mr. Glencannon saw a fourteen-foot shark, securely hooked and thrashing about in the depths like a Whitehead torpedo on a rampage.

"'Eave 'im in! 'Eave smartly now — 'eave, blarst yer, 'eave!" Mr. Montgomery was screaming. "Don't give 'im no slack or 'e'll bite the bleddy line! 'Eave! Hup! Tyke a turn around that bit.... There, that's got 'im! Run along to the galley, one o' yer, and fetch me the cook's 'atchett."

The hatchet forthcoming and the shark having been given what was good for him, his corpse was dragged to the deck and the *Inchcliffe Castle's* company gathered around in wonderment and awe.

"A-weel, noo that ye've slauchtered it, what are ye plonning to do with it?" Mr. Glencannon posed the question skeptically. "If ye shud hoppen to osk me, Muster Montgomery, I'd say ye've got a white eelephant on yere honds, or e'en worse!"

"Oh, yus? Well, I didn't 'appen to arsk yer!" retorted Mr. Montgomery, swelling with the cosmic pride of a fisherman in his catch.

"'Owever, I don't mind telling yer that I intend to tyke out 'is backbone and myke a very 'andsome walking stick of it. And when we get 'ome to London, I'll sell the walking stick fer two quid at least, so you can just climb aboard yer ruddy white hellerphant and go fer a gallop to 'ell on 'im!" He removed his jacket, clicked open his knife and with great fixity of purpose fell to his task.

"Braugh!" shuddered Mr. Glencannon, watching him. "Nosty work! Butcher's work! . . . Butcher's did I say? No, great swith, I meant fishmonger's!" And still shuddering, he hastened to his room for a stimulant.

In half an hour, though, amply fortified, he returned and stood watching, while the Mate delved deep in the beast's internal anatomy. Once, with keen professional interest, he even stooped, peered, and with his hand explored the space where the shark's engine room should have been. "Frichtful!" he murmured, wiping his fingers on a convenient fireman. "Ghoulish!"

It was shortly after this that Mr. Montgomery sprang up from his labors, waving on high an object just retrieved from the gaping cavity.

"A watch! Blyme, why 'ere's a watch!" he cried. "Yus, a fine gold ticker! Look at it, gempmen — just look at it! Belonged to some poor cove which the ruddy beggar ate, and 'ere's orl that's left of 'im. Well, 'pon my word, I believe it's a Lloyd's Watch! Yus, see, yer can still read it: 'Pre-er-presented by the Society of Lloyd's to F-r-a . . . wait-Frazer McFidd'!"

"McFidd?" repeated Mr. Glencannon. "Frazer McFidd? Why, the name soonds faintly Scottish! Weel, weel, weel, I wonder who the puir fellow was! — Did any o' ye e'er hear o' him?"

"No," Mr. Montgomery answered for the crowd. "But when we get to London I'll go right to Lloyd's and get this 'ere

McFidd's 'ome address. Then I'll take this watch to 'is widder, I will, and I betcher she'll stump up with a 'andsome carsh reward!"

"I dinna doot she can afford it!" chuckled Mr. Glencannon, his mind filled with ecstatic thoughts of one hundred thousand pounds per year.

IX

The morning following the *Inchcliffe Castle's* arrival in London, Mr. Montgomery donned his best suit and his bowler hat and hooked his shark-spine walking stick over his arm. "I'm going to Lloyd's in Leadenhall Street about this 'ere watch," he announced to the others, still gathered around the breakfast table, "and then, if the widder lives in London — well, I'll be back by noon with a pocketful of oof!"

"Godspeed!" Mr. Glencannon wished him piously. "I'll be awaiting reports o' yere mission with throbbing heart and bated breath."

Now as to the heart throbs there is no telling, but certain it is that when Mr. Montgomery strode into the saloon at lunch time, Mr. Glencannon's breath was monumental.

"Well," announced the Mate triumphantly, "I found 'er, and look!" One by one he slapped five ten-pound notes upon the table. "Yus, gempmen, she stumped up fifty ruddy quid, as yer can see! Great fat cow the size o' a coal barge, she is, and filthy-reeking-foul with money! Got a gorgeous horffice of 'er own in Grosvenor Gardens. Well, when I tells 'er my story and 'and 'er the watch, wot do yer s'pose she done?"

"Why, she bruk into tears," said Mr. Glencannon, with the calm assurance of an eyewitness.

"Oh, no, she didn't! She pushed a buzzer on 'er desk and in came a little weazened cove in a frock coat and spats. "Enery," she says to 'im, 'oh, 'Enery, wot do yer think! Oh, 'Enery, 'Enery, 'Enery, the proof 'as come at larst!' Then she turns to me and says, 'Mister Montgomery, shyke 'ands with Mister Woolstocking. Mister Woolstocking is my Managing Director,' she says. 'Hexcept fer one single tiff, one lovers' quarrel, Mister

Woolstocking 'as been my dear friend and valued associate ever since the earliest days of this 'ere business,' she says, 'and now I want you, Mister Montgomery, to be the best man at our wedding.'

"'Yus, indeed,' says this 'ere 'Enery Woolstocking, smiling from ear to ear and very cordial. 'I'll be really glad to 'ave Mister Montgomery as our best man — yus, conger-eely glad, as I used to say in the old days in Ropemakers Fields!'

"Well, they slipped me the fifty quid and, when I left, the little cove was sitting on 'er lap and she —"

"She was weeping!" Mr. Glencannon broke in hoarsely.

"Weeping?" scoffed Mr. Montgomery. "Weeping? She wasn't weeping at any price! As a matter of fact, she was larffing to beat ell!"

THE MEAN MAN OF GENOA

T he Reverend Mr. Eric Stainforth, elderly Rector of the English Church of the Pilgrims, of Genoa, stood in the cold March drizzle at the head of the ramp which leads down from the Via Carlo Alberto and considered without enthusiasm the curving panorama of harbor and sea that spread so grandly before him. He was feeling his years and the weather in his bones; and besides, he was thinking about Mr. Binney. As he shifted his gaze to the crowded waterfront, Mr. Stainforth was unable to restrain a sigh. Nearest at hand and dominating the scene, her bright tricolored funnel markings dimmed by scudding wraiths of mist, the mighty *Rex* loomed above the modernistic concrete planes and angles of her adequately advertised berth. Off to the left rose a spidery tangle of masts and rigging where a couple of Danish barques were loading; beyond them, a big black American freighter and a pale gray Norwegian discharged cargo at the Magazzini Generali, while at the far side of the Molo Vecchio lay two idle tramp ships flying the Red Ensign of the British Mercantile Marine. "Ah," murmured the Reverend Mr. Stainforth, viewing the limp banners through spectacles dimmed by fog, "the blood and — er entrails of old England! Well, I fancy it's aboard them that my painful duty lies."

As he had guessed, one of the British vessels was indeed the Inchcliffe Castle *of London.*

Descending to the quay and making his way along it amid thundering motor lorries and clanking electric trains, he came at length to the Vecchio mole. As he had guessed, one of the British vessels was indeed the *Inchcliffe Castle,* of London, while the other was the *Eskmouth,* of Leith. The *Inchcliffe* being the nearer, he turned up his coat collar, furled his dripping umbrella and started up her swaying, breakneck ladder. "Well, I'll — I'll try to manage the thing in a decent way," he promised himself, miserably. "I'll play the mendicant friar and not fall back upon Binney's nasty threats except as a last resort — if then! But — Oh, I do wish he'd handle this business himself, as long as he's too mean to buy a — a new one!"

He paused uncertainly on the rusty, deserted deck; then, hearing voices from somewhere forward, he moved in their direction. Halting at the door from which the sounds emerged, he tapped on it with his umbrella handle and emitted a discreet but nervous cough.

"Ye lie, ye lie, ye lie!" roared one of the voices bloodcurdlingly.

"Oh, do I, I do, do I?" bawled the other. "Why, blast ye, MacCrummon, if ye dinna cease dealing off the bottom, I'll snatch oot yere tripes with my bare hands!"

There was a thump, another, and a chorus of rasping, strangling snarls. Despite his age and a certain natural diffidence, the Reverend Mr. Stainforth was keenly sensitive of the obligations of his cloth and he knew where his duty lay. Pushing open the door, he stepped within and beheld two gentlemen clutching each other's throats from opposite sides of a card-strewn table. Their feet were entangled in their chairs and the chairs were bolted down; thus, although each strained mightily at his antagonist's windpipe, the horrid tug of war seemed destined to end in a draw.

"Gentlemen, gentlemen! For shame!" Mr. Stainforth admonished with a fervor which he customarily reserved for the pulpit. "Please! Oh, please, gentlemen!"

Without relaxing their holds on throats and chairs, the pair turned their eyes in the clergyman's direction and viewed him at length, hostilely. Finally, the one who looked the less like a walrus licked his lips and stertorously addressed the other.

"Glencannon," he demanded, "who is yon obnoxious auld sweer?"

"I've no' the slichtest idea," wheezed Mr. Glencannon. "But whoe'er he may be, he doesna look owerly honest. 'Twud be no more than prudent o' us, MacCrummon, to relax our holds lang enough to put yon money and the whusky oot o' his reach. Afterward, o' course, we can resume."

"Ah, tut, tut, my dear fellow!" protested Mr. Stainforth, hastily unbuttoning his waterproof and displaying his clerical collar. "You need feel no anxiety as to my, er . . ."

"Losh, a parson!" gasped Mr. Glencannon as he and Mr. MacCrummon, letting go simultaneously, fell back into their chairs. "Come, come, sit ye doon and join us, reeverend sir! There's a clean glass on the sideboard, so pour oot yere — (Foosh! Kick me, wud ye, MacCrummon? Oh, aye, aye, pairdon me.) — I mean, sir, there's a looking glass ower the sideboard, so just help yersel' to a look in it and mak' yersel' entirely at hame. Ye see, sir, Muster MacCrummon and mysel' were just whiling away the time with our daily limbering and stretching exercises, so I'm sure ye'll forgive our seeming boorishness when, feeguratively speaking, the butler brocht in yere — a-hem! — yere — card!"

"Ouch! Hell's horns!" barked Mr. MacCrummon, suddenly grasping his shin with one hand and reaching for Mr. Glencannon's throat with the other. "Why, ye treacherous, black —"

Mr. Glencannon seized the outstretched hand, planted his own elbow on the table and, appeared to strain mightily. "Cards, cards, cards!" he hissed from the far side of his mouth, jerking his head toward the pasteboards strewn upon the oilcloth. "Gather them up, ye dolt!" Then, turning to Mr. Stainforth with a charming smile, "Indian wrestling, we call this, sir! It's great sport and a capital exercise for the elbow muscles. Och! . . . There, see? MacCrummon's got me doon!"

"Well, well, well!" beamed the clergyman, sinking into a chair and wiping off his spectacles. "I can't tell you how happy I am to find that I was — er — under a slight misapprehension. . . . By the way, my name is Stainforth; I'm rector of the Church of the Pilgrims, up there on the hill in the Via San Giuseppe."

"I'm honored to meet ye, sir," said Mr. Glencannon. "No doot ye'll be interested to learn that that vurra eminent and austere divine, the late Reeverend Strathallan Glencannon, o' Craigellachie-on-Spey, was one o' my family. A mon o' pious works, his great zeal finally got the better o' him and he was transported to Tasmania for sheep stealing in 1853. Muster MacCrummon and mysel', however, are both Chief Engineers."

"Eh? . . . Engineers? How interesting! Perhaps I should explain that as one of the very few English clergymen here in Genoa, I make it my pleasant duty to visit aboard the British ships which so frequently seek haven in this port. Thus, I —"

"Haven?" Mr. Glencannon interrupted him, frowning perplexedly. "Losh, Sir, we're no seeking haven! What the *Inchcliffe Castle* is seeking is freight, and I can assure ye that MacCrummon's ship, the *Eskmouth* yonder, is doing likewise."

"Aye," nodded Mr. MacCrummon, reddening somewhat as the Ten of Clubs fluttered out of his sleeve. "We're seeking freight — the vurra same charter that the *Inchcliffe Castle* is seeking. But while our respective owners are yaggling ower the terms with the people here in Genoa, Muster Glencannon and the rest o' us are left to rot from sheer monotony. We're fair distracted for lack o' distraction. Oh, I promise ye, sir, it's a frichtful bore!"

"Ho, yes, yes, but here's an idea!" exclaimed Mr. Glencannon, brightly. "Both you and mysel' are profoond Presbyterian theologians, MacCrummon, so noo that this reeverend gentlemon is here, what d'ye say to whiling away the time with a guid auld three-cornered releegious argument?" He wheeled upon the minister and shook a horny finger under his nose. "O' course, sir, I've no the slichtest idea o' yere denomination or what gospel ye preach, but just to start the ball a-rolling, I'll tell ye to yere face that all its doctrines were conceived in error, founded on fallacy, propagated by falsehood and are, in short, puerile, idiotic and utterly ossinine balderdash. Haw, let's hear ye try to refute that!"

Mr. Stainforth winced perceptibly, but the other's words had given him an opening, and he made for it. "You seek a pastime? . . . A distraction?" he demanded eagerly. "Indeed, gentlemen, that's precisely what I've come aboard to offer you! For surely, there's no finer, no more satisfying distraction than good music — organ music! Surely, there's no better way of passing the time than sitting in a church listening to it! . . . Now, please don't think I am attempting to proselytize, gentlemen. No! I'm simply extending an invitation — a most cordial invitation — to our Sunday service, to hear our organ — to enjoy this grandest, most inspiring — er — harmony."

"Oh, losh, why that will be delichtful!" breathed Mr. MacCrummon, ecstatically.

"Aye, delichtful indeed!" echoed Mr. Glencannon. "I'd almost as soon listen to a weel-played kirk organ as to a bagpipe. The one trouble is, the distraction which ye so kindly offer is for Sunday, and today's only Thursday. That leaves a dreary muckle o' time to be passed in the meanwhile."

The Reverend Mr. Stainforth stirred in his chair and mentally braced himself for the plunge. "H'm, yes, that's so — it hadn't occurred to me," and he felt himself blushing at his

"I'll tell ye to yere face that all its doctrines were conceived in error."

own gentle fib. "But, I say, look here, I've a suggestion! Now frankly, gentlemen, our organ is not as — er — young as it used to be. It leaks here and there, and several parts of it are broken. A number of the notes don't work at all. As a matter of fact, there's an entire chord missing. Well, wouldn't you like to exercise your mechanical talents and at the same time occupy your leisure, by setting it to rights between now and Sunday? Come, gentlemen, I'd — I'd appreciate it awfully!"

"Fix it? Foosh!" snorted Mr. MacCrummon, indignantly. "So that's yere game, is it? Ye want us to pay the piper with the sweat o' our brows do ye? Weel, I thocht I smelled a rat when ye came in! Just let me tell ye that e'en if I was an expert certificated master organ tinker, which I'm not, I'd no' raise a finger to help ye, under the caircumstances!"

"No, and neither wud I," declared Mr. Glencannon, staunchly. "Much as it gawps me to agree with MacCrummon, I must say I think ye oozed yere way in here under false pretenses and that yere methods stink mildly o' fraud. Why do ye no' hire some o' the local Dagos to patch up yere auld hewgag for ye? Are ye so parsimonious that ye begroodge them the money?"

The old gentleman's mouth opened but no words came. He shuddered, covered his eyes with his hand and quailed miserably. But at length, "Please, please!" he begged. "You're right, you're absolutely right! I did come here under false pretenses! But —"

"Explain yersel', sir," invited Mr. Glencannon, relenting somewhat.

"I'll tell the truth, as I should have told it at the outset!" The Reverend Mr. Stainforth swallowed, glanced from one to the other of them and then seemed to look off into the distance. "First, forgive me if I explain that until recently my career in holy orders has not been much of a — er — success. I served in the colonies, you see, and my health was poor. But about a year ago I was called here to Genoa and I felt that my humble efforts would at last bear fruit. Here, at least, I had a real church with a real organ; I saw real work to be done and I felt my energy renewed and equal to it. The only drawback" — he clasped his hands — "the only drawback was — Mr. Binney."

"Binney?" demanded Mr. MacCrummon. "Not John Binney?"

"John Binney?" echoed Mr. Glencannon. "Ye mean the Binney o' the Anglo-Genoese Exporting Company? Why, he's the vurra same bondit who's dangling that charter before my owners, Clifford and Castle, and MacCrummon's owners, the East Lothian Shipping Company! Both our firms are cutting each other's throat to get the business, both our ships are lying here eating their heads off to be ready to snaffle up the first cargo, and — here we sit!"

"That is the Mr. John Binney." Mr. Stainforth smiled sadly. "I fancy I need not tell you that he is a mean, headstrong and overbearing man. He is the warden of my church, its senior trustee, my temporal lord and master and — the thorn in my side!"

"Heaven help ye!" breathed Mr. Glencannon, sympathetically.

"I know that it will," said Mr. Stainforth. "But from the very beginning, Mr. Binney and myself did not see eye to eye. Our church is comfortably endowed, but he'd never relinquish the purse strings, even for necessary repairs. The walls and ceilings should be redecorated. The poor old organ has been getting worse and worse. I begged him to buy a new one, but he laughed at me. I've begged him to have this one seen to, but he always puts me off. Why, in the past year, at least six young ladies of our congregation have indignantly resigned as organist after the second or third week of it!" He spread his hands. "Last Sunday, in the midst of a beautiful service, the organ moaned, wheezed and died. 'Oh, never mind,' said Mr. Binney in that cynical way of his. 'It got us through the Offertory, didn't it?' All week he has refused to call in repairmen, but this morning he telephoned me from his office. . . . Need I tell you what his orders were, gentlemen?"

"Ye — ye mean to say he told ye to come here and trick us into fixing it for nothing?"

"Precisely! And he suggested that if I were not able to cajole you, I should use threats. 'The two lines are fighting each other for my business,' he said. 'You can tell those engineers that a little extra service from one of them may help me decide which company gets the charter, and then he'll get the credit. But if neither of them will co-operate — well, then you can promise them that their owners will hear about it from me when I award the contract elsewhere!"

"Ah, swith!" fumed Mr. Glencannon. "Why, the penny-pinching blackguard is no more nor less than a blackguardly penny pincher! MacCrummon, I vurra weel ken that ye're a mon devoid o' principle but, for mysel', I refuse to be browbeaten in this matter. Foosh to Binney, foosh to his threats and foosh to his organ, say I!"

"Aye, and ye micht as weel say foosh to yere job, as lang as ye're in a fooshing mood!" Mr. MacCrummon reminded him, gloomily. "Mind ye, I wudna fix it if I cud and I cudna fix it if I wud, but either way I'm sunk, and so are you. Oh, an organ is a vurra complicated contraption, Glencannon! It's fuller o' guts than a Borneo bushmen's banquet; once we tuk it apart we'd ne'er be able to put it back together again, so yon swine Binney has got his knife in us any way ye look at it!"

"A feeg for the mechanical difficulties!" said Mr. Glencannon.

"It's the principle, the principle, that decides me!"

"Ah, m-m, well, so then you've decided," mused Mr. Stainforth, sadly. "Not that I blame you in the least — no, no, of course not! But I can't help thinking it's — it's too bad, after all my work and hopes. I really thought that this time I'd get things going, do you see? But more and more the congregation have complained of our atrocious music, and lately more and more of them have been motoring down to Rapallo and those places to worship. I'm beginning to feel afraid, er — a little bit afraid that, that . . ." His voice quavered, and quite suddenly he turned his head away.

"Ah, noo, my vurra dear sir, control yersel'!" Mr. Glencannon hastened to comfort him, at the same time taking advantage of the clergyman's emotion to down a dollop from the bottle which his exploring foot had long since prudently hooked over from beneath MacCrummon's side of the table. "Noo that we've read between the lines, noo that we understand cairtain things ye've been too proud to explain, we'll tak' a try at it this vurra day. . . . Won't we, Muster Mac?"

"Weel, I'll assist ye, but I'll no' be responsible," conceded Mr. MacCrummon, tepidly. "I'll help ye tak' it apart and thereby enlarge the scope o' my mechanical knowledge; but here and noo, Glencannon, I warn ye in a witness's presence that ye'll ne'er succeed in putting the dom thing back together again. I willna share the blame."

"Blosh!" said Mr. Glencannon. "And dinna ye know enough not to say 'dom' in the presence o' the clergy?"

"Then — then I really can count on you?" asked Mr. Stainforth.

"Aye, sir, indeed ye can!" Mr. Glencannon assured him, bluffly. "As soon as we've stomached the revolting mess which will shortly be sairved for lunch, Muster MacCrummon and mysel' will ascend to yere little kirk on the hill and go in search o' that lost chord."

As the Reverend Mr. Eric Stainforth descended the *Inchcliffe Castle's* ladder, he saw that the sky had cleared. Strolling shoreward along the Molo Vecchio, he gazed up at the sunny amphitheater of Genoa and found it good.

"Honest men!" he murmured. "Rough diamonds, perhaps, but — honest men!"

From somewhere behind him came muffled, angry voices.

"Ye lie, ye lie, ye lie!" one of them was shouting.

"Oh, do I, I do, do I?" retorted the other. "Weel, tak' a smell o' that fist and see how ye lik' it, ye nosty scut o' a black Dunvegan MacCrummon!"

II

Shortly before three o'clock that afternoon, Messrs. Glencannon and MacCrummon, the one bearing a tool bag, the other a long steel cylinder of compressed air and both of them notably high in alcoholic content, ascended the hilly streets of Genoa to the Church of the Pilgrims, which is in the Via San Giuseppe. There they found the Reverend Mr. Stainforth and a pink-cheeked but petulant young lady whom he introduced as Miss Cheevers, the organist.

"Ex-organist, you mean," said Miss Cheevers sharply, tapping her heel on the floor tiles. "I told you last Sunday I was fed up with your horrid old organ and your horrid old Mister Binney. Didn't I, Padre?"

"Yes, yes, my dear, of course you did!" said the clergyman, soothingly. "But these gentlemen are here to make the organ as good as new, so I asked you to come up to explain — er — just what's wrong with it."

"H'mph! The walrus and the carpenter," observed Miss Cheevers, eying the pair coldly.

"At yere service, Muss!" bowed Mr. Glencannon, permitting his gold fillings to sparkle magnetically. "We're no' exockly organ experts, but with yere charming co-operation we vurra soon will be. If ye'll just describe the organ's symptoms, we'll proceed to diagnose its diapason, snip the tonsils oot o' its *vox humana* and do whatever else is necessary. Noo, feerst of all, Muss Cheevers, what are all the china knobs on the sides?"

"Stops," said Miss Cheevers, acidly.

"Ah, stops indeed," nodded Mr. Glencannon. "But what mak's it go?"

"It doesn't go," snapped Miss Cheevers. "That's the whole trouble."

"Aye, precisely! But what are the names o' all these gadgets?"

Miss Cheevers shrugged. "Oh, the fugara, the flauto amabile, the viola d'amore, the tibia clausa, the contra-oboe, the aeoline, the quintaten and a lot more names a walrus couldn't remember. . . Well, cheerio, Padre; I've got to get back to the office!"

"Haw!" chuckled Mr. Glencannon, gazing after her as she flounced down the aisle. "A most attractive young lady! She has explained the whole thing so clearly that our job shud be rideeculously simple. So noo, Muster Stainforth, if ye'll leave us alone with our labors, I think I can promise ye results by five o'clock at latest."

"Eh? Five o'clock?" repeated the minister, incredulously.

"Five o'clock?" snorted Mr. MacCrummon.

"Aye, five o'clock and pairhops e'en sooner. I suggest that ye bring Muster Binney alang to see for himsel' the triumph o' mechanical genius."

When the minister had gone, "Foosh!" gasped Mr. MacCrummon. "Are ye stark, staring drunk, Glencannon? Canna ye see that yon organ has got more gadgets in it than a Chinese submarine? How in the heel d'ye expect to fix it by five o'clock?"

"By starting richt the noo," said Mr. Glencannon, producing from his tool bag a flashlight, a screw driver and a monkey wrench. "Noo, feerst, I'll ask ye to step ower to yon air pump and work up some pressure while I fuddle aboot on these keys. Whup, there! Steady, mon! Why, anybody wud think ye'd drunk the whole quart for lunch, instead o' a mere half o' it! Pump! Pump! There — that's better!"

He ran his fingers up and down the keyboard. From here and there in the gloom behind him came eerie moans and asthmatic wheezes as the air passed through the age-clogged pipes.

"Terrible!" he muttered, scratching his head. "'Tis more serious than I'd thocht, MacCrummon. Apparently there's a stoppage in the . . . But I see ye're too befuddled to be o' much use, mon! Go mak' yersel' comfortable in yon pew and sleep it off! I fear I'll have to unship a few bulkheads off this contraption single-handed, and tak' a look inside."

"Weel, be it on yere head!" mumbled Mr. MacCrummon resignedly, settling down to doze while Mr. Glencannon launched a frontal attack upon the console.

First he removed a panel and flashed his light into the musty-smelling interior. He saw cobwebs, fuzzy drifts of dust, crumpled scraps of paper and several stone-hard objects which he decided were mummies of ancient chocolate creams. "Haw!" he chuckled, examining his discoveries. "Just what I suspected! Noo I shall have to mak' a guid, thorough job o' it!" The screws of the remaining panels were rusty and their heads broke off. Undeterred by this, Mr. Glencannon seized his wrench and smashed away the woodwork, tossing the fragments over into the choir stall.

"What' the heel are ye doing?" mumbled Mr. MacCrummon, disturbed by the din.

"Fixing an organ," came Mr. Glencannon's voice from somewhere inside it.

"Oh!" said Mr. MacCrummon, dropping off to sleep again.

For something over an hour, then, the church echoed the sounds of splintering wood, rending metal and muffled oaths. At length Mr. Glencannon crawled out of the console, dusted himself off and surveyed with satisfaction the barricade of debris strewn on the floor around him.

"Weel, is it fixed?" yawned Mr. MacCrummon, starting up the stairs a bit uncertainly. "They've — I've — ye've — we've no' too much time left, mon!" He ascended four steps, went down three, then turned around and came up backward; scowling at his wrist watch. "I — I mak' it a forter-to-quive — er, four-fighty-forve — er, wait! The — exoct — time — is — noo — exockly — fifteen — minutes — before — five — exockly. But, great swith!" he gazed at the scene of havoc around the consol. "How — how in the world do ye e'er expect to put it back together again?"

Mr. Glencannon frowned and gnawed his walrus mustache. "Weel, pairhops I shud have numbered the pieces, at that," he admitted pensively.

"Ye'd have run oot o' numbers," declared Mr. MacCrummon.

"Then I'd have started numbering backward. But in any case, there noo remains nowt to be done except to disconnect yon pump, hook up the air cylinder and give her a test under pressure. I foncy a jet o' aboot three hoonderd poonds to the square inch shud — Ah, guid afternoon, Muster Stainforth! Ye're just in time for the final tryoot!"

"Er — oh, are we? Good! Mrs. and Mr. Binney, may I present Mr. Glencannon, of the *Inchcliffe Castle?* And this is

Mr. MacCrummon, of the *Eskmouth*. Er — so you've really located the trouble, Mr. Glencannon?"

"What was it?" cut in Mr. Binney, a small, crabbed gentleman with gray hair carefully pasted across a bald spot and a fountain pen and three patent pencils protruding from his handkerchief pocket. "H'mph, well, it looks to me as though you'd put things to a frightful mess. Exactly what was the matter? Come, speak up!"

"A-weel," said Mr. Glencannon, keeping one eye on Mr. MacCrummon, who was connecting the air cylinder, "the stops wudna go, the goes wudna stop, the fugara was jammed into the flauto amabile and the contra-oboe was turning counterclockwise and vice versa. But noo, if ye'll just hold tight while MacCrummon turns on the steam, we'll see what wonders science hath wrought . . . Ready, Mac? Sock it to her, lad! Full speed ahead!"

There was a high, menacing whistle, followed by a savage hiss of air. The windboxes throbbed and creaked with the unaccustomed pressure. The floor trembled, and throughout the church there was a tense atmospheric vibration like that which precedes a typhoon.

Mr. Glencannon raised his hands on high. "Hark!" he whispered hoarsely, bringing his forearms down upon the clavier and pressing twenty keys at once. There was a shattering bellow, an earthquake shock that rocked the church on its foundations. A cloud of dust flooded the crimson twilight. Then came a ripping, tending roar, a volley of pops as the pipe valves blew out, and a shower of plaster as they ricocheted off the ceiling. A complete bank of pipes teetered dizzily, tore itself loose from the wall and crashed down into the chancel. It was destruction. It was desolation. It was even as when Jericho's ramparts crumbled to the trumpet blast.

"Hoot, MacCrummon, did ye hear it?" cried Mr. Glencannon, *vox Celeste*. "'Twas the Lost Chord — 'lik' the sound o' a great Amen!' Why, in all my musical career, I ne'er heard a —"

"Oh, you didn't, didn't you?" snarled Mr. Binney, savagely dusting the calcimine off his bald spot while the hysterical Mrs. Binney was assisted into the vestry by the Reverend Mr. Stainforth. "Well, it'll be a long time before you hear the end of this, you — you vandal! Why, as soon as I can write a letter to Clifford and Castle, putting in my claim for damages and notifying them that the charter goes to an Italian line, you'll —"

"Letter? Letter?" Mr. Glencannon interrupted, blandly. "Oh, yes, that reminds me!" From his pocket he produced the crumpled scraps of paper he had retrieved from within the organ. "I really must congratulate ye on yere letter-writing ability, Muster Binney! This one ye wrote to Muss Jane Bowen, who seems to have been organist sometime last year, is a vurritable gem o' poesy. And this one to Muss Claire Butler, dated August the second, has a heart throb in its every burning line. These four, to a lady named Williamson, but whom ye usually addressed as Huggy-Wuggy Peachy-Lips (signing yersel' Dweat Big Honey Bear) were worthy o' a better fate than being tossed into the organ through the hole behind the music rack, with all the rest o' them. Losh, 'twas no wonder that the organ wudna play — and e'en less that no decent young lady wud play it! Why, ye nosty auld — Ho, ye thief! Put that bottle back in my tool bag, where ye found it! That's my private whusky — and besides, mon, remember where ye are!"

"Yes, yes, but please!" Mr. Binney wilted down onto the organ bench and fanned himself with a sheet of music. "Come!" he whispered, hoarsely. "How many letters have you got and what's your price for them? Quick!"

"A-weel," said Mr. Glencannon, "including the flaming epistle ye wrote to Muss Cheevers last Sunday, there are eighteen letters, each o' them worth a fortune. But in view o' the expense ye'll be put to, buying a new organ for the guid Muster Stainforth and having the church redecorated and all, I'll mak' ye the vurra modest price o' fifty poonds apiece."

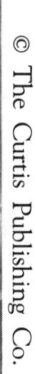

Mr. Binney wilted down onto the organ bench and fanned himself with a sheet of music. He whispered hoarsely, "How many letters have you got?"

"Phew! That makes nine hundred pounds. All right, all right hand 'em over and I'll give you a check right now."

"Oh, there's no great rush aboot it," said Mr. Glencannon, easily. "Noo that ye've definitely decided to give Clifford and Castle that charter, I'll be coming doon here to Genoa vurra frequently. I'll deleever ye one letter C.O.D. each trip. In that way, ye see, we'll be sure to string oot a vurra profitable business connection for a lang, lang, time. So noo I'll bid ye guid-by, Muster Binney — merely cautioning ye in parting no' to steal too many farthings oot o' the Sunday collection plate!"

THE DONKEYMAN'S WIDOW

That night the tropical fireflies turned in early, leaving the job of lighting Java to a full and capable moon. It rose, cool and dripping, from the sea off Banyuwangi, soared over the row of volcanic peaks which jut like an albacore's fins from the island's backbone and bathed the city of Semarang in the same soft blue that pervades a submarine noon. The visibility was astounding. You could pick out every window of the neat Dutch houses in the hilly suburbs, every tree where the suburbs dwindled to country and the hills grew into mountains. By lunar magic, the granite tower at the canal entrance was made to glow as brightly as the beacon which crowned it, while on the stern of the ship moored nearest in the roadstead you could even distinguish two rows of white letters which spelled "*Inchcliffe Castle*, London."

This vessel had her hatches open to air her empty holds, and out of her dank interior poured a medley of smells which clung to the surrounding water in a most discouraging aura. Upon her lower bridge, garbed for the climate in bright batik sarongs, her Master, her Chief Engineer and her Wireless Operator sat gasping in the miasmas of many long-forgotten cargoes and scowling at the moon in silence broken only by occasional bouts of bickering among themselves.

"Ah, foosh!" snorted the Engineer, scratching a match on the rust-pitted deck and applying it to the soggy heel that festered in the midden of his pipe. "I must confess I find the effluvium vurra depressing. At feerst I thocht it was the tidal mud; then suspected that a dead buffalo's owerripe cadaver had drifted oot to pay us a visit; but noo, Muster Levy, I reecognize it as unmistakably and characteristically you."

"Wot? Me? Oh, blyme, Mister Glencannon, 'ow can yer say such a thing?" protested Sparks, a callow, sallow youth upon whom nature had bestowed a lavish meed of nose, ears, and pimples. "You know as well as I do it's the ruddy ship which —"

"Eh? Ship? Heh? Now, just you hold on a minute!" blustered Captain Ball. "Why, I mean to say, if you mean to say that my ship smells frowsty, you can get to hell off it and go pounding your silly key aboard some Greek or Portugee, and inhale 'em to your heart's contamph, contemph, content, kerhem! No, Mister Levy, no! Whether I'm carrying beef bones, wet hides, phosphates or what-have-you, my ship's holds are sweet as a knot, and I'll thank you please to remember it. The only sole reason I ordered the hatches open is to dry 'er out, on account of them eight hundred tons of tapioca we start loading in the morning."

"Topioca? Braugh, how revolting!" shuddered Mr. Glencannon, striving politely but inadequately to muffle a seismic belch. "Och, the thocht o' e'en a spoonful o' topioca is enough to mak' my innards crawl and cringe. But — eight hoonderd tons o' it! Och!" From the shadow of his chair he produced a bottle containing a well-known sedative and gulped rather more than the prescribed dose of it.

"Well, now, just what's the matter with tapioca, heh? Please answer me that!" Captain Ball challenged testily. "Why, when tapioca's properly boiled, like Missus B. always boils it, each little lump puffs up nice and plump and slimy, like a drowned kitten's eye; it's practically little or no trouble to mashticate, and besides —"

"Yus, yus, tapioca is delicious, yer absolutely right, sir!" chimed in Mr. Levy, eager to reinstate himself. "Of course, Captain, speaking personally, I 'aven't got the misfortune to 'ave false teeth, like you, but even aside from the chewing part, I agree with you that —"

"Who asked you to agree with me?" bellowed Captain Ball, swelling to such a diameter that the sarong burst from his paunch and revealed him like an unveiled statue mottled with tropical heat rash. "Who wants you to agree with me, heh, and who cares a ratholeful of wet ashes whether you've got false teeth, shark's teeth, snake fangs or a set of ruddy unicorn tusks? If ever I want to know what kind of teeth you've got, I'll knock out some samples and see for myself — yes, and, any time I want you to agree with me, I'll order you to, d'yer understand me? Ga-hapf! Ga-humpf! I am forced to warn you, Mister Levy, that this mutinous attitude of yours is —"

He was interrupted by a burst of maudlin song from across the moonlit waters:

> *"Whin upon yer port soide's seen*
> *A steamer's starboard loight o' green*
> *There's nary a thing for ye to do*
> *For green to Port keeps clear o' you."*

"Listen!" exclaimed Mr. Levy, brightly. "Why, it sounds to me like the donkeyman!"

"No, really? The Captain and I were under the impression it was the Westminster chimes," grunted Mr. Glencannon, peering over the rail at a figure teetering in the bow of a proa just sliding into the *Inchcliffe Castle's* shadow. "Aye, it's Tom O'Halloran, richt enough; I gave him pairmission to go ashore to post a letter to his wife, but he appears to have contracted an acute attack o' the Javanese jeebies."

"Well, I 'ope 'e wasn't stricken before 'e bought a 'arf-dozen of them little two-volt flarshlight bulbs and a spool of Number One hinsulated copper wire," snickered Mr. Levy, still trying to shoo the conversation away from himself. "Yer see, 'e arsked me to 'elp 'im wire up that scale model of the ship e's been building, but —"

"Look sharp, nayger!" the donkeyman admonished the native in the stern sheets. "Don't ye know the 'rules of safety at sea? —

> "If to starboard red appear
> 'Tis yer juty to keep clear;
> Steer as judgment says is proper;
> — Port! — Starboard! — Back her! — Stop her!"

The proa scraped against the foot of the *Inchcliffe's* ladder, and after a profane and stumbling interval its passenger appeared on deck, singing lustily:

> "Whin both loights ye see ahead,
> Port yer helm and show yer red;
> Green to green — red to red,
> Purfick safety — go ahead!"

Suiting his action to the song, he lurched toward the firemen's quarters, bumping into things as he went.

"Lawks, look at 'im!" chuckled Mr. Levy, patronizingly. "I'll bet five quid 'e never make's the fo'c'sle!"

"Done!" Mr. Glencannon snapped him up. "Captain, sir! Will ye please bear witness that he said 'never'? 'Never' is a dangerous word, Muster Levy! Haw, ye gowk, ye've as guid as lost yere five quid already, and may it teach ye to phrase yere wagers more meeticulously!"

Just then, through a slight error in navigation, Tom O'Halloran mistook the open No. 1 hatch for the fo'c'sle doorway. From the hatch coaming to the bottom of the hold was a drop of thirty-four feet, five inches. He was still singing when he hit.

II

The Port Doctor, who had come out in the police boat with the *Commissaris van Politie*, was writing the death certificate: "Thomas O'Halloran; *van Britsche nationaliteit; van beroep donkeyman. Overleden; doodsoorzaak, een gebroken nek....*"

"Ah, precisely, a gebroken neck!" grumbled Captain Ball. "Well, ger-humpf, I mean to say, he had no gebusiness to go gefalling down there in the gefirst place!"

The police officer shrugged and tore a page out of his notebook. "Here's a list of what he had in his pocket; we've searched him thoroughly and ransacked all his duffel. But tomorrow, Captain, you'll have to get the British Consul to make a complete official inventory of the poor chap's belongings, and have him send them under seal to the widow in London."

"Ah, yes, yes! Don't I know it?" sighed Captain Ball, mopping his brow with the tail of his sarong. "I s'pose there'll be forms in dublicate, forms in trublicate and forms in I-don't-know-what-the-hellicate to fill out, before this mess is settled. Oh, I tell you, gentlemen, things have come to a pretty pass, when a British seaman's neck ain't equal to a mere little tumble like what this fellow took! Faugh! Why, in my time, by gad, we used to fall further than that for the sheer sport of it, and that's why the Empire is where she is today!"

"Ah, indeed?" murmured the *Commissaris*, politely. "*Nou, Doctor, laten we maar aan wal gaan en er een gaan pakken.* . . . We bid you all a very good night, gentlemen!"

As Mr. Glencannon stood at the rail watching the Dutch officials descend the ladder, he was joined by Mr. Levy. Sparks was smiling unctuously and rubbing his thin, pale hands.

"Weel, what are ye smirking aboot?" the Engineer demanded. "Dinna ye ken that this is a vurra solemn occasion?"

"Solemn fer you, per'aps!" conceded Mr. Levy, nudging him slyly. "Don't ferget, Old Walrus, that you owe me five pounds!"

Mr. Glencannon wheeled upon him horrified. "What?" he croaked. "What? Oh, ye vompire, ye ghoul! Try to collect a bet on a dead mon, wud ye? Weel, I give ye notice here and noo that I'll never pay ye! Never!"

III

After her call at Semarang, the *Inchcliffe Castle* picked up a consignment of rubber at Batavia, and then turned her blunt snout into the West for London and home. The long weeks of the passage were marred by an increasing bitterness between the Wireless Operator and the Chief Engineer, Mr. Levy stigmatizing

Mr. Glencannon as a welsher devoid of all honor, and Mr. Glencannon countercharging Sparks with attempting to steal the pennies off a dead man's eyes. Mr. Levy, his mind razor-keen for all figures save those of speech, hotly denied ever attempting to steal anything less than a shilling in his life and demanded to know wot the 'ell mere pennies had to do with the five pounds Mr. Glencannon owed him. He appealed for justice to Captain Ball, who reluctantly agreed to take the matter under advisement. But it was not until they were well into the Thames Estuary, the pilot on board and the smoke pall of London looming ahead, that the skipper handed down his decision.

"I have — ker-hem — have given this question much profound thought," he announced, pontifically. "While I wish to have it clearly on record that I do not approve of gamboleering on this here ship in any way, shape, form or manner, especially when it's a question of a dead man, the dead being sacred, even though the late defunct was drunk as a parson at the time of his untimely taking off, and while, of course, secondly, that doesn't affect the question at issue in any way, shape, form or manner, still, thirdly — er — er... Oh, yes! You were asking me about that bet! Well, as I see it, Mister Levy certainly offered to bet that O'Halloran would never get to the fo'c'sle. Mister Glencannon certainly accepted the wager. O'Halloran never got there. Well, Mister Levy, I'm very much afraid that you're the winner."

"Ah, swith!" cried the Engineer. "I'm the victim o' a technicality! O' coorse he ne'er got to the fo'c'sle! How cud he, when he fell into the hold on the way? As a strict Presbyterian, I didna want to wager in the feerst place, but if I'd dreamed I was betting with a flint-hearted Sherlock who was oot to swundle me with a cheap play on words, I'd have hoisted up the corpse with a derrick sling, dragged it into the fo'c'sle and won the money mysel'!"

"Yes, yes, capital plan! But as it is — well, you've got to fork over five quid to Mister Levy."

Mr. Glencannon counted out the banknotes with the air of a man peeling adhesive plaster from the more sensitive areas of his anatomy. "Here, ye necrophile!" he invited, sepulchrally. "Tak' yere pennies from a dead mon's eyes, and may ye sleep with yere conscience — if ye can!"

The Donkeyman's Widow   137

The Inchcliffe Castle *picked up a consignment of rubber at Batavia, and then turned her blunt snout into the west for London and home.*

But strangely enough, as on that first night home from the sea the *Inchcliffe Castle* lay in the Limehouse Commercial Docks, Sparks and his conscience continued to be most congenial bedfellows while the Engineer tossed and turned and cursed and groaned, feverish and wide-eyed. For although Mr. Glencannon prided himself on being a good loser, and often modestly dragged in references to his sterling sportsmanship in the course of conversation, it applied only within reasonable limits. Any loss exceeding sixpence ruined his temper, destroyed his appetite, upset his liver, brought spots before his eyes, plunged him into black melancholia and crowded his brain with a multiplicity of schemes for murdering the winner and stealing back the stakes. Also, as a matter of course, it gave him a prodigious thirst. It was this fact and its attendant complications which now interfered with his slumbers.

"Hame again!" he moaned plaintively in the darkness. "Hame in London, after dreary weeks at sea with nary a drap to drink! Hame in a vurritable paradise o' pubs — and me with a monumental theerst and less than a quid to slake it! A-weel!" He shook his fists in futile rage. "May those five poonds scorch a hole in his soul, and may a tree grow oot o' his back!"

Next morning, gaunt and shaky, he worked for hours camouflaging certain swindles in his coal account, and in the afternoon descended to the engine room where by the light of sooty oil flares he drew up a list of necessary repairs and refitments. It was not until dusk that he was free to peel off his overalls and emerge upon deck for a breath of rainy London air.

"Ah, losh!" he sighed, gazing up at the lowering sky against which were silhouetted the warehouses, chimney pots and gasworks of Limehouse. "How happy I ocht to feel tonicht, to be back in a cauld climate — a white mon's climate — a — a — whusky climate!" Suddenly, across the river on the Rotherhithe side, a great electric sign blazed forth its message of solace to mankind. As Mr. Glencannon read it, his voice was hushed with awe and a wave of nostalgia swept over him. "'Duggan's . . . Dew . . . of . . . Kirkintilloch. . . . Duggan's . . . Dew . . . of . . .'" He plunged his hand into his pocket and fished up a palmful of coins. "Twelve — foorteen — fufteen sheelings, thruppence, ha'penny," he counted, huskily. "Ah, mockery! 'Tis barely enough for a guid start — and a start withoot a follow-up is only a bitter oggravation!"

"Duggan's . . . Dew . . . of . . . Kirkintilloch," the sign repeated in letters of fire; then the letters vanished, and their place in the firmament was occupied by a mammoth bottle. Even as Mr. Glencannon watched it, spellbound, the bottle tilted itself tantalizingly in his own, personal direction and gushed an amber, cascade of Highland nectar that would have floated the *Inchcliffe Castle*. It was the last straw!

With a hoarse cry, he swarmed up the ladder and dashed along the upper deck to the wireless room. Pausing only to don a set of brass knuckles, he flung wide the door and hurled himself within. "Ghoul!" he shouted. "Body snatcher! Give me back my five poonds, or — or . . ." To his vast disappointment, Mr. Levy was nowhere in sight; in fact, from the mingled aromas of shaving soap, hair oil and shoe polish that pervaded the room, it was obvious that he had recently betaken himself ashore. More crestfallen than ever, Mr. Glencannon was about to quit the premises when on the shelf beneath the porthole he saw that which gave him pause. It was the model of a ship — the miniature counterpart of the S.S. *Inchcliffe Castle* herself.

"Ah, swith — 'tis puir Tom O'Halloran's!" he exclaimed. "The Widow O'Halloran's, rather; for it shud have been sent hame to her from Semarang. Why, yon scut o' a Levy hasn't a micht o' richt to keep it!" He switched on his flashlight and examined the little ship closely. It was, he saw, some four feet long, built accurately to scale and apparently complete to the most minute detail of gadget, gear and fitting.

"A braw neat job!" he muttered admiringly. "It's worth ten quid if it's worth a bross bawbee. I dinna doot the widow can sell it and . . . Sell it? Sell it? But how cud she sell it? Why, I'll tak' it ashore the noo, mak' a roond o' the pubs and sell it for her mysel'! 'Twill be an oct o' Christian chority to which I'll most geenerously contribute my talents and my time. My only charge o' coorse, will be for my expenses, plus a numminal sairvice fee and the usual commission."

He found the model heavy and awkward to handle, particularly as the jigger stay between its masts prevented his carrying it under his arm. After a certain amount of backing and filling he negotiated the doorway and then, holding his burden crosswise in front of him like a scullion bearing a roast pig on a platter, he proceeded down the gangplank and into the rainswept highways and byways of Limehouse. His forward vision was obscured by the model's superstructure; but trusting his instinct to guide his footsteps, he soon found himself in a crowded barroom. Unfortunately, as he saw when he took his nose out of his glass, the establishment catered only to seafaring folk who, though they gathered around to admire the model, were poor prospects for its sale.

"Aye, gentlemen," Mr. Glencannon explained solemnly, "'tis the sole leegacy o' one o' our dead colleagues to his puir bewidowed widow. I wish I'd the money to buy it from her mysel', but as it is" — he shrugged — "weel, I've swallowed my pride, and in sweet Chority's name I'm hawking it from one pub to the next in order that dear Tom O'Halloran's sweet young widow may not know the bitter pangs o' want."

"Eh?" A venerable white-whiskered gentleman who had been slumbering under a settee in the corner lurched abruptly to his feet. "O'Halloran, you say, sir? Not — surely not Tom O'Halloran? Ah, lads!" he harangued the company in a fine pulpit quaver, "Tom — Tom O'Halloran! He was my pal!" Hiccuping something about the glorious day of resurrection when the sea shall give up its dead, he wilted to the floor, pillowed his head on a cuspidor and gave vent to hollow sobs.

"There!" said Mr. Glencannon, a catch in his voice. "There's the proof o' how Tom had friends on all seven o' the seven seas! But aloss for his little blonde widow, all his friends are puir sailormen, lik' you —" he bowed to the assembly, "lik' mysel', and lik' yon ancient oxygenarian whaling captain there. For if I canna sell this model, o' what avail is all our friendship, and what's to become o' her?" He picked up his glass, saw it was empty, shed a tear into it, and set it back on the bar. The barmaid, whose heart and mascara were melting, hastened to replenish it.

"There — that drink is on the 'ouse, sir," the publican assured him, feelingly. "And wot's more, I'd — I'd like to contribute ten shillings for the benefit of the poor chap's widow."

"Spoke like a man! That's the spirit!" applauded one of the guests. "'Ere's five bob to join it. But wait — I'll just pass the 'at and take up a collection!"

Mr. Glencannon stood as one stunned, viewing the proceedings and listening to the clink of coins. The collection, as far as he could estimate as he pocketed it, exceeded three pounds, not including the more obvious counterfeits. So great was his emotion that he was able only to stammer his thanks. He gulped his drink and was about to depart elsewhere on his mission of mercy when he was smitten by an inspiration. Going over to the ancient mariner, who was still weeping in the corner, "Come!" he whispered, shaking him, "I'll tak' ye aroond to see the widow!"

"Widow?" The other's bleariness was dispelled by a faunlike leer. "Widow?" He sprang to his feet with surprising alacrity and followed Mr. Glencannon into the street. Once

The Donkeyman's Widow 141

"I'm hawking it from one pub to the next in order that dear Tom O'Halloran's young widow may not know the bitter pangs o' want."

there, however, he suffered a relapse, leaned against a hydrant and burst into tears again.

"Ah, noo, noo!" Mr. Glencannon urged him. "Pull yersel' together, Captain, and save yere sobs till we need them! I've a vurra neat little scheme by which we can aid O'Halloran's widow and at the same time mak' a tidy profit for oursel's."

"Profit?" queried the ancient mariner, drying his eyes with his beard and then dusting off his hat with it. "Pray explain yourself, my dear Lady Rutherford!"

"Great swith!" snorted Mr. Glencannon, kicking him on the shins exasperatedly. "Will ye please try to concentrate, ye dissolute auld whale butcher? Ye will? Guid! Weel, then, I've no doot ye obsairved that back there in yon boozing ken, it was yere ain vurra dramatic display o' grief that set the tide o' sympathy flowing. If it worked there, can ye teel me why it willna work elsewhere?"

"I'll bite. Why?" demanded the ancient one, vacantly. "Oh, by the way — who's this Hal O'Tommeran everybody's talking about these days?"

"Ah, foosh, sir!" Mr. Glencannon chided him. "Tom O'Halloran was yere auld shipmate, yere ain dear pal! Ye said so yersel'!"

"No, did I?" demanded the other, chuckling mischievously in his whiskers. "Fancy that! I suppose I must've been having one of my spells, like. I never heard of O'Halloran in my life. By the way, Mister O'Halloran, my name's Lionel Futter. I'm a theatrical scene shifter, when there's any theatrical scene shifting to be shifted, which this here lousy season there ain't."

"Ah, dearie me!" groaned Mr. Glencannon, "I'm dizzy! I'm confused! I'm flobbergasted! But — weel, I suppose it mak's no difference in the working o' the scheme. Listen! All ye've got to do is precede me into the next pub and order a drink. In aboot ten minutes, I'll happen in and tell the sad tale o' the donkeymon's widow. When I say the name 'O'Halloran, 'twill be yere cue to let yere great grief get the better o' ye. They'll probably tak' up a collection spontaneously; but if they dinna, we can easily talk them into it. At the end o' the evening we'll divide fifty-fifty and turn ower the balance to the widow."

"Sure, fine!" agreed Mr. Futter. "O'Halloran! O'Halloran! O'Halloran! . . . Lead the way, Miss Purdy; I'm just rehearsin' my part."

IV

Mr. Glencannon was awakened by bright, rainwashed sunshine pouring into his room on the *Inchcliffe Castle*. He was troubled by a slight headache, which he could only ascribe to some fine print he had read on a label the week before, and was vaguely disturbed by his inability to recall the night's events in detail. Even a quarter-hour's drowsy mental probing failed to fill in all the gaps.

"Ah, weel!" he consoled himself, sliding out of his bunk and pouring a tumblerful of what might have been a gargle if it hadn't been whisky. "What matter the details, when the main fact remains?" The main fact consisted of fourteen pounds, sixteen shillings, six pence piled on the dresser; as nearly as he could remember, eight pounds of it had been paid for the model by a pub keeper in parts unknown, while the remainder had been raised by popular subscription in a blurry succession of bars. For a moment he wondered how he had avoided paying Mr. Futter his share; then he remembered that at one time in the evening they had tired of lugging the model from pub to pub and endeavored to float it down the rushing torrent of a gutter; the model refusing to float, the ancient mariner had plunged in to retrieve it and run hopelessly aground. The last Mr. Glencannon had seen of him, he was lying gripped by the suction of a sewer grating, his white beard whirling around his neck in the mad vortex of the maelstrom.

"Weel, I'll have a tidy little sum for the widow, e'en when I deduct for my expenses," mused Mr. Glencannon, scrubbing his teeth. "O' coorse, strictly speaking, the expenses were neegligible, but I canna blame her for that."

As he shaved, he was wondering just how much he would be justified in charging. Five pounds appealed to him as a fair figure, but — "Oh, why o' coorse!" he reminded himself. "I must no' forget the five poonds I was already oot! If it hadna been for her husband's inexcusable awkwardness in bloondering into the hold, I'd ne'er have lost the bet. Plainly, then, 'tis chargeable to his estate."

But as he put on his necktie, he reflected that even ten pounds deducted from fourteen pounds, sixteen shillings, six pence still left a comfortable balance. "Weel, noo, I wonder!" He addressed his image in the mirror. "I wonder whether, after all, 'twere fitting to go polluting her preecious meemories o' him with sordid thochts o' finonce? 'Twud it no' be kinder, sweeter and ten times more geenerous to say nothing aboot money at all and merely convey to her his last words?"

The longer he mulled it the better did this solution seem, so he devoted the greater part of the day to composing a suitable oration *in extremis*. This embraced a wide range of subjects and concluded with a clarion warning against the perils of tapioca to the men of the British Mercantile Marine; but as he read it over, finding it not without merit, he suddenly bethought himself of Mr. Levy. Although the Wireless Operator had not returned aboard, Mr. Glencannon realized that when he did so, and found the model missing, he was certain to wax exceeding wroth; indeed, he was even capable of running to Mrs. O'Halloran with scandal, slur and slander. The Engineer decided to forestall him by visiting the widow at once and establishing his own probity and good will beyond all possible cavil. Thus, as soon as he had finished his tea, he hurried ashore, and threading his way through narrow Limehouse streets in which cats averaged three to the garbage pail, arrived at the O'Halloran residence. This was a two-story brick cottage with pink lace curtains in the windows; on the top step stood a beef tin, trimmed and gilded in the likeness of the ducal coronet of Windsor, from which projected the stumps of several veteran geraniums.

"H'm. Vurra neat!" mused Mr. Glencannon, thumping on the door with a polished brass knocker which he recognized as the handle of a bridge telegraph which had disappeared from the *Inchcliffe Castle* some months previously. "Aye, and aside from the neatness, it's a guid bit more lavish than ye'd expect on the meager pay o' a donkeymon. If I had a suspicious nature, I'd be inclined to . . ."

The door opened and revealed the largest quantity of woman that Mr. Glencannon had ever seen in one place at one time. This mountainous specimen placed her arms akimbo and surveyed him with marked disfavor. "Go 'way!" she ordered, giving off dense vapors of gin. "Wotever ye're selling, I don't want none!"

"My dear Moddum!" Mr. Glencannon doffed his cap and bowed, "I dinna come to sell ye anything, but to give ye something. Ye see, I . . ."

"No, I won't accept none o' yer rotten free sample brushes, neither!" snapped Mrs. O'Halloran, sidling away from the door some forty inches in order that she might slam it without bruising her hip.

"But, Moddum, please! I'm Muster Glencannon, Chief Engineer o' the *Inchcliffe Castle* — yere dear deceased dead husband's superior officer —"

"Mister Glencannon?" The mountain gasped, giggled coyly, and erupted another Vesuvian waft of gin. "Not Mister Colin Glencannon, wot poor Tom orlways hadmired and talked about so much? Well, good lawks, come in, come in, sir, and may 'eaven fergive me fer mistyking yer fer a ruddy 'ouse-to-'ouse mop-and-mouse-trap monger!"

He followed her into a sitting room furnished with red plush chairs of the size and style commonly used by performing elephants in the higher income brackets and safely boarded one while she filled two glasses with a colorless liquid which she poured from a gin bottle. "I farncy yer've come to tell me about poor Tom," she said, adjusting her southern hemisphere to the chair opposite him. "Of course, Clifford and Castle's horffice give me the sad news when it 'appened, but they didn't 'ave none of the detyles. Was 'is poor corpus badly mucked up, Mister Glencannon?"

"I'm ha-hapf-happy to assure ye that it wasn't," gagged Mr. Glencannon, glancing about him for a fire extinguisher and then at the gin bottle to make sure it wasn't brass polish. "He appeared lik' a mon who's gone peacefully to sleep, except, o' coorse, that he was looking rather fixedly ower his left shoulder."

"Ah, yus — cautious to the very end! My Tom was never one to let nobody sneak up on 'im from be'ind — no, not 'im, Mister Glencannon! 'E was a smart lad and a good provider!" She sighed and gazed appraisingly at the room around her. "This 'ere little 'ouse is orl paid up for; I don't owe a ruddy penny on it, even fer the three more gauges," she explained, proudly.

"Indeed?" said Mr. Glencannon. "Pairhops ye'll pairdon me for wondering just how he monnaged it on his wage o' nine poonds a month?"

"Oh, that," simpered Mrs. O'Halloran, hoisting up approximately a shovelful of her left cheek to produce the effect of a wink and at the same time playfully stamping on his foot. "Lawks, Mister Glencannon, I hexpect I don't 'ave to hexplain to a canny Scotch gempman like you that Tom 'ad lots of irons in the fire! 'E was in with a good, slippery crowd, Tom was, and almost every port 'e visited, 'e'd manage to pull orff a little deal of some kind. Er — she hesitated — "this larst trip, though — well, candiedly, he was hexpecting great things to come of it, Mister Glencannon! But . . ." She spread her hands helplessly and sighed.

Mr. Glencannon shifted in his chair. "A-weel," he said, "if ye find yersel' financially embarrassed, Mussis O'Halloran, I micht arrange to advance ye a poond or two to tide ye ower, although . . ."

"Oh, 'eaven bless yer, no, it ain't nec's'ry!" she assured him. "As a matter of fack, Sir John Castle and Mister 'Azlitt 'as offered me the position as chief charlady in the company's horffices any time I care to haccept it. No, it — it ain't that." She refilled the glasses and took a thoughtful snifter from her own. "D'yer know," she said, musingly, "Tom orlways wished 'e could 'ave you in on some of 'is little deals, Mister Glencannon. 'The Chief's a smart one, Veronica,' 'e used to say to me time and again. 'There's no flies on Mister Glencannon! If 'e was only a little more honest, wot a partner 'e'd make!'"

"Ah, noo!" protested Mr. Glencannon, wounded to the quick. "I think I can almost truthfully say that in all my lang career I've ne'er been detected in a single shady act!"

"That was hexackly, Tom's point!" Mrs. O'Halloran coincided. "Still, if 'e'd only declared you in on that there Semarang deal, I'm sure everything'd 'ave turned out all right."

"Semarang deal?"

"Yus," said Mrs. O'Halloran, confidentially. "Now, I wouldn't breathe a word of this to another soul, but as long as it's fell through there's no 'arm telling yer that Tom and the boys 'oped to pull orff a very 'andsome profit on a pair of precious stones. Hemeralds and roobies, I believe they was —anyway, one of the parties Tom was in touch with 'ere in London 'ad a friend out in Java 'oo 'ad come by these stones one way or another. But the Dutch police and orl their narks was 'unting fer 'em 'igh and low, and the poor chap didn't know 'ow to get rid of 'em. Well, it was orl arranged for this cove to meet Tom at wotever port in Java the *Hinchcliffe Castle* might call at, and Tom would do the rest."

"Ye mean he'd tak' the jewels and smoogle them into England?"

"Heackly! But though we've been orl over Tom's stuff which the Consul sent 'ome with a fine-tooth comb, cutting open the linings of the clothes and I don't know wot orl, there ain't a single sign of a jewel in it."

"A-weel," murmured Mr. Glencannon, fearing that the gin had melted his bridgework and taking another sip to wash it down, "the police and the Consul made thorough sairches at the time, so I venture to suggest that yer husband ne'er got in touch with the proper party."

"Ah, but we know 'e did!" said Mrs. O'Halloran. "'Ere, 'ere's a letter 'e posted to me on the very day 'e was so crooly took orff."

The letter read:

Dear Veronica I hope you are not bak on the drink and wats more if I heer tork about you carrying on with any man when I get bak I will nok his dam blok orff and yours 2 well we are now at Semrang Java it is a stinking hole but everything is orl fixt up you no wat I mean so it will be cleer sailing home green to green and red to red purfick safety go abed like it says in the old sea song ha ha ha well I hope you are not bak on the drink and wats more if I heer tork about you carrying on with any man when I get bak I will nok his dam blok orff and yours 2
Yours very truly
Thomas Robert Emmet O'Halloran

As Mr. Glencannon read the letter a second time, he could feel his heart pounding. "Mussis O'Halloran," he said hoarsely, setting down his glass, rising to his feet and moving toward the door, "it's possible, as ye say, that yere husband octually had the stones in his possession when he wrote this letter. But it's obvious, aloss, that the wages o' sin is death. So noo, Mum, I'll leave ye alone with yere grief, merely reminding ye that yere husband's trogic end is one more proof o' that wise auld provairb, 'Honesty is the best policy.'"

Once in the street he set off at a rapid pace, made slightly erratic by the benzol content of the gin. "Rubies!" he muttered. "Emeralds! 'Green to green — red to red' — why, he was e'en singing it, that nicht when he came back aboord! They're the port and starboard lichts o' the model, plain as day! I must buy it back from yon pub keeper at any cost and — and . . ." He halted dead in his tracks and clapped his hand to his brow. "Foosh!" he gasped. "Buy it? How can I buy it? Why, domned if I've e'en the faintest reecollection o' where I sold it!"

Still vainly cudgeling his brain, he entered a bar and called for a stimulant. This served the double purpose of soothing his gin-lacerated larynx and giving him an idea. "Why, o' coorse!" he exclaimed. "Psychology! If, as they say, a somnambulist or a person in a tronce will always cover the same ground a seecond time, why will it no' work in the present instance? If I drink as much the noo as I drank last nicht and then simply turn mysel' loose to wander as my instincts direct, I'll return to the vurra place I sold it! Ho, Muss!" — he signaled the barmaid — "a dooble o' the same, please and then keep on pouring them till ye see I'm properly psychic!"

V

It was a peculiarly psychic evening and Mr. Glencannon, questing from pub to pub through the dark and misty streets of Limehouse, became increasingly aware of supercosmic forces sloshing around within him. He saw whole squadrons of flaming whisky bottles suspended in the sky, looping and swooping, tilting and gushing above the oily black bosom of the river. At times he felt that his spirit had quitted his body and was soaring freely in the outer spaces; at others, he was conscious that a brass-knuckled fist, strangely like his own, was successfully combating the hostile vibrations of poor outcast souls who babbled about a widow's fund and accused him of misappropriating it for drink. He saw faces vaguely familiar, as from some previous incarnation; but when he winked at them jovially and inquired if they'd heard the one about the donkeyman's widow, he found himself tongue-tied and unable to go on with the story. He even felt a tantalizing, dreamlike doubt that there was such a story. Once, wondering what ailed his tobacco, he was surprised to find his pipe stuffed with sizzling white whiskers, a few of which were still attached to epidermic morsels of somebody's chin. "Strange! Strange!" he muttered. "I'd say it was a sign from my father's ghost, except that the dom auld rip had a red mustache and wudna reecognize me anyway! If I'd e'er heard o' a mon named Lionel Futter, I'd say they belanged to a mon named Lionel Futter, but I ne'er heard o' a mon named Lionel Futter, so dinna be ridiculous. Who's ridiculous? Why, blost yere impairtenance, I am, sir; in fact, I reecognized ye the moment I set foot in the place! I've been sairching aboot for ye all evening, and noo that ye've found me I'll be so kind as to ask ye please to accept these twelve poonds and give me back my ship model!"

Through the hazes of infinite distance he saw himself pay over the money and have a drink on the house; then, personally and triumphantly bearing the model before him, he fared forth into the night, his voice raised in song:

"*Red to green and green to red
Red to green to red to red and so forth and so on.*"

"Haw, it's lik' the Jewel Song from *Frowst* or any o' those Eyetalian operas!" he exulted as he boarded the *Inchcliffe Castle* and lurched to his room. He set the model on the dresser and considered it gloatingly. "Noo for the red port licht, which will certainly be the ruby, and then for the green emerald to starboard. I — er — ah, horrors!"

For he saw that the model had no port and starboard lights, and in that instant realized that she'd never had them. From the dim depths of his memory came a voice — Mr. Levy's voice — as he'd heard it that moonlit night in Semarang. "I 'ope 'e bought them little two-volt flarshlight bulbs," Mr. Levy was saying. "'E arsked me to wire up that model of the ship 'e's been building. . . . ."

His hands trembling as with palsy, Mr. Glencannon explored the model from stem to stern, from masthead to keel. He tapped its solid portion with his knife, explored its ventilators and funnel with his finger, and shined his torch beam into its tiny doors and portholes. But — the stones were not there. His twelve pounds were lost, forever and for aye!

Snatching up a bottle which might have contained whisky, and did, he drained a good quarter of it; then, seizing the model, he kicked open the door and staggered toward the rail. At that very moment, the psychological strain under which he had been laboring proved too much, and he lapsed to the deck in an advanced state of spiritual disembodiment.

Some hours later Mr. Levy, returning aboard, found him snoring in the scupper, his back propped against the rail, the model crosswise in his lap.

"Ho, yer rotten thief!" fumed Sparks' "Steal a poor widder's model, would yer? Yus, and me planning to tyke it up to 'er 'ouse tomorrow. Well, I just got 'ere in time! Come, get up out of here, yer narsty Scotch grave robber, before yer catch yer death o' the peenoomonia — though, at that, I oughter leave yer 'ere to freeze!"

He dragged Mr. Glencannon across the deck, boosted him over the doorsill and heaved him into his berth. "There!" he sneered. "There's the one 'oo called me a ruddy ghoul — the one 'oo said I'd steal the pennies orff a dead man's eyes! Well" — he dug into his pocket and brought up a handful of change — "well, I'll show yer 'oo'll steal pennies orff a dead man's eyes!" He selected a couple of broad coppers and was about to lay them upon Mr. Glencannon's tight-shut orbs when he thought better of it. "No!" he chuckled. "Why waste even tuppence on a cove like you?" From among the coins in his palm he picked out two dark, glossy objects the size and shape of half-lumps of sugar. "'Ere's a present from the dead man 'imself — the bits of colored glass to fit over the port and starboard lights, which poor Tom O'Halloran give me just before 'e went ashore that night!" He placed them on the Engineer's eyelids and, with a final sneer, departed.

When the sound of his footfalls had died away in the distance, Mr. Glencannon stirred, smiled and very slowly opened his eyes. For an instant he was blinded by red and green fires that sparkled, blazed, smoldered and then blazed again. He removed the two objects and held them up to the light. They glowed like magic coals in an alchemist's furnace.

"A-weel, ye little beauties!" he scolded them good-naturedly. "After the trooble and expense ye've caused me, 'tis too bad ye're no' another twenty carats larger! But — ye'll do! Aye, ye'll do!" Tenderly, carefully, he tucked them under his pillow — the emerald to starboard, the ruby to port. Then he kicked off his shoes, ripped off his trousers, switched off the light and dropped off to sleep, murmuring:

> "Green to green . . . Red to red . . .
> Foosh to the world!
> I've . . . gone . . . to . . . bed."

At the Sign of the Brass Knuckle

Some three thousand years ago, a squadron of Phocaean ships put out from Asia Minor and sailed westerly for many weeks. Entering a region of strange, wild winds and leaping, muddy waters, the navigators judged the ultimate edge of the world to be not far beyond and prudently took shelter in a cove. Their rigging was gale-frayed and rotten; so, gathering certain fibrous plants which grew on the hillsides roundabout, they cleared a ropewalk through the pines, built huts along both sides of it and settled down to the tedious job of twisting new cordage. They called their camp Massalia. Today it is called Marseille. The ropewalk is the Rue Canebière.

Teeming thoroughfare of the greatest seaport on the ancient Mediterranean trade route, the Rue Canebière is a peacock alley, a blazing pageant, of half of humanity's races. The native Marseillais, born boasters and proud boosters all, swear that you have only to sit long enough on a Canebière café terrace to see every person you have ever known stroll past you on parade. This pleasant local legend has been dished up in hundreds of guidebooks, retold by thousands of tourists and rewritten by countless authors of that perennially popular tale about the young man who deserted from the French Foreign Legion until, what with the efforts of them all, gossips' civic fable has come to be accepted as sober, gospel fact.

Mr. Colin Glencannon, Chief Engineer of the British tramp ship *Inchcliffe Castle*, had repaired ashore accepting it wholly and expecting to meet large numbers of convivial friends. But the longer he sat outside the Café Marius and the more of the Café Marius's *pastis* he got outside of, the more skeptical he became. "Ah, foosh and foosh again!" he growled, peering blearily across the stack of saucers which marked his rather considerable score. "Neegers, Chinks, Arabs, Chinks, Neegers — all the mongrel riff-roff o' the Red Sea, the Indian Ocean, the Gulf o' Oman and Newark Bay — but ne'er the familiar face o' a white mon in the lot! Weel, I suspected from the ootset that this street was a swundle, and noo I dom weel know it!" He ordered another *pastis* (high-velocity synthetic absinthe, by-product of the great poison gas and ammunition factories around the Étang de Berre) and gloomily consulted his watch. "Eight o'clock! A-weel, as lang as I canna find a friend in all the dreary town, I'll choke doon a few more sowps o' this liquid French pastry and tak' a bite to eat. Then I'll go aboord the ship and while away the evening playing solitaire with a bottle o' Duggan's Dew. Aloss, alock, and whurra, whurra! There's no pang which gnaws a mon lik' loneliness!"

He sat back and resumed his search of the passing faces. From time to time beggars, catching his eye, approached near enough to be kicked on the shins, and were. Once a furtive gentleman oozed up to the table, whispered something in his ear and slipped him a pink and perfumed card reading "The Jollity Nigcht Club. 14 Lady Hostesses 14. Anglish Spoking." Mr. Glencannon rose, knocked out three of the furtive one's front teeth, and settled disconsolately into his chair again. He observed with chagrin that for some reason people were vacating the near-by tables and moving farther back on the terrace. This made him feel lonelier than ever.

"Ah, noo, my worthy friends!" he turned and harangued them reproachfully. "I'm only a visiting stranger in sairch o' someone to talk to, yet ye shun me lik' a leopard bruck oot with the spots! Tsk, tsk, tsk! I think ye're vurra unkind, vurra unpolite! But upon reflection, I'd rather talk to mysel' than to a pack o' fulthy swine, and noo, just to show ye, I will!"

Limbering his vocal cords with another *pastis*, he launched into a dramatic word picture, complete with sound effects, of the Argyll and Dumbarton Highlanders fighting their memorable action at Festubert, in 1915. He mimicked the shrill skirl of the pipes, the deafening bursts of the shells and the horrid screams of the wounded as the red field was won. Then, weeping copiously, he intoned the full Presbyterian burial service, fired a volley and trumpeted "The Last Post" over the graves of the glorious dead. Finally, standing stiffly but slightly slantwise at salute, he raised his voice in "God Save the King." He was doing nobly with it when he descried on the fringe of the gathering crowd two tough-looking individuals who were likewise saluting. He bit off the anthem in the middle of an ear-piercing note, seized a water carafe by the neck and viewed the interlopers askance. One of them, a veritable giant, was so inky black, so thick of lip, so flat of nose and kinky of hair that Mr. Glencannon shrewdly suspected him of owning Negro blood. His companion was approximately white, but he so closely resembled a baboon that there could be no doubt about his being a Liverpool Irishman. Mr. Glencannon had spent the greater part of his life in tramp ships' engine rooms; he knew a fireman when he saw one, and now he saw two.

"See here, ye dom scum!" he addressed them in his best professional manner. "Are ye mocking me, or what?"

"Mocking ye? Indeed, and that we're not, sorrh!" protested the simian one. "Me and this nayger are patriotic British subjicks, the same as yersel'. . . . Sure and we are, ain't we, Claude?"

"Rawther!" said the Negro, loftily.

Mr. Glencannon, now seeing four of them, realized that here, at last, was an opportunity to vent his pent-up ire. "Aye!" he bawled, "I know ye're British and, what's more, I know yere skulking breed!" He dashed his cap to the sidewalk and stamped upon it. "Foosh! They told me I'd meet my friends and fellow kirk members on this sorra street! Instead, I encounter nowt but a gang o' smutty ashcats that have joomped their ship, lost their papers, and noo disgrace their Kung and Kong, er, King and country by carousing droonk and disorderly on the public causeways o' a great furreign city!"

"Oh, bless ye, Chief!" Instinctively the Irishman addressed Mr. Glencannon by his proper title. "Ye're roight about our having no papers, else whoy would me and Claude have signed aboard that stinking Greek? Torpeteered nine miles off Martigues, we was, and us with a cargo of munitions for Alicante, Spain. But in the fortnight since, we ain't even been eating decent meals, much less getting drunk, sorrh! . . . Ain't that hivven's own truth, Claude?"

"Rawther!" agreed the gentleman of color.

At this unexpected tale of distress, Mr. Glencannon was moved to sympathy. "Oh, weel, that's different!" he said. "If ye've no' had a drink for a fortnicht, ye'll o' coorse be ravenously theersty. Er" — he took his foot out of his cap, took the shoe off his foot, polished his sock with the cap, scaled the cap across the avenue and set the shoe on his head — "er — d'ye know what I'm going to do for ye noo my puir lads? Why, I'm just going to advise ye to move alang aboot yere business, because stonding here watching me drink will only be an aggravizing tantalization, or words to that effick — ick — eck!" The shoe slid off and clattered upon the table. Retrieving it he cocked it rakishly over his ear as though it were a Glengarry and tied the laces under his chin.

"Bit o' a breeze tonicht!" he observed. "Weel, guid luck to ye, lads!"

"But now please, sorrh!" persisted the Irishman. "We're in desperate bad straits, me and Claude, and I wonder if ye wouldn't be a proper sportsman an stump up a franc or two when we've shown ye our tricks?"

"Tricks?" repeated Mr. Glencannon. "What tricks? D'ye mean ye're prestidigitators, moontebanks or summat such?"

"Oh no, sorrh!" said the other. "We eat fire, nails, swords — in fact" — he grimaced — "that's dom near all we've had to eat for a week! But look, Chief." He produced an electric light bulb from his pocket and a ten-inch knife from somewhere under his coat. "Is it worth five francs o' yer money to see Claude eat this bulb and me swally this knife?"

"Haw!" and Mr. Glencannon pushed back his shoe in amazement. "Surely ye're jesting! Why, guid losh, m'lad, if the neeger actually eats yon boolb and if ye really swallow that knife, I'll no' only give ye five froncs, I'll give ye six! . . . Aye, seeven, even!"

"Done!" said the Irishman, eagerly. "Here, show him, Claude!"

The Negro wrapped the bulb in his handkerchief and smashed it against the edge of the table. Then, crooking his finger in the genteel manner of an old maid eating comfits, he picked up the fragments one by one, placed them on his tongue, and calmly crunched and swallowed them. Meanwhile, his companion tilted back his head, opened his mouth and slowly slid the knife down his gullet until only the wooden handle protruded. Letting go of it, he spread his arms and rolled his eyes triumphantly at Mr. Glencannon.

The Engineer toyed with his drink, yawned, and then fell to thumbing a charge of tobacco into his pipe. "Weel, come, come, lads — let's see ye do yere tricks!" he invited. "What's all the delay?"

"Argh?" Indignantly, the Irishman unsheathed the knife from his esophagus while the Negro sputteringly ejected a loop of filament which had lassoed his palate. "Eh? Wh-what was that ye said?"

Mr. Glencannon scratched a match on the sole of his sock and lighted his pipe before replying. "Noo, noo, my fine fellows!" — and in his eye was a canny glint — "dinna ye try to impose on me! Ye boasted ye'd swallow that knife. Weel, if ye've swallowed it, why is it noo in yere hond? And ye claimed that this blackamoor cud eat an electric licht boolb — but the entire bross part o' it still lies richt there in his hondkerchief!"

"But — but — holy saints, Chief! What d'ye expect for yer money?"

"I expect ye to swallow the knife and the neeger to eat the boolb with no hondles, bross, or other parts left ower! Guid losh, mon, a contract is a contract!"

"Oh, so ye mean yer won't pay us?" The Irishman's knuckles whitened as he gripped his knife and his big baboonlike face was not good to see. Neither was that of his towering black companion.

Mr. Glencannon made sure that the water carafe was within convenient grabbing distance. "Noo dinna bluster, dinna threaten, ye oogly brutes!" he warned. "Ye've caused a crowd to collect and feerst thing ye know there'll be a policeman. I foncy I don't have to infoorm ye that getting arrested in Fronce withoot papers or passports is a vurra serious business and —"

"*Circulez! Débarrassez!*" A policeman came shouldering into the crowd.

The Irishman's knife vanished within his sleeve, and for an instant his fist vibrated beneath Mr. Glencannon's nose. "Mister, I'll git ye for this, or me name's not Hogan!" he rasped. Then he and the Negro slunk away in the strolling throng on the Rue Canebière.

"Braugh!" shuddered Mr. Glencannon. "They're dom near as uncouth as the pair o' scuts that desairted from my ain stoke-hold yesterday! Ah, dearie me! I didna come ashore tonicht to mingle with thugs and gallows birds!"

He ordered a double portion of bouillabaisse with lobster and a *pastis* to whet his appetite pending its preparation. He was discussing this drink when he became aware that a newcomer had seated himself at the next table. Idly turning to consider him, Mr. Glencannon saw that he was a florid person with a well-developed paunch, a neck some three sizes larger than his head, ears like crullers and a face which bore marks of collision with rapidly moving objects, such as fists in six-ounce gloves. All in all, he looked like an ex-pugilist turned publican.

"Swith!" murmured the Engineer. "If I hadna lost all hope o' e'er meeting a friend on this cheerless street, I'd swear yon loompy specimen was guid auld Horace 'Dumbbell' Dillon. But o' coorse, richt the noo, auld Dumbbell is stonding behind his bar in The Physical Culture Café, in Bexhill Street, London — and by this time next week I'll be stonding there in front o' it!" As he thought of The Physical Culture and the many pleasant hours he had whiled away therein, a wave of nostalgia surged over him. It was a rendezvous of good fellows, a cozy little spot with fresh sawdust on the floor to hide the blood stains, and for many years it had been Mr. Glencannon's headquarters whenever the S.S. *Inchcliffe Castle's* affairs brought him to the port of London. "Aye," he mused, "one always meets one's friends and cronies, time ne'er hangs heavy, in auld Dumbbell's Physical Culture! I canna remeember a single evening withoot bottles thrown, heads cracked and the whole thing ending up in a guid auld slugging kicking, stomping, gouging riot! No wonder the place is prosperous. Weel, as I say, I'll soon be back there — and after the favor I did for auld Dumbbell last time, I know he'll welcome me as though I owned it!" Smiling reminiscently, he thought of the morning, many months before, when he had chanced to encounter Mr. Dillon in the corridor of the Wapping Stairs Police Court; he himself had just been discharged with a reprimand, but Mr. Dillon, who was manacled between two policemen, explained that unless he could scare up twenty-five pounds bail at once, he would be locked in the ruddy stir. The charge — he sniffed deprecatingly — was mayhem, a trivial thing; but the magistrate had taken a narrow view and, well... could Mr. Glencannon oblige a friend with twenty-five pounds? Mr. Glencannon, whose faith in the probity of publicans was unbounded, produced the money on the spot, then, because the *Inchcliffe Castle* was sailing at noon for the Orient, he hurried off, the other's protestations of gratitude ringing in his ears.

"O' coorse," he mused, "it's been seeven months I've been away, so I suppose I canna decently ask him to pay me less than foorty per cent interest per month for the accommodation. Foorty per cent o' twunty-five mak's ten, seven times ten, makes seeventy, plus the original twunty-five, brings it up to ninety-five poonds.... Weel, just to mak' it easier for him to feegure, let's put it in roond numbers and call it an even hoonderd."

Suddenly conscious of being stared at, he turned toward the lumpy one. The fellow's face was wreathed in an incredulous smile. "Colin!" he gasped joyfully, springing to his feet as at the clang of the bell. "May 'eaven strike me stiff if it ain't old Colin Glencannon!"

"Aye, himself and none other!" beamed the Engineer. "Weel, weel, weel, Dumbbell, so it really is you! Sit, ye doon, mon, sit ye doon! *Psst! Psst! Garsong! Deux plus pastries, silver plate,* and — oh, I say, Dumbbell, have ye had yere supper yet?

No? *Alors, then, Garsong! Bring encore un dooble bully base fer this Moonseer, savvy?*"

"Ah gor-blyme, Colin, it's a fair treat to set me eyes on yer!" sighed Mr. Dillon. "I've been piddling up and down this 'ere ruddy road orl evening, 'oping against 'ope I'd see a familiar face from 'ome. But, I say — wot's that yer wearing on yer 'ead — a shoe?"

"A shoe? On my head? Oh, haw, haw, haw, how droll!" Mr. Glencannon reached over and poked him in the ribs. "Ye're in yere cups, Horace! Come, lad, try to control yersel'! Teel me, how are ye enjoying yere holiday, here in the sunny South o' Fronce?"

Dumbbell Dillon winced. "'Oliday?" he repeated cynically. "This ain't no 'oliday fer me — it's an escape. Since I seen you last I — I got married, Colin. Married to the wrong woman!" He made a helpless gesture. "Ah, Colin, Colin, never marry out of yer class, like wot I done, old boy; and if ever yer do, may the merciful 'eavens 'elp yer!"

Mr. Glencannon stirred uneasily. "But — Dumbbell! D'ye mean to say ye married that barmaid ye had in The Physical Culture that looked lik' three Joan Crawfords?"

"No" — Mr. Dillon moaned over his *pastis* — "the woman I married looks like four Katherine 'Epburns."

"Och, puir fellow!" murmured Mr. Glencannon. "Come!" and under the impression that the mussels in the bouillabaisse were lumps of coal, he fished them out and hurled them into the window of a passing tramcar. "Come, Dumbbell, do ye scup up a gutfull o' this nice, steaming fish gurry and then ye can teel me all aboot it."

Mr. Dillon scupped manfully and with a right good will; in fact, a casual observer would have said that he was hungry. "Well, it wasn't no time before she tried to change the 'ole character of the place," he explained. "Instead of leaving The Physical Culture a decent gempmen's pub — why, would yer believe it, Colin, she wanted the place to cater to — to women?"

"Oh, scondalous, scondalous!" breathed Mr. Glencannon. "Yere charming little dive was tough enough already, withoot having hostesses! How did it all end, Horace?"

"It ended by me taking it on the lam, as our American cousins put it," said Mr. Dillon, simply. "I soon realized I couldn't stick it with 'er at any price. But I couldn't afford to 'ave 'er sue me fer desertion, so when it was time fer that there case to come up that you bailed me out on, I told 'er I'd surely get three years in choky if I stayed fer trial. I jumped my bail, left 'er to run things as she ruddy well pleases, and come down 'ere to start life anew."

"Ye — ye joomped yere bail?" demanded Mr. Glencannon, weak with apprehension but plunging desperately into action. "Weel, Horace, noo that ye speak o' it, yere little debt, plus interest and charges, comes to a hoonderd quid. And as I know that under the hoppy caircumstances o' our meeting here, I canna possibly pairsuade ye to let me pay for my share o this vurra deleecious dinner, I've had eighteen pastries besides a dooble ration o' stew."

Mr. Dillon scupped clear to the bottom of his plate, pushed it aside and sat back before replying. "Colin," he said, evenly, "I 'aven't got a bleddy centime to me name. Pay for my dinner and lend me two thousand francs to tide me over, there's a good chap!"

"Eh?" In that awful instant Mr. Glencannon felt that he was about to faint. "W-what's that?" he managed to croak. "D'ye mean to say that ye're — ye're broke? But what aboot The Physical Culture, mon?"

"Oh, that!" said Mr. Dillon, his lip curling with righteous scorn. "Why, the Missus 'as changed the name of it, 'ired a dance horchestra and a troupe o' singsong girls, and it's making money 'and over fist! But, well, I'll tell you wot, Colin; I ain't no saint and I never was, but money made out of night clubs, cabareets and all them sort of deadfalls is dirty money, and I don't want no part of it! Me, I'm starting life anew, like I told yer. Some day, I 'ope to pay orff me debts."

"Oh, ye do, do ye?" snarled Mr. Glencannon, half rising and banging on the table. "Weel, ye domned hypocrite, yere sweet and pretty sentiments aboot dirty money are all vurra sweet and pretty, but I want my hoonderd poonds! I insist and demond that ye pay me! I want money, money, money — clean money or dirty money, it's all the same to me!"

Mr Dillon considered him pityingly. "Well, Colin, if that's 'ow yer feel, nothing could be easier!" he shrugged. "If yer conscience will permit yer to accept dirty money, I'll cheerfully assign my full 'arf share of the place to yer. It's making more profits than it ever made before — it's worth five 'undred dirty pounds if it's worth a dirty farthing!"

"Eh?" Mr. Glencannon brushed the tongue of his shoe out of his eye and leaned forward intently. "Eh? Ye really mean ye'll — But foosh, ye scut, I wasna born yesterday, nor e'en the day before! There's something fishy aboot this! What the heel cud I do with a nicht club, anyway?"

"Well, ye might go and sit in it, fer one thing," suggested Mr. Dillon, placidly. "But, of course, Colin, if yer think my proposition is fishy — well, it's all I've got to offer, so I'm afraid yer out that 'underd quid!"

Mr. Glencannon gulped so indignantly that his Adam's apple thudded against his breast, bone. "Blost it, it seems to be a case o' Hubson's choice!" he fumed. "O' coorse, I fully realize that if there were no skull-doogery aboot this thing, a half share in yere hurdy-gurdy should, as ye say, be worth a pretty penny. But fronkly, Horace, although I've ne'er heard more than a dozen people describe ye as a swundler, I canna recall e'er hearing a single soul go oot o' his way to call ye honest."

"All right, look 'ere!" Mr. Dillon tore a piece off the menu and scribbled on it. "'Ere's a legal deed, with everything in black on white, which makes ye 'arf owner. But this is just to prove my good faith; this very night I'll write the Missus to 'ave the lawyers draw up the formal papers. Now, then, 'ere — 'ow does that suit yer?"

Mr. Glencannon scanned the document closely. It made things clear, no doubt about it. Already, in his mind's eye, he could see himself quitting the sea and settling down in comfort in London as coproprietor of a good rough-and-rowdy resort. "A-weel, it seems to be in order, I must say," he admitted, striving to conceal his jubilation. "I — I . . ." His emotions got the better of him. "Here, Horace, auld pal!" he said, hoarsely, "I pledge ye my gratitude in this final drink!"

"Well, chin-chin!" said Mr. Dillon, lifting his *pastis* politely. "And now, if yer'll just lend me the loan of them two thousand francs . . ."

"Ah, but dom it, Horace, mon! If . . ."

Mr. Dillon sighed, retrieved the paper and prepared to tear it up.

"Stop! Stop! Here ye are!" Mr. Glencannon restrained him, counting out the money. "Guid heavens, lad, canna ye see I'm only being jocular?"

When Mr. Dillon had taken his leave, Mr. Glencannon sat for a moment watching his lumpy form disappearing down the now almost empty Canebière. "Why, the puir gowk must be crazy to mak' me a present lik' this!" he chuckled. "But, o' coorse, come to think o' it, I've often heard it said that he's been punch-droonk e'er since the historic one-round beating he took from Bombardier Wells." He folded the precious document away in his wallet. "'Tis the turning point o' yere fortunes, Glencannon!" he gloated. "Here ye sat, cursing this gay thoroughfare, little dreaming that all the time it was yere pathway to riches! For noo ye're half owner o' The Bross Knuckle Café, at 32 Bexhill Street, London, E.C., and from the name o' it, a braw disreeputable den it must be! ——Half owner noo, yes — but it shud tak' ye no time at all to swundle Mussis Dillon oot o' her share o' it!" He raised his glass, and found it empty. "Waiter! Where's that waiter? . . . I'll see that the sairvice is better than this in my little place! Garsong! Psst!"

There was an answering "Psst!" from the sidewalk and and an eager, ratlike gentleman appeared at his elbow. "Yess, sir! Postcarts! Verree special! Verree artistique!" he hissed, opening a handful of photographs fanwise and sliding them under Mr. Glencannon's nose. As the Engineer scowled at them, he could feel his gorge rise. "Ah, foosh and for shame!" he snorted. "Why, what do ye mean, ye lout, trying to sell me stuff, lik' this?" The vendor endeavored to shove the cards into Mr. Glencannon's pocket, and though the kick that landed on him was delivered by a stockinged foot, the sentiment behind it was devastating. He limped off around the corner, dripping curses.

"Strange!" murmured Mr. Glencannon, massaging his twinging toes. "The hat check girl must have snotched it off me when I wasna looking! Weel, it's an excellent way to cheat the customers, at that, so I'll just mak' a note o' it for The Bross Knuckle.... Ah, waiter, there ye are! Fetch me one more pastry and I'll call an end to this glorious evening!" He ran his eye up and down the stacks of saucers, each one representing a *pastis* at four francs. There were approximately twenty-five of them. The two double portions of bouillabaisse with lobster would come to a hundred francs additional. "Weel!" — he patted his wallet — "what do I care? I — I — Ach, horrors!" For the wallet wasn't there! He had been robbed! That postcard seller . . .

His first thought was to flee, but then he realized that the strain of the evening had sadly affected his legs. Miserable, hopeless, he sat there on the deserted terrace, his forehead a-glisten with the cold sweat which trickled down from under his shoe. "Aloss, life is like a piston!" he soliloquized. "Ups, doons, ups, doons — but it's the doonstrokes that do the damage! What though I am a café proprietor? The proof o' it was in my wallet, and the wallet is gone! If Dumbbell neglects to write to his wife, I'll be ruined, ruined! And whate'er else happens, I'm in for a drubbing and a nicht in the clink when they ask me to settle my reckoning here!"

From somewhere in the distance, up a side street, came shouts and the thin shrill of police whistles. Simultaneously, the knife swallower and the Negro strolled around the corner, spotted Mr. Glencannon and moved with studied casualness toward his table. The Engineer reached for the carafe, observing as he did so that the sinister companions were covertly panting for breath.

"The police is after us!" rasped Hogan. "We're going to sit at yer table fer a minute — and if ye so much as bat an eye, I'll do ye in!" They settled down — the Irishman, head in hands, studying the menu and the Negro taking cover behind a newspaper which he snatched from the next table.

Two black-caped agents came pounding around the corner and halted uncertainly on the curb. "That way, Moonseers!" called Mr. Glencannon, pointing toward the Cours Belsunce; then, when they had vanished, "A-weel, my charming

Hogan and my excellent Claude," he said, with unwonted affability, "what little boyish pronk have ye two cutthroats been up to noo?"

The Irishman expelled a long breath. "Well," he confessed, "we — we was up there in an alley laying for you, don'tcher see, when this other bloke happened along. We bashed him over the head and stole his money. But oh, sorrh, I can't tell ye how grateful we are to ye for . . ."

Mr. Glencannon restrained him with an impatient gesture. "Dinna thonk me," he said hollowly. "Anything I can do toward the confusion and deetriment o' this dom city, I'll do and do glodly!" He fell silent, glancing from one to the other of them and chewing the *pastis*-flavored bristles of his walrus mustache. "Er," he cleared his throat, "I hope ye were able to feelch a really worth-while sum?"

"It's enough to get us out of here — if we only had our papers!" said the knife swallower, wistfully.

"Weel," said Mr. Glencannon, "how wud ye lads lik' to go back aboord the ship with me noo and sail for London in the morning?"

"London?" There was a throb in Hogan's voice. "London, says you? How'd we like to sail for London — in the morning?" Ah, but come, Chief — it's yerself that's mocking us now!"

Mr. Glencannon shook his head and smiled benignantly. "No' at all!" he declared. "We're shy a trimmer and a firemon in the stokehold, and as for yere papers, dinna worrit!"

"Ah, whoy bless yer soul, Chief; I — I can't hardly believe it!"

"Weel, ye can consider it all settled," said Mr. Glencannon. "Let's have a drink on it!"

"Right ye are, Chief! But, begging yer pardon, sorrh, the drink has got to be on us! Now that we've got money, we want to pay!"

Mr. Glencannon seemed about to protest, but then shrugged in genial condescension. "Oh, vurra weel!" He smiled. "Have it yere ain way, lads! I'm the last mon in the world to domp the spirits o' a party. Ye can e'en pay my whole dom bill, if ye insist!"

"Well, we do insist!" said Hogan, grandly. "Sure we insist — don't we, Claude?"

"Rawther!" said Claude, with enthusiasm.

II

If Mr. Glencannon intended to ditch his saviors en route to the ship, either the state of his health or the manner in which the precious pair stuck to him must have caused him to change his mind. Whatever the reason, all three of them arrived in poor order aboard the S.S. *Inchcliffe Castle* just before the dawn.

The stokehold, shorthanded, was busy making steam. Hogan and Claude were booted below by the junior Engineers and given slice bars and shovels to sober up on. Mr. Glencannon, who, strangely enough, was now beginning to droop, retired to his room for a few hours' repose.

During the ensuing days, as the *Inchcliffe Castle* crawled along the coast of Spain, through the Strait of Gibraltar and out into the Atlantic, the Engineer was prey to a profound preoccupation. It deepened as they neared the shores of home. "Aye," he mused, "for e'en if Dumbbell really has fixed things legally, as he promised, what will Mussis Dillon's attitude be when I show up to tak' ower my share o' the place? From what he said o' her, it's plain she's an evil-tempered auld hellcat, no doot an alcoholic; and ladies o' that kidney are notoriously deeficult to hondle. My fine sense o' chivalry will prevent me cracking her ower the head, so pairhops I'd just better kick her doon the stairs. But — no doot she's got the place weel guarded by thugs, bullies and chuckers-oot, and what will they do to me? Ho, dom, Glencannon ye're faced with a vurra deelicate problem o' etiquette!"

He was still mulling it at supper that evening when Mr. Montgomery, who had been watching him eat, interrupted his train of thought.

"Lawks!" the Mate exclaimed. "Yer orlmost as 'andy with that knife as that there Liverpool bucko yer brought aboard at Marseels! Why, 'im and the nigger are a pair of blinking wonders! This arfternoon, during the first dog watch, they was down there on No. 2 'atch putting on a show fer the other 'ands that fair beat anything I ever seen in a bleddy music 'all!"

"Ker-hem! Er — I mean to say, what was they doing?" inquired Captain Ball. "I hope it wasn't nothing vulgar and off color, like them performing seals I saw at the King's Lane Theater, last time we was in London. Why, would you believe it, gentlemen, six of the nasty brutes was cavorting around on the brightly lit stage absolutely stark naked!"

"No, no, it wasn't nothing like that, sir!" Mr. Montgomery assured him. "First the Irishman shoved a knife down his maw. Then he pulled it out, took a swig o' petrol, struck a match on his teeth and — POOF! — 'e belched flyme and smoke clear up to the ruddy mast'ead, 'e did!"

"Humph!" grunted Captain Ball. "I hope it didn't damage the paint?"

"No, sir," said Mr. Montgomery. "'But that wasn't orl! When it come the nigger's turn, blyme if 'e didn't eat a busted helectrik bulb, bite the 'andle off a teacup and swaller a 'eaping 'andful o' Number Three linoleum tacks!"

"Well, ker-hem, a vessel at sea is no place for horseplay, Mister Mate, and you'd ought to've put a stop to it then and there. Now I s'pose I'll be getting letters from the office raising hell about the ship using too many stores."

"Well, to tell yer the truth, sir, I — I was clean swept off my feet by it orl! Them two chaps could work up an act that'd bring 'em ten quid a week, easy! Somebody ought to take 'em in 'and, that's wot I say!"

Without a word, Mr. Glencannon rose, left the saloon, hurried to the fiddley and descended the neck-breaking ladders into the clamorous sample room of Hades that was the *Inchcliffe Castle's* stokehold. Among the lost souls there engaged in feeding the fires, he distinguished Hogan and Claude. "Come!" he shouted, leading them over into the comparative quiet of the starboard bunker. "I've guid news for ye! Yere arteestic careers are noo assured!"

"Artistic careers, sorrh?" repeated the Irishman, permitting the corner of his sweatrag to drop from between his teeth. "Whoy, I can't even draw a straight loin!"

"No, but ye've other talents!" said Mr. Glencannon. "Noo, look! In Marseels, I accepted an interest in a hurdy-gurdy in payment o' a bad debt. It has occurred to me that ye and Claude wud mak' a vurra attractive attraction in the floor show. We'll arrange aboot the wages later but, to begin with, I'll let ye keep fifty per cent o' everything ye can steal from the customers. We dock sometime tomorrow afternoon; so if ye care to accept the proposition, I'll tak' ye aroond there with me and put ye to work, tomorrow nicht. Is it a go?"

"Indeed and it is, sorrh!" said the Irishman, joyfully. "It's just the chance me and Claude have been hoping and praying for for months — eh, Claude?"

"Rawther!" said Claude.

"Weel, ye can consider yersels engaged," said Mr Glencannon. "But oh, by the way, lads — I've ne'er been to the place yet, mysel', but I have reason to believe it's no' exockly refined; in fact, to put it fronkly, it's a vurra tough dump. What's more, my partner and mysel' probably willna see eye to eye aboot certain matters, so there may be a bit o' a fracas."

"Ah, lovely!" grinned the Irishman, spitting on his hands and doubling them into fists, while Claude picked up a lump of coal and munched it with gusto.

At a late hour the following evening, Mr. Glencannon and his bodyguard came ashore in the Limehouse Commercial Docks. Walking westward parallel to the river, they arrived in one of those regions, now common in most great cities, where yesterday's howling slums are rapidly being converted into today's snootiest colonies of fashion. Bexhill Street had not yet achieved complete respectability and, for the time being, squalor and opulence shared the thoroughfare as incongruous neighbors. At the far end of the street, where of yore The Physical Culture Café cast squares of light and occasional customers across the sidewalk, Mr. Glencannon saw a red-and-yellow-striped awning beneath which a uniformed doorman stood sticking his chest out.

"Ah, swith!" he murmured in amazement. "Yon's a gilded palace if I e'er saw one — aye, a palace o' sin, for I mustna be deceived by its looks! Weel, there's the place, lads!" he proclaimed. "If ye'll just stick close to me, noo, I'll ask this fellow to announce me to my partner. Ho, lackey!" he addressed the functionary, "Is Mussis Dillon in the club yet?"

The other eyed him with distaste. "Wot's it to yer?" he demanded. "Beggar orff from under this hawning, orl three of yer!"

"Ye're fired for insolence!" Mr. Glencannon told him briefly. "Go inside, tak' off yere uniform and get yere pay from the purser!"

"Eh?" the doorman snorted. "Fired am I? Well, now, just 'oo in 'ell do yer think yer are, Mister? Fer two ruddy pennies, I'd —"

"Claude, I'll thonk ye please to attend to this," said Mr. Glencannon; and then, when Claude had done so, "There! Noo let's just drog him into the vestibule so's he willna clutter up the sidewalk, and mak' oursel's known. Here, you!" he summoned a waiter. "Tak' my compliments to Mussis Dillon, and teel her Muster Colin Glencannon, Esquire, wud lik' to see her here in the lobby withoot delay."

"Missus — Missus 'oo, sir?" and as he took stock of the visitors the waiter's teeth chattered. "Why, there isn't no Missus Dillon 'ere, sir! If you'll just step outside a minute, I'll . . ."

Shouldering past him and bowling over several dress-suited individuals who sought to bar their way, the trio strode between red plush portieres into a room of dim lights, many tables, snowy shirt fronts and gleaming shoulders. At the far side of the dance floor, an orchestra of Argentine Gauchos from the pampas of Whitechapel was just oozing into a tango.

"Weel, weel, weel — guid evening, everybody!" shouted Mr. Glencannon, clapping his hands lustily and skidding across the dance floor with his bodyguard at his heels. "Weel, here we are again, friends, here we are again! Is everybody hoppy, is everybody gay? Ah, that's fine! That's woonderful! That's marvelous! And noo, friends, as lang as Mussis Dillon hasna showed up yet, I'm taking the liberty o' onimating the proceedings with a new and vurra novel novelty which I have retained at ruinous expense!" He dragged the band leader from the platform and stepped up into his place. "Ladies and gentlemen!" he announced. "I have great pleasure in presenting

"I'll let ye keep fifty per cent o' everything ye can steal from the customers."

to ye that famous team o' society entertainers, Glencannon's Merry Collegians — Oxford Paddy Hogan and Cambridge Neeger Claude! Give, Hogan, give!"

Hogan swigged from a flask, scratched a match on his teeth and gushed flames like a volcano. "Marvelous! Marvelous!" shouted Mr. Glencannon, applauding wildly. "Come on, people, give the lad a hond! . . . Oh, dinna ye worrit aboot yon ceiling draperies — they're only imitation silk and the fire will burn itsel' oot in no time! Noo, friends, I'll just ask, Claude here, to . . . Ah, Mussis Dillon, I presume? Weel, weel, dear Moddum, I'm charmed, indeed, to mak' yere acquaintance!" He bowed gallantly and touched the back of her jeweled hand with a mustache like a shoebrush. "Ye see, I — But, foosh — what's this?" Glancing around him in dismay, he saw that the place was full of policemen! It was a raid!

With rare presence of mind, "Ho, constables!" he shouted. "I demond that this disorderly joint be arrested as a disorderly joint! They sell intoxicating beeverages here, Sergeant, and if ye dinna believe me, ye've only to smell my breath. . . . And as for you, Moddum — why ye shameless auld harpy, I'll ne'er relent in my crusade against sinks o' this sort until the last o' them has been raided, padlocked and banished from the British Isles!"

"Shall we take him in charge, Lady Birkitt?" asked the Police Sergeant. "I can't make out whether he's drunk, crazy or both."

"Noo, wait a minute!" protested Mr. Glencannon. "There's something crooked going on here! Moddum, are ye no' Mussis Dillon, and is this no' Dillon's Bross Knuckle Café?"

Lady Birkitt favored him with an icy stare and turned to address her guests. "For some reason, our charming visitors seem to have confused our little club with a rowdy sailors' boozing ken which a ruffian named Dillon used to conduct next door. I had trouble with him for months and finally asked the police to close him up as a public nuisance. One night about two weeks ago, he rolled in here drunk and swearing vengeance and — well, I suppose this is it!"

"Oh, yus? Well, we'll see about that, yer ladyship!" the Sergeant rumbled ominously. "There's nothing we'd rather do than handle beauties like these three! Hup! Take 'em in charge, men!"

As the constables were frog-marching them down Bexhill Street, "Oh, bless me soul, sorrh!" exclaimed Hogan, suddenly. "Whoy didn't I remember it before?"

"Remeember what?" snapped Mr. Glencannon. "D'ye mean ye knew that Horace Dumbbell Dillon was making me the tool o' his vengeance and swundling me all alang?"

"Dillon? . . . Never heard the name till tonight, sorrh! No, I mean about the name o' that place! Claude and I should have known by the street address that it wasn't The Brass Knuckle at all!"

Mr. Glencannon scowled at him suspiciously over the burly blue shoulder of his escort. "Not The Bross Knuckle? What do ye mean, ye scut?"

"Whoy," Hogan lowered his voice, "it's a funny thing, sorrh, but — ye'll remember that noight in Marseels whin Claude and I er — managed to git hold of the money to pay for yer dinner and all them drinks with? Well, in the wallet we found a strip of paper, like torn off a bill of fare. There was a lot of writing on it we didn't bother to read, but I do remember seeing 'At the Sign of the Brass Knocker — 32 Bexhill Street, London.' 'Knocker,' it was — not 'Knuckle.' He must have been the very bloke ye got yer share of the café from — and tonight ye must have took us to the wrong place, don'tcher see? If I'd only thought of it sooner, sorrh, we —"

"Hup! Whoa! Grab him!" barked the Sergeant. "Steady, you ruddy Scotch walrus — come along peaceful!" He snapped the handcuffs on Mr. Glencannon's wrists. "If ye want to fight with yer little playmates, yer've got orl night ahead of yer in the same cell to do it!"

The Scot From Scotland Yard

The tale has been told of the night in Semarang, Java, when Thomas O'Halloran, donkeyman of the S.S. *Inchcliffe Castle*, quaffed deeply of the gin which comes in tall gray jugs, was delivered aboard in a *prau*, attempted to walk across the open hatch of No. 2 Hold and sustained what the Dutch port doctor described in his report as *een gebroken nek*. The deceased's wages had been only eight pounds five shillings per month, but he had done rather tidily in the smuggling line and so left a two-story brick cottage in Limehouse, London, three hundred and seven pounds in cash and two hundred and twelve pounds of widow. This copious lady was given a job in the offices of the *Inchcliffe Castle's* owners, where, until high noon of a recent Saturday, she rendered invaluable service in polishing the brass sign at the entrance, preventing visitors from seeing whoever they wished to see and finding the managing director's eyeglasses for him whenever he dropped them to his wastebasket or lost them on his nose. She is the heroine of the following brief but romantic account, which begins with a knock at the door of Captain Ball's cabin on the *Inchcliffe Castle*, home from a traipse down the West African coast and discharging the gleanings thereof in No. 4 of the London Commercial Docks.

"Ker-hem, ker-huff — come in!" called Captain Ball.... Ah, here you are, Mr. Glencannon! Well now, first of all, if you'll just be good enough to take that there chair over there — er ... No, no — I mean to say, leave it where it is, but sit in it, sit in it! ... Ah! That's better! Well now, first of all, Mr. Glencannon, the reason I sent my steward down to the engine room for you is because I want to talk to you as man to man — ker-huff! Let me say, first of all, that I fancy I don't have to justify my motives to you, and so I won't waste any time beefing around the bush, which you ought to know me well enough to know is not my habit anyway. Oh, I'm just a plain, direct speaker, Mr. Glencannon, even blunt, and when I call a spade a spade, I call it a spade, see what I mean? Blunt! Ha-exactly! Well now, I feel it in duty to speak to you about that chap's big fat lolloping widow who works in the office that busted his neck in Batavia — no, Surabaya — now wait a minute, wait a minute; we was loading sago — no, rice — no, no, tapioca — Semarang! Ha —Semarang! We was loading tapioca and he busted his neck in Semarang, and his name was O'Halloran. Well, Mr. Glencannon, I guess you have already guessed that I am referring to Missus O'Halloran, the fat lady who is his widow. Well now, I don't wish to seem blunt, Mr. Glencannon, but all the same I hereby solemnly warn you that you'd better stop playing fast and loose with Missus O'Halloran!"

"Eh?" gasped Mr. Glencannon. "Mussis O'Halloran? I play fast and loose with — Mussis O'Halloran? Ah, swith, sir! Surely ye must be joking!"

"I am not joking," said Captain Ball. "In matters such as this, it would seem to me that levity would scarcely seem seemly. No, Mr. Glencannon, no — I mean to say — er — that is, I mean what I say!"

"But foosh, sir! It's too rideeculous!"

Captain Ball shrugged. "Oh, is it? Well, maybe! All I know is that every time I've gone to the office since we've been in port, she's buttonholed me on the way out and gushed a lot of gush about you, to say nothing of rolling her eyes, et and cetera! And surely, you won't attempt to deny that the time you and I went up there last trip, you — chuckled her under the chin in the anteroom? Ha — I saw you, Mr. Glencannon, I saw you! Now, what's your answer to that?"

"Ho, dom!" groaned Mr. Glencannon, reddening. "Alos, sir, as to that, I canna but admit it, to my shame! If I'd e'er dreamed she'd tak' it seriously, I'd have put on my bross knuckles feerst! But, captain," — he leaned forward eagerly — "dinna ye remeember why it was that I stooped to that bit o' unfoortunate horseplay? Dinna ye recall that I was spoofing her aboot the rumors that she was going to wed a policeman? Weel, then!" He sat back triumphantly. "Doesna that vurra fact vindicate my motives?"

"It may vindicate your motives, yes, but it don't get you out of the jam," said Captain Ball. "For all I know, she may have been being courted by the whole London Metropolitan Police Force, including horses, air-raid constables and the Thames River patrol, but the fact remains she's now got her big fat eye on you. Ah, *la woman is fickle-o*, as the Eyetalians put it; I'm afraid I can't give you an exact translation of the phrase, but the gist of it is that 'woman is fickle,' if you see what I mean."

"Aye, I do see what you mean," said Mr. Glencannon, with a shudder. "I see, besides, that Mussis O'Halloran's a vurra dangerous woman of a vurra dangerous age! I accept yere warning in the spirit it's meant, sir, and I'll keep oot o' her sicht from this time forth!"

"Umph! Well, you'd better not do anything of the sort!" said Captain Ball. "Oh, hell's bones, no, that'd be fatal! 'Absence makes the heart grow fonder,' Mr. Glencannon, and don't you jolly well forget it!"

"Ah, but dearie me! Then what in the wurrld am I to do, Sir?"

"Well" — Captain Ball sat back and crossed his hands upon his paunch — "if you'll take my advice — ga-huff — you'll go ashore and see her right away — not ostentagiously, of course, but casual-like, as though it was casual. Hazlitt wants you to report at his office, anyway, so he can put you on the carpet about them coal bills from Las Palmas, so before he's ready to start yapping at you, just wait outside in the anteroom and talk to her. Find out for yourself exactly what's what and where the land lays."

Mr. Glencannon sat silent for a moment; then he sighed, rose and walked slowly from the room.

II

"Well, good lawks!" Mrs. O'Halloran's upper works bulged and palpitated over her reception desk like a cluster of toy balloons at a fair. "Lawks and lor 'lumme if it ain't Mr. Glencannon 'imself! 'Owe are yer, Mr. Glencannon, 'ow are yer; though if ye're feeling 'arf as 'ealthy as ye're looking 'andsome, yer couldn't arsk fer more!"

"I am vurra weel indeed, thonk ye, moddum," said Mr. Glencannon, with reserve, "barring, o' course, those manifold infeermities which creep upon all folk o' yere ain age and mine, to remind us, aloss, that the cauld grave awaits."

"Br-rh! 'Orrors! Please don't talk like that or yer'll remind my late 'usband, Gord rest 'is soul, though I suppose by this time there ain't much left of the rest of 'im, wot with the worms and wigglers and orl."

"No," agreed Mr. Glencannon. "I foncy he's been reduced to lowest terms, especially as he was buried in the truppics. But speaking o' husbands, Mussis O'Halloran, I wud be remiss in coortesy, indeed, were I no' to inquire as to the progress o' the — er — little *affair de cur* ye were having, last time I was in London. I allude, o' course, to yere romance with the policemon."

"Oh, that!" Mrs. O'Halloran blushed and looked away. I — well, candiedly, Mr. Glencannon, as to that, I 'ardly know to say."

Mr. Glencannon's eyes narrowed warily. "Am I to understand that ye've undergone a change o' heart, Mussis O'Halloran?"

"Well, yus and no. Jymes and I are still as good friends as ever — in fack, 'ardly an evening goes by without 'im dropping in at my 'ouse when he comes orff juty, so's 'e can tyke 'is shoes orff and rest 'is feet whilst I stews 'im a dish o' tea. But —"

"But swith, dear moddum, it all soonds vurra domestic and congenial! Do ye mean he's never made ye a definite proposal?"

"Well, 'e's never wrote me no compromising letters, if that's, wot yer mean, but 'e's arsked me to my fyce to marry 'im time and again. No, no, it ain't that" — and again Mrs. O'Halloran averted her gaze. "The trouble is — well, to tell yer the truth, Mr. Glencannon, the trouble is 'is nyme!"

"His name! Why, what is his name and whate'er can be the motter with it?"

"The meaning of it's the matter with it," said Mrs. O'Halloran. "I 'esitate to mention it aloud, even to a dear old friend like you."

"Indeed?" Mr. Glencannon stirred uneasily. "Indeed? Weel, suppose ye spell it, then."

Mrs. O'Halloran hesitated and then shook her head. "It ain't even such a nyme as a genteel lydy would know 'ow to spell," she said. "Much less would she care to 'ave it printed with a rubber stamp on 'er wisiting card and go through life being called by it. Ah," she sighed, "why couldn't 'e 'ave 'ad a lovely, 'igh-clarss nyme like Glencannon, fer instance?"

Mr. Glencannon winced. "Oh, but after all, what's in a name?" he scoffed. "If the fellow really cares for ye, surely he cud be pairsuaded to change it!"

"Chynge it? Chynge it wot to?"

"How can I say, moddum, until ye've told me what it is the noo?"

Mrs. O'Halloran steeled herself to the ordeal. "I 'ate to repeat — no, no, I mean, to pronounce it!" she corrected herself hastily. "Still, if I must, I must! 'Is nyme is Belcher!" She hid her face in her hands.

"Belcher? H'm!" Mr. Glencannon nodded judicially. "Aye, weel, it is, as ye say, a rather indeelicate appellation, no doot aboot that. Am I to assume, from yere inteense aversion to it, that he is in the habit o' suiting the — er — action to the wurrd?"

"Oh, no, not Jymes!" Mrs. O'Halloran assured him. "As a matter of fack, 'e's taciturn to a fault."

"Weel, that sumplifies things," said Mr. Glencannon. "The only real problem, then, is to think o' a name that wud be sotisfactory to you and that ye cud pairsuade him to adopt. Noo, let's see, let's see! I suppose it wud be desirable from his standpoint, oot o' reeverence for his ancestors and all, to have the significance o' the auld family cognomen more or less presairved in the new. Weel, what wud ye say to Burpee? Or better still, McGurk?"

"Burpee! McGurk! McGurk! Burpee! M'm — well, Mr. Glencannon, I s'pose it orl depends on the expression of yer fyce when yer says em, but both of them nymes sound just a bit too — realistic for me."

"Ah! Then what aboot Winchester or Colt or Lee-Enfield — all o' them the names o' justly ceelebrated repeaters, if ye get the point? Again, proceeding alang a similar line o' thocht, what aboot Parrot or Ditto? On the other hand, if ye'd prefair a really romontic name which conveys the deep inner feeling o' what we're striving to express, what wud ye think o' Heartburn? 'Mussis Police Constable James Heartburn' — ah, losh, moddum, there's a beautiful lilting name for ye!"

"Well, they're orl better than Belcher, I must say," Mrs. O'Halloran conceded. "But wot really worries me is whether I could ever get Jymes to consent to a chynge. It'd 'ave to be broached to 'im very indirect and subtile or 'e'd fly orff the 'andle an 'oller 'is ead orff! 'E's a stubborn bloke, and being on traffic juty, 'e ain't one to listen to reason. Ah, me," she sighed and slumped back dispiritedly, "if only 'e 'ad a nyme like Glencannon in the first plyce and was a worldwise, interlectual gent like you!"

"Er — indeed, quite so, quite so!" muttered Mr. Glencannon, turning deathly pale. "However, Mussis O'Halloran," he went on desperately, "if ye anticipate deeficulties, pairhops I micht try to help ye to bring him to reason."

"Would yer really? Ah, ye're a saint!" Impulsively she grasped his hand and pressed it warmly. "Yus, ye're a very angel from 'eaven! Now, listen, Mr. Glencannon, dear! Tomorrer's Saturday. Well, come and 'ave tea at my 'ouse, Number Eleven, Catsmeat Yard. Jymes will be there — and though I 'aven't got much 'ope, we'll see wot you can do!"

III

The following afternoon Mr. Glencannon had polished the buttons of his uniform and brushed the snuff off the breast of it, preparatory to going ashore, when a prudent inspiration caused him to lay it aside in favor of his dark-blue civilian serge.

"Ah, swith," he muttered as he stepped through the dockyard gate, "'tis lucky I bethocht me o' her weakness for unifurrms! Seeing me thus in the garb o' an ordinurra mortal may wean her from her mod infotuation!"

In response to his knock, the door of No. 11 Catsmeat Yard was flung open and Mrs. O'Halloran greeted him with outcries of feigned surprise. "Mr. Glencannon, of orl people! Wot a 'appy chance!" she screamed. "Come in, come in, Mr. Glencannon, do!" She ushered him down the dark, narrow hallway, nudging him and jerking her head at a police helmet hanging by its chin strap on the Argentine cowhorn hatrack. "Step into the parlor," she invited. "I want to myke yer acquainted with another dear old friend."

As Mr. Glencannon entered the room he tripped over a black receptacle which he at first supposed to be a coal scuttle; then, discerning a similar object looming beside it, he recognized a pair of shoes. Vast as were the dimensions of this footwear, he could not suppress a gasp of astonishment as he beheld the owner. Reclining upon a sofa, and with his white-stockinged feet occupying an armchair at the far end of it, was sufficient policeman to populate the guilty nightmares of London's entire underworld, with enough left over to supply Birmingham, Liverpool and Manchester.

"Mr. Glencannon," said Mrs. O'Halloran, "I'd like to interjewce yer to Police Constable Belcher. Mr. Colin Glencannon is chief engineer in one of our ships," she explained, "while Police Constable Jymes Belcher is a police constable. 'Is number is Number Sixty-one-eighteen."

Police Constable James Belcher, No. 6118, stirred slightly, but did not trouble further to acknowledge the introduction. "Me feet 'urt," he growled at no one in particular.

"There, there, Jymes, don't fret!" Mrs. O'Halloran comforted him. . . . The poor dear wants 'is tea, that's wot's 'is trouble."

She winked at Mr. Glencannon. "I'll just leave you two boys to 'ave a nice little chat together whilst I go out and slop up something in the kitchen."

The engineer returned the wink and settled into a chair. "Aweel, constable," he said genially, "I deduce from yere unifurrm and a chonce remark drupped by our charming hostess that ye're connected with the police. Fine weather we're having, isn't it?"

"No," said Constable Belcher.

"Ah, I get yer point exockly!" Mr. Glencannon agreed, exuding charm from every pore. "Spring days are notoriously treacherous — in fact, o' all times o' the year, this is the season when we must guard our health. Noo, constable, it is weel known that a pinch o' bicarbonate o' soda after meals is a —"

"Me feet 'urt," said the policeman. Ponderously he heaved himself to a sitting posture, and treated Mr. Glencannon to a long, searching scrutiny. "Humph!" he grunted. "Now just turn yer side face. . . . Hup — not so far, not so far! . . . There, hold it! H'm! H'm! 'Ave yer got any scars, any teeth missing, any tattoos or other special identifying marks? Come, my man, speak up!"

"No, I have not," said Mr. Glencannon, squirming uncomfortably, but not forgetting his mission or the necessity for tact. "As a motter o' fact, constable, I can say with all truth and modesty that I'm a pairfict physical speecimen. Thanks to my temperate habits and rigid prunciples o' diet, I've been spared e'en those afflictions to which nine people oot o' ten are —"

"Me feet 'urt, that's my trouble," said Constable Belcher; then, in a sudden burst of confidence, "It's the damn calluses."

"Aye! Calluses! Precisely! Noo, just let us suppose, just for the sake o' supposition, that yer name, instead o' yer feet, was Callus. Weel, foosh, mon, wudn't ye be willing and eager to change it to McCallister?"

"Change me name! Oh, ho!" Constable Belcher glowered at him suspiciously. "So you believe in using false names and aliases, do yer? Wot did you say yer own name was? Glencannon?

The Scot From Scotland Yard

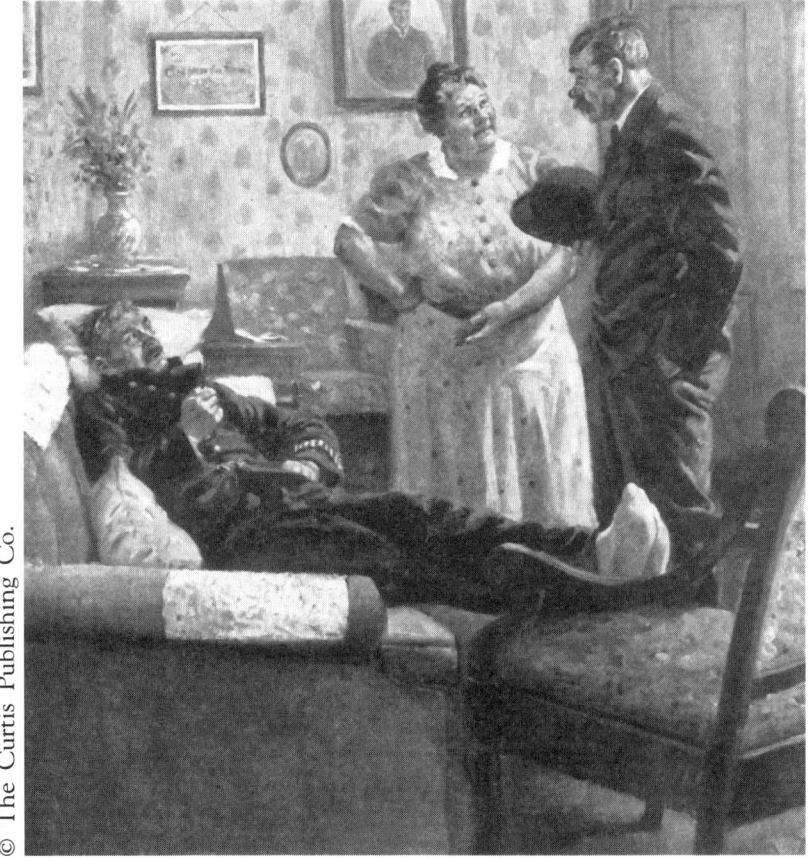

Police Constable James Belcher stirred slightly, but did not trouble further to acknowledge the introduction. "Me feet 'urt," he growled.

Ye're quite sure about it? And yer occupation's mercantile-marine orfficer? H'm!" He unbuttoned his tunic pocket, produced a notebook and a sheaf of printed circulars and fell to studying them. From where he sat, Mr. Glencannon could see that the circulars were illustrated with full-face and profile portraits of sullen gentlemen who wore numbered placards pinned to their lapels.

"H'mff — yus, 'ere it is!" muttered Constable Belcher. "Now, look ere, my man!" He shook a finger like a truncheon beneath Mr. Glencannon's nose. "I'm going to arsk you a few questions, and I warn you to be very, very careful about your answers. I don't want no ifs, ands and buts. I don't want no evasions; I want a simple yus or no, understand me? Right! Now, first of all, do you or don't you know anything about six cases of Japanese silk that was feloniously removed, transported and stolen out of Stillman and Sons' Ware'ouse, Number Fifteen, Clive Road, between one o'clock and five twenty A. M. on the fourteenth instant?"

"No," said Mr. Glencannon. "But I can give ye a guid live tip aboot the theft o' a mandolin, a patent anchor and a pedigreed sow at Majunga, Madagascar, on July eleeventh last."

Constable Belcher consulted the circular and then, leafed through the others. "M'mph! That there's a different case," he grunted. "'Owever, we've got it well in 'and and an arrest is expected shortly. But now I s'pose yer'll try to tell me that yer 'aven't got any information regarding a seafaring chap named Nelson, first name unknown?"

"Nelson? Nelson? Ah, noo, constable, I'm hoppy to say I can be of assistance to ye! Nelson's feerst name was Horatio and he died at sea aboord H.M.S. *Victory,* off Cape Trafalgar, on October the twenty-feerst, Eighteen hoonderd and five."

Constable Belcher scratched his head and then reopened his notebook. "Deceased, ten, twenty-one, eighteen-five," he mumbled as he wrote. "Well, it don't check up! There's something fishy 'ere! Still, though, the commissioner or nobody else can't say I 'aven't done a jolly neat bit o' work in finding out this crook Nelson's first name!"

"Ah, but feerst names are o' minor importance!" said Mr. Glencannon, returning to the fray. "And so, for that motter, are last names. A fig for names, say I! 'A rose by any other name wud smell as sweet!' Come, come, constable; surely ye'll admit that!"

"I'll admit nothing," growled Constable Belcher. "Absolutely nothing! Anyway — f'mff — that smell you smell ain't figs, it's fried kippers, so wot the flyming 'ell's the matter with yer? . . . Veronica! " he bawled plaintively. "Oh, Veronica! I wants me bit o' tea!"

"Coming, Jymie, coming!" Mrs. O'Halloran entered with a tray laden with a ham, a platter of herrings, a plate of scones, three teacups and three bottles of gin. "Draw up to the tyble, you poor 'ungry dears, and scowff it whilst it's 'ot!" she invited.

The herrings were hot, the scones were hot and heavy, but the gin, which had been hewn from the solid alcohol by the hostess' own fair hand, was hot or cold, light or heavy, or all four at once, depending upon the reaction of the particular nerves and ganglia it happened to rupture on the way down. Now, Mr. Glencannon had always taken an intelligent interest in table beverages, and so was intrigued by the multiple-phase principle upon which this gin functioned; indeed, he had never experienced anything quite like it before, and he felt his connoisseurship challenged. Thus, while Mrs. O'Halloran screamed and ate and Constable Belcher ate and drank, he quietly proceeded to conduct a series of experiments with a view to determining several points concerning it. By the time he had established its value in tonsillectomy, dental anesthesia and pyloric ventriloquism, he had forgotten what the other points were, but he went on experimenting anyway. He felt, somehow, that his researches were leading him nearer and nearer to an epoch-making discovery, a great truth. And suddenly, sure enough, the pale green haze in which he seemed to be floating concentrated itself into a flash of blinding white light and lo, the Glencannon Law was revealed! It was so firmly based in logic, so beautifully lucid, so austerely plain, that he wondered why no one had stumbled upon it before. According to this law, as expressed mathematically, the more gin, x, he drank, the drunker, y, he became. There was, he realized, no gainsaying it. The thing was irrefutable, ironclad, impregnable! He was striving for nonscientific terms in which to expound it to the assembled laity, when, from miles across the table, came Constable Belcher's voice:

"Me feet 'urt! They 'urt, they 'urt, they 'urt like 'ell! Feet or wheels, wheels or feet, that is the burning question! Bicycles 'ave two wheels and so 'ave motorbikes. Taxicabs 'ave four wheels and there's millions of 'em. Busses 'ave six wheels. Vans 'ave eight wheels. Lorries 'ave twelve, fourteen, even sixteen wheels, to say nothing of the bleddy trailers." He paused and downed another teacupful of gin. "Roller skates 'ave wheels," he resumed, "costermongers' barrows 'ave wheels. Yus, gorblimy! The 'ole great city o' London 'as got wheels, wheels, wheels; while me" — he thumped himself on the chest with a sound like a cooper hammering a barrel — "while me, me, me — day arfter day arfter day — I just stand there, stand there, stand there! On me feet, feet, Feet!" He collapsed into his chair and sat mopping his beaded brow with a crumpled police circular.

"Aye, feet!" murmured Mr. Glencannon, politely. "Or, as ye so cleverly phrased it, 'feet, feet, Feet.' Weel, after all, I suppose feet are as satisfactory to stond on as anything. Else why?"

"Else why what?" inquired Mrs. O'Halloran, in the bright, interested manner of the perfect hostess.

"Else why feet," said Mr. Glencannon. "I wonder if by any chonce ye hoppen to be fameeliar with that great pooem o' the late Muster Kipling's entitled 'Boots,' beginning — er:

> "Boots, boots, boots, boots,
> Boots, boots, boots, boots,
> Boots, boots-"

"Lawks, please don't recite that!" Mrs. O'Halloran shuddered coyly. "That there 'orrible 'ollering part, where the poor bloke goes orff 'is chump, orlways gives me the creepers!"

She poured herself a modest spot of gin. Mr. Glencannon was about to do likewise when he saw that Constable Belcher had captured his teacup and was brushing the outside of it with fine gray powder from a phial. Puzzled, the engineer was preparing to launch a rather complicated witticism about a bull in a china shop painting the lily on the cup that cheers, when:

"Sh-h! 'E's trying to bring out yere fingerprints!" Mrs. O'Halloran whispered. "Oh, 'e's a conscientious constable, Jymes is! Crimes and clues is orl 'e thinks about, when 'e ain't thinking about corns and calluses. More's the blinking shyme 'e ain't been permoted to plain-clothes detective years and years ago!"

"Aye, years and years and years," murmured Mr. Glencannon, viewing the proceedings with apprehension. Although he was reasonably certain that no warrants were out against him within the London police jurisdiction, he could not help but reflect that the world was wide and that the fingerprint system was rapidly achieving international scope. He was relieved, therefore, to see that the constable's efforts with the teacup brought negative results, and he realized with gratitude that the gin must have gnawed its way through the crockery and evaporated the tell-tale traces on the exterior surface. He contrived to spill some of the contents of his bottle onto his napkin and with it surreptitiously polished the handles of his knife and fork. Then, as an additional precaution, he swallowed the remainder.

"There, noo!" he muttered. "That will boffle e'en the bloodhoonds!"

"Wot blood'ounds?" inquired Mrs. O'Halloran.

"Blood'ounds? Blood'ounds? I never said nothing of the ruddy sort!" roared Constable Belcher into the teacup. "The number I arsked for was White'all One-two-one-two, which is the telephone number of New Scotland Yard. Do I get it or do I don't?"

"Haw, look at him! Why, I do believe he's fuddled!" chuckled Mr. Glencannon. "The puir alcoholic is trying to try to drink gin oot o' a teelephone! I wonder if by any chonce ye hoppen to be fameeliar with that great pooem o' the late Muster Kipling's entitled 'Gunga Gin,' beginning — er:

> "Boots, boots, boots, boots,
> Boots, boo —"

"Lawks, please don't recite that!" Mrs. O'Halloran shuddered coyly. "That there 'orrible 'ollering part, where the poor bloke goes orff 'is chump, orlways gives me the creepers!"

Constable Belcher bit a crescent out of the teacup, ejected it with evident distaste, and frowned at her reprovingly. "Why, yer said them very same words before," he growled. "Do stop repeating yerself, Veronica!"

"Repeating meself? Me?" Mrs. O'Halloran uttered a piercing scream, snatched up the ham by the femur bone and smote him over the head with it. "Oh, yer narsty vulgar brute!" she cried, smiting him again. "Oh, yer great, 'ulking lout of a traffic policeman, yer! Wot d'yer mean, using such language in front of a genteel gempman like Mr. Glencannon?" She continued to hammer him with the ham.

Taking advantage of this hiatus in the tea party, Mr. Glencannon rose, tiptoed into the hall, collected his bowler and vanished into the dank Thames fog.

"Foosh!" he breathed. "I'm oot o' her clutches for the moment at least, but if I dinna dilute the gin that's smoldering within me, my liver will start peeling!"

He turned into a crowded pub just off the Commercial Road, ordered a double Duggan's Dew and set about the dilution in earnest. Almost at once he could feel the Glencannon Law beginning to reassert itself, and by the time he had run off the second test (x^1) he estimated his condition as approximately y^3. Turning abruptly upon the gentleman to his left, who was tapering off on beer, "Let's see yer full face, my mon!" he ordered.

"Eh?" The beer drinker thumped his glass down truculently.

"'Oo the 'ell are you?"

"Noo, noo, my mon, keep a civil tongue on yer head!" Mr. Glencannon cautioned him. "It's I who's osking the questions aroond here and the onswer is, yes and no. Do ye or do ye not know anything aboot the sixteen cases o' Joponese silk that was feeloniously removed, transported and stolen oot o' Stillman and Sons' Warehouse on the foorteenth instonce? Speak up!"

The beery one's knees gave way and he grasped the bar for support. "Oh, gorblimy, guv'nor — no, no, of course I don't! I'm no bleddy thief, guv'nor. Anybody in the neighborhood can tell yer that! Just arsk the landlord, Alf Cherry, ere — 'e knows me!"

"Yus, yus, inspector, I can vouch fer this 'ere chap," the publican intervened. "'Is nyme is Willy Biddlecroft, and 'e's the parish gryvedigger."

"Has he got any tattoo marks or scars missing?" demanded Mr. Glencannon.

"Oh, lor lumme, sir, I couldn't tell yer that! 'Ave yer, Willy?"

"No, no, cross and double-cross me 'eart!" cried Mr. Biddlecroft, doing so with fervor.

"H'm! Humph!" Mr. Glencannon scribbled in his notebook. "Weel, I want Whitehall One-two-one-two, five, seven, nine, ten, slogging up and doon again, boots, boots, boo —

Er — no, no, wait! The mon I'm after is a seafaring mon named Nelson and his feerst name is positively no' Horatio. My name is James Belcher and my noomber is Sixty-one-eighteen. But yer name's only Wully Biddlecroft, ye silly auld goat, so run awa' and dig a grave for yersel', and stop wasting my time! A-humph! . . . Noo then, you!" he bawled at the gentleman on his right. "Let's have a look at yer profile!" Receiving no answer, he brought his eyes into focus and saw that the gentleman was no longer there. Indeed, a careful investigation disclosed that, save for himself and the publican, the recently crowded barroom was now deserted.

"Ah, ha!" he sneered. "'The wicked flee when no mon pursuiteth!' Why, at least a dozen o' them have left their drinks untasted on the bar!" He rectified this omission as rapidly as possible then confronted the dismayed landlord. "Weel, my fine fellow, I must say ye've got an ugly gang o' gallows birds for customers! I've had my eye on this disreeputable shebeen for a lang, lang time and noo ye're aboot to lairn to yer cost that ye canna harbor criminals and get awa' with it!"

The publican turned pale around the gills and hastily filled Mr. Glencannon's glass to overflowing. "'Ere, inspector," he said, "this one's on the 'ouse and as many more as yer can stummick. I wantcher to feel that ye're orlways welcome 'ere, inspector; yus, I 'ope yer'll feel free to drop in at any time, sir. Er — of course" he winked and lowered his voice — "of course, if yer could just manage to let me know in advance when ye're coming, I'll arrange to 'ave a little extra refreshment for yer." He smirked and winked again. "A nice veal-and-'am pie with a five-pound note in it, fer instance! What d'yer say to that?"

"I say veal is nosty and ham gives me hives. What's more, unless ye pay me ten poonds cash doon the noo, I'll run ye in for attempted bribery!"

"Yus, yus, of course!" Trembling, the publican dug into his till and counted out the money. "'Ere yer are, Inspector Belcher! It's a pleasure — a pleasure, I assure yer!"

Mr. Glencannon stuffed the notes into his pocket, downed his drink and set forth in quest of pastures new. "Haw!" he chuckled, slamming the door behind him. "It looks lik' a rough nicht for the thieves and publicans!"

IV

"Yus, yus, inspector, I can vouch fer this 'ere chap," the publican intervened. "''Is nyme is Willy Biddlecroft, and 'e's the parish gryvedigger."

When Mr. Glencannon awoke next morning, he found himself in his bunk on the *Inchcliffe Castle* and seventy pounds in bank notes on the top of his dresser. At first he was puzzled as to how he and they had got there, but as he sipped a light breakfast, he gradually pieced together a spotty recollection of his nocturnal exploits.

"A-weel," he mused, "seeventy poonds is seeventy poonds, and seeventy poonds is a vurra tidy sum indeed. But I fear, aloss, that I've only got mysel' deeper in the mess I set oot to get oot of. Feeguring ten poonds per pub, that means I must have exocted treebute from seeven pubs. Weel, it's a foregone conclusion that some o' the ootraged landlords will run yammering to Scotland Yard with complaints o' blackmail. Then, o' course, yon Belcher's name will be mud, he'll be sacked from the police foorce, and Mussis O'Halloran will set her cap for me in deadly earnest! Ah, foosh, Glencannon, foosh!" He finished his breakfast at a gulp. "Ye're so dom clever that yer brain is too great for yer other capacities! It leaves ye shorthanded, understaffed!"

Consulting his watch with his right eye, the lid of which was the easier of the two to keep unstuck, he was surprised to see that it was eleven o'clock.

"Weel," he murmured drowsily, "we puir sons o' toil can at least be thonkful for the sweet repose o' the Sabbath. But I

The Scot From Scotland Yard 187

wonder — aye, I wonder what troobles and tragedies the forthcoming week will bring?" His head sank down on the pillow and, in spite of certain hollow, crumpling sounds as the bowler's brim collapsed, he drifted off into a fitful slumber.

All day Monday he worried. In Tuesday's newspapers he noted with dismay that a police officer, whose name was not divulged, had been summoned before the commissioner to answer charges of extortion preferred by several Limehouse publicans. On Wednesday he read in panic that "the complainants, when confronted with the accused constable, were unanimous in declaring that he bore no slightest resemblance to the man who, masquerading as a detective, blackmailed them last Saturday night. They then furnished a detailed description of the actual culprit, and his arrest is expected shortly."

"Ah, dearie me!" groaned Mr. Glencannon, quaking. "Why, the unscruppulous scuts have exonerated Belcher and raised the hue and cry after me! Me! Me, o' all people! No doot at this vurra moment they're hunting me lik' a wild beast! Whurra! I'd dom weel better keep mysel' oot o' sicht!"

He slipped a brace of bottles into the pockets of his overalls, scurried below and crawled into the shaft tunnel. There he spent the better part of the next two days, skulking in the darkness and communing with the stern tube gland. It was on Saturday morning, just as he had come up to his room for fresh supplies, that he heard a nervous tap at his door. Before he had time to dive under the bunk, Jessup, the steward, entered on tiptoe.

"Beg pardon, Mr. Glencannon," he whispered tensely. "There's a bloke come aboard to see yer that I don't 'arf like the looks of. It's none of my business, of course, but if yer should 'appen to arsk me, I'd say 'e was a ruddy plainclothes policeman. Well, sir, I told 'im — er, er —"

Mr. Glencannon followed the steward's horrified gaze and beheld a colossal figure looming in the doorway.

"Belcher! Why, my dear Belcher!" he exclaimed weakly, at the same time glancing at the dresser to make sure that his brass knuckles were available. "Swith, auld mon, if it wasna for yer face, yer foorm, yer feet, and the general look o' ye, I'd ne'er have reecognized ye in civilian clothes! Come in and tell me the news, lad, while I show ye a vurra neat little trick with a bottle and a corkscrew!"

"Umph!" The policeman stooped, turned himself sidewise and edged into the room. He sat down on the bunk, which creaked under his weight. "Me feet don't 'urt," he observed, hoisting them aloft, bracing them against the opposite bulkhead and surveying with satisfaction the new tan Oxfords which encased them. Then, recalling himself to business: "But now, see ere, my man! I've got an anonymous letter 'ere that was sent to me by somebody that didn't sign 'is name. I want yer to tell me, yes or no, whether yer recognize the 'andwriting."

"No," said Mr. Glencannon emphatically.

"Unh? Well, but wait till yer've seen it, cantcher? 'Ere, now look at it."

Mr. Glencannon looked. The letter read:

MR. JAMES BELCHER, NO. 6118,
IN CARE NEW SCOTLAND YARD,
VICTORIA EBANKMENT, LONDON.

Dear Mr. Belcher Sir: Saturday night I was in 2 different pubs when you come in looking for Sailor Nelson about them 16 cases of silk Well Mr. Belcher Sir when I heard you say it was 16 cases and not 6 it conformed my suspicions that Nelson had double crossed me on that deal as well as several others because he said it was only 6 cases and paid me my share according Well Mr. Belcher Sir I am not in the habit of narking on my pals but I reelize now that Sailor Nelson is no pal of mine no he is a dirty rat and what he needs is about 15 or 20 years in quod to teach him British sportsmanship His Christian name is Walter Nelson and he lives at No. 11 Hildreth Road Hoxton on the second floor Well Mr. Belcher Sir when you arrest Nelson also ask him about the West India Dock Road robberies last month and also the 2 pawn shops that was broke into in Rotherhithe also that lorry load of cigarettes and tobacco that was stole out of that Houndsditch garage you will remember the job I mean as there was rather a stink about the watchman getting done in Well Mr. Belcher Sir as it is getting late I must close

Yours respectfully
An Honest Citizen.

Mr. Glencannon looked up from the letter. "I can assure ye I ne'er saw that handwriting before in my life," he declared righteously.

"H'mph! Well, now, can yer think of any bloke answering the following description — er" — he brought out his notebook —"middle age, medium height, stocky build, ruddy complexion. Talks with a Scottish accent. Wears a walrus mustache, is probably a ship's officer, and is reported to be partial to a whisky known as Duggan's Dew of Kirkintilloch?"

"M-m-m, no, I canna say that I can," said Mr. Glencannon, his ruddy complexion fading to gray, his walrus mustache drooping like a weeping willow, and the Duggan's bottle rattling dismally against the glass as he poured himself a drink.

"Well, no, and neither can I," growled the policeman. "And it's a damn funny thing, too, because I could almost swear I'd seen such a bloke someplace recently." He closed his eyes, pressed his hand to his brow and then shook his head. "No, it's no use, no use!" he sighed. "Oh, if I could only collar that bird, what a fine thing it'd be — right on top of my promotion and orl!"

"Yer — p-p-promotion?" Mr. Glencannon managed to stammer. "Ah, swith, auld mon, I — I congratulate ye!"

"Well, that's exactly wot the commissioner and everybody else is doing," said the policeman complacently. "'Ere, just 'ave a squint at this!" He passed over a multigraphed sheet which read:

CITATION AND SPECIAL PROMOTION

BELLSHEAR, James, No. 6118, is promoted this date from Constable, Traffic, to Detective, 2nd Grade. Working on his own time and initiative and in spite of a plot to discredit him on false charges, Bellshear tracked down and arrested an important criminal, broke up a dangerous gang of thieves and recovered stolen property valued at many hundreds of pounds. Detective Bellshear's conduct should serve as an inspiring example to the entire force.

"Bellshear? Bellshear?" Mr. Glencannon stared at the name and repeated it incredulously. "Weel, whoosh and whoosheroo! Is that the way ye spell it?"

"Yus, but I'm getting jolly well sick and tired of arnswering that question! 'Ow in the 'ell does everybody think I spell it — with a Q or something?" Abruptly, Detective Bellshear pulled out his watch and scowled at it. "Eleven thirty-five! Well, come on!" he ordered gruffly, rising to his feet. "I've got a police car waiting."

"Eh?"

"Come on, I said, and be quick about it! Don'tcher realize that ye're wanted?"

"W-w-wanted? Wh-wh-what f-f-for?"

"To be best man at the wedding. Veronica O'Halloran becomes me bride at 'igh noon today!"

The Loving Cup

One morning, as the S.S. *Inchcliffe Castle* lay at Cape Town, loading cargo for London and way ports on the West African coast, her Chief Engineer, Mr. Glencannon, received a postcard with the following message:

DEAR COLIN

Saw in shipping news *Inchcliffe* is in port and would like to see you old man. Have splendid job out here in the subherbs do come out here and have lunch with me old man and maybe a nip or two of the right stuff, what ho? Take No. 8 bus passing Victoria Basin Docks and tell conductor to let you off at Sunnyvale Meadows, walk through gate and inquire for me in building with ivy on it.

I am, etc., yours very truly,

Your friend,
ANGUS BRAID.

Though having known him but casually, Mr. Glencannon recalled Mr. Braid as a marine engineer of rather more than average capacity when someone else was buying the drinks, and so was mildly puzzled at this unwonted bid of hospitality. Wondering what the catch might be and whether or not to accept, he observed that a postscript had been scrawled on the margin of the card and, turning it sidewise, read: "Did you hear about MacCrummon since you got here?" As the import of this query bore in upon him, he snorted, sprang to his feet and rapped out a fearful oath; his brow beetled, his jugular swelled, and his mustache bristled like that of a bull walrus endeavoring to swallow a stingray tail-first. "MacCrummon?" he snarled. "MacCrummon — here? Ah, foosh! Is there no place on earth I can go withoot running a-foul o' the black Dunvegan scoondrel? What's he doing in South Africa?" He stood for a moment, breathing through distended nostrils. "The only way to find oot is to find oot — before he can do me dirt!" Snatching up his cap, he stamped down the gangway and across the busy docks to the Greenpoint Road, where he boarded a No. 8 bus. "A-weel," he panted, settling into a seat, "forewarned is forearmed — but I must be vurra canny, vurra cautious and vurra caircumspect all the same!"

For a while he sat reviewing the long, bitter feud waged between himself and MacCrummon; then, in an effort to dismiss the sinister creature from his mind, at least temporarily, he turned his attention to the landscape. What with the towering heights, the white town and the purple sea, he found the prospect magnificent. Across the flat top of Table Mountain lay a great steamy cloud, its edges billowing out over the emerald-green lucerne fields below and drenching them with beneficent moisture. "Yon looks lik' guid, rich grazing land," he mused. "Indeed, I'm surprised to see so few cattle pewling aboot in the pastures. I wonder if . . ."

"Sunnyvale Meadows!" the conductor called. "'Ere's yer stop, Mister!"

Descending, Mr. Glencannon found himself before a massive iron gate, open upon a driveway flanked by lawns where peacocks proudly strutted. Some distance along the driveway was a group of white marble buildings which vaguely reminded him of temples he had seen on the hills behind Athens. "A vurra hondsome establishment, whate'er its purpose," he pronounced. "— Aye, and a vurra prosperous one as weel, judging from the processions o' expensive motor cars wuch are plying to and fro. But — I wonder exockly what the place can be?"

He halted before a building around whose Doric columns dark green ivy twined. Carved across its frieze was

THE SUNNYVALE MEADOWS CREMATORIUM

"Ho, o' course, a dairy!" he exclaimed. "Weel, I said it looked lik' rich grazing country from the vurra ootset! But — be domned if I e'er saw a creamery half so elegant as this one! And what in the wurrld can an auld confairmed milk-shunner lik' Angus Braid be doing in it?"

He passed through the doorway into a marble entrance hall illuminated by slanting beams of softly-colored light from a single stained glass window high in the wall. The place was bare of furniture save for a desk behind which sat a beauteous damsel, gowned in dove-gray satin. At the sound of his footstep, this goddess rose, smiled and moved toward him lissomely, her ivory hands clasped before her in sympathetic solicitude. "Good morning," she throbbed, in a voice sweet as that of a nightingale gargling honey. "May I — may I be of — help?"

"Aye, my bonny plump milkmaid, indeed ye may!" replied Mr. Glencannon jovially, chucking her under the chin. "Just infoorm me where I can find Muster Angus Braid, who's yere chief bottle-washer or summat such, and I'll reward ye with a chaste but full-flavored kiss. —Nice, soniturra little place ye've got here, lass!"

The goddess dealt him a kick on the shin and jerked her lovely head toward a bronze portal at the rear of the room. "Down that passage, you louse!" she snapped. "It's the door at the end, marked Chief Engineer."

Beating a retreat in the direction indicated, Mr. Glencannon entered a narrow, white-tiled tunnel. From somewhere in the distance came the scrape of shovels, the thump of slice bars and the clang of furnace doors, as though a ship's stokehole were getting up steam. "Losh, I'm beginning to see the onswer, noo!" He nodded understandingly. "With the pasteurizers, churns, separators, refrigerators, sterilizers and all such cumplex machinery, the Chief Engineer o' a great muddern dairy plont lik' this must have a mon's-size job! And here" — he paused before the door and turned the knob — "and here is the office o' the mon himsel'."

Mr. Angus Braid, a stout, red-haired gentleman in a khaki boiler suit, looked up from his littered desk and paused in the task which currently occupied him. "Hoot, Colin!" he cried, setting down bottle and glass and hurrying forward with extended hand. "So ye got my postcard! Dom, lad, it's grond to see ye!"

"Thonk ye, Angus! Eh? Weel, noo that ye speak o' it, I believe I cud do with a muddest dollop," said Mr. Glencannon, agreeably but with a certain reserve. "— Just a drap, ye understand — just enough to moisten the bottom o' the tumbler till it starts to owerflow. There! When! Whoa, lad! — Here; I'd best sop up the excess with the blotter, before it tak's the varnish off yere desk."

Mr. Braid poured for himself and raised his glass on high. "Weel, here's to our reunion — and to yere vurra guid oppetite! — And speaking o' appetites —" he glanced at his watch — "if ye'll excuse me half a minute, Colin, I'll just step oot and arrange aboot getting the lunch started; then we can sit doon, have a guid auld gossip, and exchange news. H'm, let's see, noo; have ye got any suggestions? Is there anything in particular ye feel lik' eating, auld mon?"

"A-weel," said Mr. Glencannon, politely mindful of the resources at hand, "nothing wud suit me better than a nice cauld pitcher o' milk and eight or ten new-laid poached eggs on golden slobs o' toast spread thick with sweet butter. Yummy! Think o' it! And then, to finish off with, what cud be more delicious than a brimming bowl o' Devonshire cream and a comfortable gutfull o' fresh cottage cheese?"

"Ah! Fine! A copital menu!" Mr. Braid cried enthusiastically. "Naturally, I've none o' the things ye've enumerated, but a nice baked peacock wud exockly touch the spot! Sit doon and amuse yersel' with the whusky, Colin, while I go see if I can inveigle one in off the lawn and strongle it withoot the gardener noticing."

"A baked peacock?" repeated Mr. Glencannon. "Weel, a baked peacock wud undootedly be vurra toothsome although at Valparaiso I once ate a boiled vulture that was a wee bit on the gamey side. But, Angus, dear lad — reflect! It wud tak' ye at least four hours to bake yere peacock, e'en after ye'd inveigled it and strangled it, and four hours wud mak' it teatime."

"Four hours to bake the peacock?" scoffed Mr. Braid. "Haw! Four minutes is more lik' it! Please look ower there, Colin — I mean at yon center dial on that instrument panel — and teel me what it reads!"

Mr. Glencannon squinted his eyes at the cluster of gauges and gadgets on the wall opposite the desk. "Why, the center one reads two thoosand, five hoonderd and fifty-one," he announced. "But — two thoosand, five hoonderd and fifty-one what, Angus?"

"Two thoosand, five hoonderd and fifty-one degrees Fahrenheit, that's what!" said Mr. Braid, a note of pride in his voice. "That instrument's a remote control thermometer, hooked up with my main unit — the new model, coke-fired, reverberatory furnace whuch we just installed last week. — Wait!" From a shelf he took down a gracefully shaped vessel of antiqued bronze and unscrewed the top of it, exposing a fine white powder within. "Noo, here's a somple o' what that new furnace can do in only twenty-two minutes. I particularly invite yere attention to the lovely, fluffy texture o' the residue, whuch is unconditionally guaranteed to pass through a sifter screen o' one hoonderd and fifty meshes to the square inch. — It's a dom tidy job, ye must admit it!"

"Aye, vurra tidy!" murmured Mr. Glencannon, perplexed but polite. "Indeed, it does ye great credit, Angus. But — what is it?"

"Eh? Why, it's MacCrummon, o' course! As soon as I saw his name in the papers, after the unfoortunate occident they had doon yonder at Mossel Bay, I . . ."

"Wait!" Mr. Glencannon's voice cracked and his hand shook so violently that he was obliged to drain his glass to avoid spilling its contents. "W — what — what's this ye're teeling me, Angus?"

"Why, sumply that I wired them that if they'd ship his corpus to me, express prepaid, I'd give him a cumplimentary treatment on my ain time — thus, incidentally, testing oot our new furnace, don't ye see? Weel, when he was deleevered here, the following afternoon, I pairsonally stoked the new unit up to a temperature o' twenty-eight hoonderd and sixty degrees. Then

I opened the primary draught a trifle more than halfway and — wud ye believe it? — I ran him through in twenty-two minutes flat. The results, as ye've just seen, were wholly gratifying. But noo I'll nip ootside and snaffle the peacock; then we . . ."

"Angus!" Mr. Glencannon restrained him. "Do I understand that MacCrummon got — killed?"

"A-weel," shrugged Mr. Braid, "if he didn't, I'm afraid I've put him to considerable inconvenience!"

Mr. Glencannon paled and glanced fearfully about him. "— And this place?" he demanded. "Is it — is it lik' those dreadful Hindu *ghats* beside the Ganges at Benares?"

"No, and ye can see for yersel' it isn't!" said Mr. Braid, a trifle stiffly. "The Sunnyvale Meadows Crematorium, Limited, togeether with its subsidiary, The Sunnyvale Meadows Intramural Necropolitan Foundation, is the most muddern and efficient mortuary processing and disposal establishment in the entire Union o' South Africa. When I deemonstrate what I can do with a peacock in approximately four minutes, ye'll . . ."

"No!" pleaded Mr. Glencannon, turning slightly green. "Somehow I — I dinna think I cud stoomach a peacock today. P-p-p-pour me a drink, Angus, w-w-will ye?"

Mr. Braid peered at him solicitously and hastened to unlimber the bottle. "Here, Colin! Oh, forgive me, lad, for breaking the sod news to ye so abruptly. I didna realize that ye and MacCrummon were such close friends!"

"We weren't." Mr. Glencannon's voice was hollow. "Indeed, I willna conceal from ye that we were mortal enemies. No blacker scoondrel e'er drew breath than him whose pitiful oshes repose in yonder urn! But, weel, auld Davie MacCrummon was a worthy foe, when all is said and done. Somehow — somehow life willna be the same withoot him!" He bowed his head for a moment, his glass pressed to his lips; then with a manly effort, he tilted it back and lo! the glass was empty.

"Colin, yere sentiments do ye prood!" Mr. Braid applauded. "I can see withoot osking that ye'll render him one last earthly sairvice."

"— Meaning whuch?" asked Mr. Glencannon, cautiously. "Didn't ye just noo say ye'd, er, processed him free and cumplimentary?"

"Oh, absolutely! I mean that ye'll convey his oshes to London and hond them over to his puir dear wife."

"His wife? — Whuch wife, Angus? He had five that I know of."

"He had seeven," said Mr. Braid. "I mean the one that lives at Number Twenty-three, Mutton Mews, The Lower High Street, Hoxton. As she was his last spouse o' record, it follows that all the others are automatically bigamists, and as such can have no valid or tenable claim in law, *auribus teneo lupum,* to his relics, chattels or suppositories."

"True!" agreed Mr. Glencannon, who knew his Blackstone as one of the poorer grades of Welsh coal. "But while, o' course, I cudna refuse to undertake the meelancholy mission ye suggest — e'en though, as ye're weel aware, carrying cadavers in any form is likely to bring bod luck to the ship — 'twill be two months at least before the *Inchcliffe* gets to London. — Why do ye no' symply send the urn by post?"

"I was plonning to, but I found there's no end o' red tape and expense when ye try to ship human oshes in the mails. Then I saw in the paper that the *Inchcliffe* was in port, due to sail hame shortly, and I knew ye'd forget yere auld sea superstitions and be glad to save the puir widow a-muckle o' trouble and money. — Can I write her this vurra day, Colin, informing her o' yere laudable spirit, and saying that ye'll phone her as soon as ye get to London?"

"Aye, write her." Mr. Glencannon nodded. "Losh, losh, I ne'er imagined I'd be shipmates with MacCrummon again and him guaranteed to pass through a one hoonderd and fifty screen sifter! — To think that ye cud tak' a braw, tough speecimen lik' him, shove him in a furnace and in only twenty-two minutes . . ."

"Ah, swith, that reminds me!" Mr. Braid smacked his lips. "How's yere oppetite the noo?"

Mr. Glencannon turned green again, but this time with faint overtones of mauve. "Oh, I find yere whusky vurra nourishing indeed," he said hastily. "This brond, Duggan's Dew o' Kirkintilloch, is really a balanced liquid food, being distilled o' pure, sun-ripened grain and, therefore, rich in vitamins, proteins, alcohol and all the other mind and body-building elements."

"Weel, let's build up our minds and bodies with a few more sowps o' it, then," suggested Mr. Braid, hospitably. "After all, Colin, the day is yet young!"

The day was drawing to a close, however, as Mr. Braid escorted his guest down the driveway toward the gate of the Sunnyvale Meadows Crematorium. Having finally succeeded in dissuading him from going to roost in a tree with a family of peacocks, he flagged an empty hearse, boosted Mr. Glencannon and the urn into the back door of it, and bade them Godspeed to Cape Town, the coastal ports of West Africa and the faraway city of London-on-the-Thames.

II

At supper one evening some weeks later, as the *Inchcliffe Castle* was snouting her northward way through the Gulf of Guinea, Captain Ball muttered an exclamation and dropped his soup spoon on the table.

"Well, by dodd!" he said raptly, beaming upon his officers with a proud, patriarchal eye. "— D'you know what?"

For a moment there was silence; then, "No. What?" inquired Mr. Montgomery, the Mate, taking it upon himself to speak for the company.

"Eh?" Captain Ball bristled slightly. "Why, that's word for word precisely what I just now asked you, isn't it? Really, ker-hem, when I pose a civil question, Mister Mate, you don't have to throw it back in my very teeth, so to say. Er," in the shelter of his napkin he readjusted them on his gums. "Um-m-m, *tsick!* — No, no; what I mean to say is, today's the third of the month, isn't it? — It is? Well, then!" he sat back, clasped his hands upon his paunch and smiled at the lamp which swung in its gimbals to the slow surge of the South Atlantic swell. "Today, gentlemen, is my twenty-fifth anniversary in the service of this line!"

"Ho, congratulations, Captain, and many hoppy returns!" cried Mr. Glencannon, and a polite echoing murmur went up from round the board. "— Although, o' course," the Engineer continued, "there'd be a hoonderd times more cause for congratulation if ye'd put in the time with decent owners, instead o' with such mean, grosping, niggling, parsimonious penny-pinching stinkers as the weel-known firm o' Messrs. Clifford, Castle and Company, Limited."

"Yes, yes, I fancy there would," Captain Ball admitted. "C and C ain't exactly what you'd call a big-hearted concern, as all of us can testify. Er, by the way, Sparks — you didn't happen by any chance to pick up a personal message for me from the office this evening did you?"

"No, sir," said young Mr. Levy, the Wireless Operator. "There wasn't nothing come over arfter the six o'clock Greenwich time signal."

"Um," Captain Ball wilted visibly. "Well, there you are! — But damme if I really didn't think Clifford and Castle would do the decent thing today, for once in their lives! It wouldn't 've cost 'em only a trifle to send me a word of greetings and, yes, of appreciation, after all these years I've served 'em. You see, gentlemen —," there was a quaver in his voice — "it'd've meant a very great deal to me, but even more to Missus B.!" He dipped his spoon in his soup and paddled it about dispiritedly; then, gruffly excusing himself, he left the saloon.

"Welp," shrugged Mr. Montgomery, "the poor old codger's feeling 'is years tonight, no doubt, about that!"

"Aye, and ye're feeling yere oats as usual, no doot about that, either!" said Mr. Glencannon. "Ye've still got yere shifty eye on the Auld Mon's job and e'en at a time lik' this, ye're too uncouth to hold yere swinish greed in check. Foosh to ye, Muster Montgomery!"

"Oh, skip it, skip it, do!" the Mate retorted, disgustedly. "Fer pity's sake, don't go to 'arping on that there subjick again! I'll admit I'm progessive and ambitious, same as any other up-and-coming young cove — and why shouldn't I? But if yer think I think it's not a ruddy rotten shame the owners didn't send him a Marconi tonight, giving 'im a gold watch and a tidy cash bonus, yer've got another think coming!"

"Indeed, I've got seeveral," said Mr. Glencannon "and in view o' their peculiarly pairsonal nature, I'd urgently advise ye to pack yere left ear in asbestos." He finished the meal in silence.

Some time later, as he lay reading in his room, there was a knock at his door and in came Mr. Montgomery. "Now see 'ere, Mister Glencannon," said the visitor, earnestly. "The rest of us 'ave been discussing about the Old Man's anniversary, and we've agreed that it's up to us to do the 'andsome thing by 'im — even though the bleddy owners didn't. Of course, we can't afford to give 'im no silver tea set or nothing like that, but we've orl noticed that there bronze loving cup yer've got there on yer dresser, and we thought . . ."

"— Impossible!" Mr. Glencannon interrupted. "What ye're aboot to suggest is absolutely oot o' the question!"

"But why? Wot is that cup, anyway?"

"Oh, it's — it's — a-weel, it's a sort o' a trophy," stammered Mr. Glencannon. "Aye, a prize, that's it! Ye see, I won it in a peacock strangling contest, conducted by the Royal South African Ornithological Society o' Cape Town, and . . ."

"— And yer mean yer wouldn't care to part with it on account of sentimental reasons?"

"— Sentimental reasons? Oh, losh, no! I mean that yon cup is worth a pretty penny, ten quid at the vurra least — and much as I am in sumpathy with yere idea o' presenting Captain Ball with a suitable token, I dinna feel that I shud be called upon to be the sole contreebutor. — In other wurrds, Muster

"Impossible!" Mr. Glencannon interrupted. "What ye're aboot to suggest is obsolutely oot o' the question!"

Montgomery, I was no' born yesterday and I crave yere pairdon while I thumb my nose at ye."

"But 'oo the 'ell's calling on yer to be the sole contributor?" demanded Mr. Montgomery. "Now, wait a minute; look! That there cup's worth ten quid, yer say — Right! The rest of us 'ave just finished subscribing nine pounds, three shillings, seven pence 'apenny to the Captain John Ball Twenty-fifth Anniversary Token Fund and 'ere's the money right 'ere! Will yer accept it fer the cup, the difference to be considered as your contribution to the fund?"

"A-weel, in those caircumstonces, I have no altairnative," said Mr. Glencannon. "But e'en though, obviously, I am bearing the lion's share o' the cost, I dinna begrudge it; indeed I congratulate ye on yere spirit in initiating this thing, Muster Montgomery." He counted the money and put it in his pocket. "When do ye plon to hold the presentation ceremoonies?"

"Tomorrer night, just as we sit down to a special surprise supper the steward's promised to throw up for us. But look, I say, Mister Glencannon!" Mr. Montgomery reached over and tapped the urn with his finger. "I don't suppose yer could manage to engrave a bit of an inscription 'ere on the side of it, could yer? Some nice bit of sentiment, I mean —something original — oh, I don't know — something like to the effect, er, 'To Captain John Ball, With Esteem, Affection And Love?'"

"Pairfict! Exockly the proper wurrding!" cried Mr. Glencannon. "I'll borrow some acid from Sparks and set to wurrk etching it immediately. And — er — Chauncey, auld mon!" — he laid his hand upon the other's shoulder — "ye're no' such a bod sort after all! Ye've made me realize ye're a true friend o' Captain Ball's — and any friend o' his is a friend o' mine!"

Having procured the acid, Mr. Glencannon returned to his room and set about organizing himself for his task. "Noo, the feerst thing is to tronsfer MacCrummon to another container o' some sort. H'm, let's see!" He looked around him. "Weel, I'm sure he'll find yon whusky bottle vurra homelike once he gets used to being inside it, instead o' the other way aroond. — It's still a guid quarter full, o' course, but I can easily rectify that." He rectified it, uncovered the urn and paused for a moment in contemplation of its contents. "Alos, puir Hamlet, I knew him weel!" he soliloquized. "— But domned if I e'er dreamed he'd turn oot snow white!" He set the bottle on the floor and endeavored to pour the ashes into it. While a certain quantity entered the neck, a considerably greater quantity spilled down the sides to the carpet. "Foosh, he's stooborn and headstrong as ever!" growled Mr. Glencannon. "— No, no, I fear this willna do; I'll have to pour him back, find something with a wider mouth, and begin all ower again." With a shoehorn, he shoveled up as much as he could from the carpet, replaced it in the urn, and scuffed the remainder with his foot. "'Twull keep the moths awa'," he said. "Indeed, seeing it's MacCrummon, 'twull dootless keep awa' hawks, eagles and vompire bats." The ashes in the bottle presented a more difficult problem; they adhered to its moist interior and though he shook it, joggled it, thumped it and cursed it in the exasperated manner of one striving to promote the flow of coagulated ketchup, his efforts were unavailing. "Ah, foosh!" he snorted. "— How vurra vexing! How utterly futile!" He tossed the bottle through the porthole. "After all, it was only a trifling quantity o' him and probably none o' his indispensable mechanism anywa'." He went forward to the galley and helped himself to a marmalade jar, a fruit tin and a chutney bottle; these were easy to pour into and accommodated MacCrummon with ample room to spare.

"Haw!" Mr. Glencannon chuckled as he rubbed the side of the now empty urn with crayon, to form an etching ground. "I hope Gabriel doesna blaw his trumpet for the final resurrection, with MacCrummon divided up in three portions! At the feerst note the impetuous scut wud come thumping and closhing together, lik' so many empty coal cars coupling up to a train!"

He did a successful job with the engraving; indeed, throughout the following day it was greatly admired by his colleagues, who stole, one by one, into his room for a preview. The presentation ceremonies that evening were equally successful, due not only to his forethought in filling the cup with whisky at the outset, but to his diligence in replenishing it at frequent intervals. Captain Ball, taken wholly by surprise, was at first dumbfounded, then delighted, then profoundly touched, then hilarious, then lachrymose and finally comatose. It was well after midnight when they lugged him to his room and put him to

Captain Ball, taken wholly by surprise, was at first dumfounded, then delighted, then profoundly touched.

bed, the cup still clutched to his breast. As they tiptoed away, he stirred slightly, set it upon the floor and dropped his false teeth into it, mumbling, "I owe it all to you, Mary!"

Some time later Mr. Montgomery, in his room, was endeavoring to remove his white canvas shoes, which he had cleaned especially for the party. The shoes had dried, hard as rocks and in some mysterious fashion had become firmly cemented to his feet. "Ouch, ow, gor-blyme!" he fumed, struggling with them. "I thought I was 'elping myself to pipe-clay, out of that there marmalade jar of 'is, but — ouch! — I wonder wot the 'ell it really was?" Simultaneously, in his quarters further aft, Mr Swales prudently fortifying himself against the morrow's hangover with what he had earlier filched from Mr. Glencannon's fruit tin as bicarbonate of soda, suddenly pressed his hands to his midriff and lurched out on deck toward the rail. And Mr. Glencannon, taking a final nightcap, was surprised to observe that the contents of the three reliquaries on his washstand shelf had greatly diminished since morning. "Uncanny — vurra uncanny!" he muttered. "— Foosh, MacCrummon, what deevilty have ye been up to noo? Why, there's scarcely a third o' ye left, so I micht as weel consolidate ye." He emptied marmalade jar and fruit tin into the chutney bottle and poured the inconsiderable surplus down the drain of the wash basin. "O' course, I'm plonning to buy a proper vase for ye, when we get to London, but if ye keep on dwundling at this rate, I can put ye in an envelope and mail ye to Mussis Mac-Crummon for a penny stomp!"

On a day some weeks later, when the *Inchcliffe Castle* had put in to Las Palmas to coal, Mr. Glencannon was visited in his room by Mr. Levy. "There's something I want to talk to yer about," said Sparks, mysteriously, closing the door and shooting the bolt. "I wish yer'd tell me whether I'm right or wrong."

The shoes in some mysterious fashion had become firmly cemented to his feet.

"Weel, on prunciple, I'll say ye're wrong," declared Mr. Glencannon. "Just exoctly what have ye got on yere mind?"

"This 'ere," said Mr. Levy, handing him a carbon copy of a typewritten page. It read:

>CAPTAIN HONORED BY OFFICERS, CREW
>Loving Cup for Ball on Twenty-Fifth
>Anniversary
>REBUKE TO OWNERS SEEN IN MID-SEA
>CEREMONY

Las Palmas, June 24. (By Air Mail.) Ignored by his employers after a quarter century of faithful service under their house flag, John Ball, Master of the S.S. *Inchcliffe Castle*, was honored by his shipmates in a touching ceremony conducted at sea, it was learned when the vessel arrived here today. No sooner had Captain Ball announced his "Silver Anniversary" and expressed his natural chagrin at not receiving so much as a congratulatory message from his owners, than a collection was taken up among his devoted officers and men and he was presented with a handsome loving cup, suitably inscribed. The *Inchcliffe Castle* is one of the extensive fleet of cargo ships operated by Messrs. Clifford, Castle & Co., Ltd., of London.

"Ho, dom!" cried Mr. Glencannon. "Dinna teel me that this thing has been sent oot, Sparks! Who — who wrote it?"

"The Mate wrote it," said Mr. Levy. "'E used my typewriter, d'yer see, and knocked out seven or eight copies — enough fer orl the London papers. I couldn't sneak this 'ere one 'ere until after 'e'd gorn ashore to post the rest of 'em."

"Ah, foosh, foosh, foosh!" Mr. Glencannon pressed his hand to his forehead and rocked back and forth in anguish. "Why, 'twill ruin Captain Ball — aye, ruin him absolutely! When the owners see it, they'll — they'll . . ."

"— They'll give 'im the ruddy sack; yus, that's exockly 'ow I figured it," Mr. Levy finished. "They'll maybe even set the Board o' Trade on his neck fer preaching insubordination prejudicial to discipline and orl like that, and then where'll 'e be? And the 'ell of it is" — he waved his cigarette-stained hand toward the dispatch, "— the 'ell of it is, every larst word of it's true!"

"Aye, and it just goes to show the cleverness o' the slimy, back-knifing villain!" groaned Mr. Glencannon. "The B.O.T. will surely suspend the Auld Mon's ticket — indeed they may e'en concel it! But in any case, C and C will fire him, and that Cockney cockroach o' a Montgomery'll get his job!"

"But ain't there something we can do?"

Mr. Glencannon pursed his lips and shook his head. "No," he said, "I fear it's too late to do anything, noo! For pity's sake, dinna breathe a wurrd o' this to the Skipper — 'twud worry him sick!"

When Mr. Levy had gone, Mr. Glencannon shook his fist at the chutney bottle on the shelf. "MacCrummon!" he rasped, "ye've brocht bod luck to the ship, as I knew from the start that ye wud! Ho, ye black Dunvegan sweer! If 'twere no' for the fact that yere widow wud sue me for domages and that ye'd pollute the ocean, I'd chuck ye owerboard!"

III

Arrived in London, Mr. Glencannon's first concern was to rid himself of the ashes. "Whurra!" he muttered, as with the chutney bottle wrapped in newspaper he hurried along the dockside toward the public telephone box. "If I can turn him ower to his widow before the owners get a chance to sack the Captain, pairhops — who knows? — pairhops I can break the evil spell and save the puir auld gentleman after all!"

He looked up Mrs. MacCrummon's number and was put through to her. When he introduced himself, she wept a little, thanked him for the noble service of which Mr. Braid's letter had already apprised her, and asked him to call at her flat in the course of the hour. Repairing to the bargain basement of a Fullworth Shilling Shop, he purchased a vase of imitation Staffordshire ware, tastefully decorated with a decalcomania of a huntsman slitting the throat of a wounded stag. The bargain basement was almost completely filled with fat ladies shoving one another about, and so he dared not attempt to transfer the ashes then and there lest someone joggled his elbow and cause him to spill what little of MacCrummon remained. Regaining the street and God's good air, he hailed a taxi and bade the driver drop him at whatever pub was nearest Number Twenty-three Mutton Mews, The Lower High Street, Hoxton.

The pub was on the corner. Entering, he installed himself in a booth, ordered refreshment; unwrapped vase and chutney bottle and . . .

"— And what's more," came a drunken and familiar voice from the next booth, "it weighs a guid thirty carats, as ye'll see for yersel' before ye're an hour older. But we've got to wait here till she phones us that the puir gowk has octually deleevered it, d'ye see?"

For a moment Mr. Glencannon sat spellbound, electrified, frozen. "MacCrummon!" he gasped. "But no — it can't be! But — yes, it is! Has he risen lik' the phoenix from the oshes — or . . . ? Ho!" He thrust his trembling fingers deep into the powder in the bottle. Suddenly — yes! — they encountered something hard! He fished it out and blew the powder from it, revealing a pebble from whose chipped surfaces, here and there, flashed rays of blue-white fire!

"— But o' course," MacCrummon's voice drifted over the partition, "I've had to wurrk it vurra cleverly. As ye dootless know, gentlemen, I.D.B. — as they call illicit diamond buying in South Africa — is an extremely ticklish proposition. But most dangerous o' all is getting the stones deleevered here into England. Weel, being rather more than average canny, I wrote to my auld pal Angus Braid, in Cape Town, and . . ."

"Sh-h-h! Shut up, Mac! Please!" warned a second voice.

"Yus, button yer chin, do!" came a third, gruffly. "D'yer want to swump this 'ole ruddy deal? If yer keep on shouting and . . . Whup! Oh! Good lawks, wot 'it yer, Mac? Dammit, man, yer 'ead's bleeding! And — and — why, yer orl covered with talcum powder — no, plaster! The ceiling must 'ave fell and . . ."

IV

With the pebble clutched in his hand and the hand thrust deep in his pocket, Mr. Glencannon returned in haste aboard the *Inchcliffe Castle*. As he made his way forward to the Captain's quarters, "'Twull be his salvation!" he told himself. "If he's oot o' a job and on the beach, as by this time I fear he is, he can tak' the stone ower to Antwerp or Amsterdam, sell it to some dealer for a foortune and earn a hondsome commission for his pains. I'll give him a full ten per cent! — Weel, maybe five. — Three, anywa'! Ho, Captain!" he cried, bursting into the cabin. "All's weel that ends weel! Feerst, pairmit me to congratulate ye, and then . . ."

"M-m? Oh, yez, yeth, yesh!" Captain Ball laid down a pair of pliers and hastily installed his teeth. "That is I mean to say, quite so! And let me thank you most sincerely for your, er, for your very good offices in the matter, Mister Glencannon! — There, there, now — don't blush, don't stammer, don't attempt to deny it! It's me who should be doing the stammering and blushing and attempting to denying, ker-hem, ker-huff! I had no business sneaking into your room when you wasn't there, I freely confess it! But if I hadn't — well, I wuldn't ever have known!"

"Ye — ye wuldn't e'er have known what, sir?"

"I wuldn't ever have known it was you who sent that news dispatch from Las Palmas. But you'd left the carbon copy of it on your washstand shelf, and so — well, my teeth have been loosening up a bit, lately, but I found that that there cement sort of stuff which you kept in that chutney bottle on your washstand sort of temporarily cemented 'em in, sort of, see what I mean? So when I just now got this letter from the Managing Director, I . . ."

"— Letter? — From the Managing Director?"

"Yes. Here it is."

Mr. Glencannon took the letter and read:

My dear John:
All the London papers printed glowing accounts of the manner in which your ship's company recently honored you. There was, of course, a mistake in figuring the length of your service with the firm, as our records show beyond question that you have been with us only twenty-four years, not twenty-five. But this is a minor detail. The important point is that the spontaneous gesture of your officers and crew proves you to be a commander worthy of, and able to earn, the deepest loyalty and devotion of his subordinates. In these days, alas, such ability is only too rare and is, therefore, a doubly valuable asset to shipowners who can point to it in their personnel.

John, the Board has directed me to send you the enclosed cheque for £100 as a token of appreciation for the valuable publicity which your qualities have brought to the firm. It will, of course, in no way affect the regular Twenty-Five Year Bonus which will be awarded you as soon as you are eligible.

With warmest personal regards, I am,
                    Yours faithfully,
                        Virgil Hazlitt.

"Weel, weel, weel!" breathed Mr. Glencannon. "— Or rather — as I said before, all's weel that ends weel! — For everybody! By the way, Captain — did ye e'er see a rough diamond?"

"Eh? — Oh, now, come, come — you're entirely too modest!" Captain Ball laughed, slapping him on the back.

THE ROMANTIC GLENCANNON